Isabel didn't know *what* she was feeling.

All she knew was that Jacob seemed furious on her behalf. It was...shocking to her.

And a wee bit flattering.

She bit her lip and stared at the red traffic light—yet another one. Jacob seemed to be attracting each and every stop along their route. She tried not to sneak looks at him.

"How long were you two a couple?" His voice was so low she had to strain to hear him. "Were you engaged to him? Did you expect to be married to him?"

Should she answer? He seemed like he was on her side. He seemed...to intrinsically believe in her.

"Sort of," she whispered. "I mean..." She glanced at him. His eyes were warm and understanding. She really felt as if she could trust him.

But this was madness. She'd only met him a few hours ago, and she was Isabel Sage—she couldn't trust outsiders.

D0187591

Dear Reader,

Thanks for picking up *Scotland for Christmas*! I loved writing about the Sage family of Edinburgh, Scotland, so much for my last Harlequin Superromance book, *The Sweetest Hours* (December 2013), that I decided to set two more stories in their romantic world.

This story is primarily a bodyguard tale. Jacob Ross is an emotionally cut-off US Secret Service agent who needs to find out how his police officer father was killed in action years ago while rescuing the kidnapped niece and nephew of John Sage, billionaire CEO of the Sage family empire. Isabel Sage is John's lonely other niece. Though she is smart, hardworking and—above all—loyal to her family, she is drawn to the gruff protector who initially hasn't been honest about his agenda with her. As a potential successor to the CEO job, it's not in her best interests to help Jacob. And Jacob certainly can't afford to fall for this gentle woman from a completely different world from his.

But the healing power of love shines through, and as they return to Scotland for Christmas, Jacob is reconciled to his family's painful past while Isabel finds the one love who truly makes her feel at home.

I hope you enjoy Isabel and Jacob's story.

All the best,

Cathryn Parry

CATHRYN PARRY

Scotland for Christmas

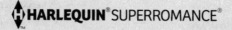

HARLEQUIN® SUPERROMANCE®

Recycling programs
for this product may
not exist in your area.

ISBN-13: 978-0-373-60889-8

Scotland for Christmas

Printed in U.S.A.

Cathryn Parry loves to travel—especially to Scotland!—at any time of year that she can manage. At all other times she lives in New England with her husband and her neighbor's cat, Otis. Cathryn is an active member of Romance Writers of America and enjoys presenting inspirational workshops to writers. Her Harlequin Superromance books have received such honors as a Booksellers' Best Award, HOLT Medallion Awards of Merit and several readers' contest nominations. Please see her website at cathrynparry.com.

Books by Cathryn Parry

HARLEQUIN SUPERROMANCE

Other titles by this author available in ebook format.

CHAPTER ONE

U.S. SPECIAL AGENT Jacob Ross was sitting in an intimate Italian restaurant in midtown Manhattan, next to a woman he wasn't interested in being with, when the text message that he'd been waiting for came in.

Jacob reached for his jacket and stood.

"Where are *you* going?" Eddie asked from across the table.

Jacob glanced at his oldest friend and ex-partner, the guy who'd ridden with him nearly every day for seven years, back when they'd still been on the New York Police Department together. Clinging to Eddie, practically in his lap, was his wife, Donna, and though she leaned forward, desperately trying to catch Jacob's eye, he was purposely avoiding the two women and their blatant interrogation.

"A job," he said to Eddie. "Sorry, but I have to go."

Eddie put down his wineglass and raised his eyebrow. He probably figured Jacob was bluffing about the text message, but would never say so in front of Donna.

"Right," said his ex-partner. "The Cifelli bust?"

The Cifelli bust was their personal code. It was

nonsense—meant absolutely nothing. Jacob and Eddie had made all kinds of fake codes and short-hand between them over the years. Since they'd been special agents in the U.S. Secret Service together, though, they'd been working under stricter protocol, as part of bigger teams with more complex oversight.

Jacob paused. He still had his phone out, in the process of texting back, but in terms of operational backup, it probably *was* best to involve Eddie. They'd both gone through the brutal Secret Service background check at the same time—from polygraphs to psychological testing, and in Jacob's case, to the dark cloud that still hung over him: the threat of further, future investigation. There wasn't much his old partner didn't know about him.

"Actually," he said to Eddie in a low voice, "it's about Sage."

"Sage?" His former partner made a soft whistle. Then he reached for his jacket. "I'm coming with you."

"Eddie, not you, too!" his wife said. "We just ordered."

"Give me five minutes, hon," Eddie said as he kissed her, and then he motioned Jacob toward the exit. Jacob led the way, weaving through a crowd of waiting diners as he pushed through the heavy glass doors.

Outside, the street was brightly lit, loud with students and tourists. The Friday after-work rush was in play, too; businesspeople hurried past, intent on getting to their subway and bus stops. The sky was spitting rain; a miserable, late-October night.

They took refuge under an awning near the sign for West Fifty-third Street. Not wasting any more time, Jacob pulled up the text message.

Eddie angled toward the screen, squinting at it. "Why are you getting a text about John Sage after all this time? What's happening, Jake?"

What was happening was that Jacob's application to the most elite and sought-after of Secret Service jobs—the Presidential Protective Division—had been put on hold. The new department psychologist had flagged Jacob's file, and not in a good way. "I got called into headquarters today with a list of questions I need to answer," Jacob said.

"You're kidding. Questions about your father?"

Jacob nodded. Eddie knew he didn't like to talk about him. He shuffled his feet from side to side, not saying anything more.

Then again, special agents were superstitious. *Nobody* liked to talk about police officers killed in the line of duty.

"Can your mom help with the questions?" Eddie finally asked.

"No." His mom never discussed it—she'd already remarried by the time Jacob's biological father had died, and Jacob didn't want to upset her by reopening old wounds.

Exhaling, he tried to relax. "I thought I'd covered this stuff in the original interviews, but there's a new psychologist on staff. She's not giving me a choice. I have to deal with it if I want to advance."

"Well, if you want help investigating anything, you know I'm in."

"Thanks. I appreciate that." Jacob just had a bad feeling in his gut about the whole thing. It wasn't as if he'd ever even met his biological father, so he didn't see how the fact that he wasn't clear on the details of his father's death was even relevant. After the new department psychologist had buttonholed him, he'd pushed aside the old anger and confusion and had tried to look at the situation objectively, like an investigator would—the way he'd been trained.

Unfortunately, very little was available online about the botched kidnapping-rescue, twenty years earlier, of the young niece and nephew of the Scottish industrialist John Sage. In Jacob's experience, it wasn't normal for information to be scrubbed like that.

"I phoned authorities over in Scotland, but they don't have dossiers anymore. They don't want to talk to me, and I think it's because they don't know what to say. My instinct tells me the case has been covered up, and I don't have jurisdiction to force the subject."

"I didn't know that," Eddie said quietly.

Jacob shrugged. There was nothing he could do to change history.

Eddie gestured to Jacob's phone. "How is Lee helping you with this?"

Lee Palmontari was ex–Secret Service, and Jacob and Eddie's boss until he'd retired. Now he owned a high-end bodyguard/driver business, mostly staffed by other retired federal agents working on contract.

"Lee is me thinking outside the box," Jacob said. "Every billionaire industrialist in the world needs to travel to New York City sooner or later, right? Who else would John Sage call for local security services during his stay?"

Eddie nodded. "Lee."

"Exactly. I left Lee a message explaining what I wanted. He just texted back saying he could help."

"How?"

"I don't know yet."

"So call him and find out."

"I will," Jacob said drily, "when you go back inside. Your five minutes are up."

"Nope. You're not getting rid of me." Eddie shook his head and grinned. "Look, Jake, I know you're angry about the setup tonight, but don't blame Donna. My wife means well—she wants you to be happy."

What did *happy* have to do with anything? Jacob just wanted to do his job and get to D.C. He *would* be part of the Presidential Protective Division. Filling the holes in his personnel file was the first step in getting there.

"You know I'm not family material. Not like you."
Jacob gave his friend a look as he punched up Lee's
contact number. Eddie just rolled his eyes.

"Hey, Jake." Lee himself picked up the call. "I
do have a side job available you might be interested
in. I can't promise anything, but…yeah, the opportunity is there."

Jacob's heart beat faster. Talking to Sage face-to-face was the answer to everything he needed. "Great.
But you know I can't take payment for it, right?"
With his already shaky work status, he couldn't
make it official—no money changing hands, nothing he could potentially get in trouble for.

Eddie slid his hands into his pockets. He knew
the risks, too.

"This would just be a favor to you, off the books?"
Jacob clarified.

"Sure," Lee said. "That's not a problem. It's just
a short driving gig, mainly."

There was something about the way Lee said
mainly that stood out to Jacob. But the promise of
a "driving gig" had already snagged him: alone,
in a car with the man who held the answers Jacob
needed.

"Okay. When and where do I pick up Mr. Sage?"

"Ah…not quite, Jake," Lee said. "The job is to
drive his niece."

"His *niece?* Why would I want to do *that?*"

Beside him, Eddie shook his head. A quick thumbs-down movement as he scratched his chin. *Ratchet it down,* that meant. *Ratchet down the intensity.*

One thing Jake had learned in his life was that intensity was not appreciated. People weren't supposed to care too much, and if they did, they were supposed to hide it.

Take it easy. Relax. Go with the flow. Withdraw. Nothing is all that important.

That's what people said to him. Sorry, but it just wasn't who he was. Everything to him had meaning. It was his weakness and his strength. That fact that Jacob cared, intensely, helped him as an investigator and a bodyguard, even though in real life, it often seemed to alienate him from everybody else.

Or maybe Jacob was just better off alone.

"Look, Jake," Lee was saying, "you're right, never mind about the job, why don't we just forget I called and we'll—"

"No," Jacob interrupted. With the phone still at his ear, he stepped away from Eddie, out from under the awning and into the street, where the rain was coming down a little harder. More of a drizzle than a spit. "Sorry. That didn't come out right. Tell me more about the…niece."

There was a pause on the other end of the line. "Are you sure you're okay with this?" Lee asked in the same tone of concern the psychologist had used earlier in the day.

Jacob scrubbed his hand over his face. He was

screwing up here, and for a stupid reason. Maybe he was just sensitive from having been fixed up with Donna's friend. It was ridiculous to even think that way—it wasn't as if Lee had suggested that he *date* the niece.

He thought back to the restaurant, and the red-head with the heavy eyeliner who'd looked at him with such expectation.

He *really* needed to get out of New York.

"Tell me about the job," he said quietly. "What does it involve, specifically?"

"Nothing you and I haven't done dozens of times before. Just three days of bodyguard security and easy driving. You're required to pick up the niece and escort her from Manhattan to the small-town inn in Vermont where she'll be staying."

"And then?" Jacob asked, his voice sounding tighter than he wanted it to be.

"And then…you drop her at the inn. It's a Friday night, and you'll stick around through Saturday. Sunday morning, you drive her back to Manhattan. Job over."

Jacob glanced to Eddie, beside him yet again, even in the rain. His eagle ears would be picking up every word.

Eddie smirked at him. "Sounds romantic."

Jacob ignored the comment. "I assume Sage will be at the inn already?" he asked Lee.

"Affirmative. That's the point of this exercise.

He's flying directly from Scotland, for the family wedding."

"A family…" Jacob closed his eyes. Eddie made a noise beside him. A cross between a snort and a laugh.

"Yes, a wedding," Lee repeated. "Will that be a problem?"

Jacob hadn't even gone to Eddie's wedding two years ago. The fact that it had been in Maryland and Jacob had been out of town on a special assignment had been a great excuse to miss it. Nobody had pushed him to go because they knew the nature of his job. Now, however…

"Nope, no problem," Jacob said. "It's all good." *Just peachy.*

"Okay. I'm told the whole Sage clan will be there. Most of them are flying over from Scotland directly. It's the, ah, nephew's wedding. He's heir apparent to Sage's empire, so, yes, you had better believe that John Sage will be present."

Jacob shifted his feet on the slick sidewalk. He saw how the stage would be set. Lee was right. This wedding would be his best opportunity to talk with John Sage alone.

But still…Jacob wasn't getting a good feeling. "What's the deal with the niece?"

There was a pause. "Are you *sure* this won't be too hard for you?"

"*Why* would it be hard?" Jacob demanded.

There was another, longer silence on the other end. "I know the Sage family is personal to you, Jake...."

And like a flash, Jacob understood. How could he have missed this? "The nephew getting married... he's the boy who was kidnapped as a child, isn't he?" The kid that Jacob's policeman father had died while protecting. "And this niece I'm driving...she's the sister? The little girl who was with my father, too?"

"No, she's not his sister," Lee said quickly. "Isabel Sage is a different niece. Jake, I wouldn't have called you without checking that first. Okay? You won't need to interact with them unless you decide you want to."

The pulse in Jacob's neck felt as if it was on overdrive. Extra hits of adrenaline.

He shouldn't be reacting this way to having to meet them. He shouldn't be letting it bug him at all. If anything, he was playing right into the agenda of the department psychologist when she'd given him that miserable set of questions.

So you never met your real father? He was Scottish, right? And you were born there, too? Why haven't you been back? And let's talk about his death—exactly what happened, and how did you process it, step by step? How does it make you feel?

She'd made it seem as though Jacob was defective when he'd told her that he didn't feel anything, because he wasn't familiar with every little detail.

That even at the time, he'd felt it only slightly. He'd tried to explain that it was an early divorce and his mother had remarried and his biological father had never been part of his life. Still…blood was blood, the psychologist had implied, and the death must have affected him somehow. And Jacob, to his shame, knew she was right.

He *would* like to know the details and circumstances surrounding his father's death. If he was honest with himself, he'd wanted to know for his whole life. He'd been almost twelve when it had happened—just a kid—and nobody had talked much about it to him.

Until now, he'd been discouraged from asking questions. He just wished that his future didn't rest on his ability to dig up answers from a reclusive Scotsman.

Beside him, Eddie cleared his throat. Jacob had forgotten he'd been listening in. Had forgotten he was standing there with a phone in his hand while he stared into space, lost in the past, furious and not knowing what to do about it.

But he owed Lee an answer.

"Jake," Lee said quietly into his ear, "if you want the job, it's yours. But only if you feel you can give Isabel Sage the professional security she deserves. Sage works with my firm because he trusts me. He knows I hire only the best. You've got to promise me you can handle the assignment—to guard and protect her—with the professionalism you were trained to do. I'm exposing myself here, big-time, but I don't need to tell you that. You know where I'm coming from. You know what I owe you."

"Yeah," Jacob said. He did know. He got what a favor this was to him, but Lee also knew he could trust Jacob with his business. Hell, he'd trusted him with his life.

"Discretion," Lee repeated. "Confidentiality. Professionalism. Remember those things and you'll be fine."

"You don't have to tell me. I live discretion and professionalism."

It was all Jacob knew how to do. He never said a word about the people on his jobs. Ever.

And if he wanted to continue on the path of doing what he was meant to do, to the ultimate prize of being allowed to guard the most important and most defensively vulnerable people in the country, then he needed to have a conversation with John Sage.

Just one hour would be enough. Whatever reservations Jacob felt about the man or his family members—he needed to put it aside in favor of his future.

The past is over, as his mother had so often said when he'd asked questions. *It's what's in front of you that counts.*

Well, that was what he was concentrating on now—what was in front of him. That was what this upcoming weekend would be about, despite the lousy choice that it was. But the choice to bail on the opportunity was even worse.

"I'll do it," he said to Lee. "I'll guard Isabel Sage. Thanks for setting this up. I mean it."

As he hung up, he felt Eddie's gaze on him. Jacob sighed. "Do you want to go with me?"

"I wish I could. But Donna wouldn't be happy if I left her and Alden for another work weekend."

Jacob nodded, thinking of Eddie's four-month-old son. "You're right."

"So you'll be alone this time," Eddie remarked, hunching deeper into his jacket. "There'll be no team behind you to back you up. That'll be different."

Jacob considered that. Secret Service protective details were huge and complex. Whenever they did bodyguard assignments for a visiting head of state or a foreign dignitary, they worked in large, interconnected teams, with command posts, operation centers, motorcade service. One-on-one coverage was unheard of. "Yeah, I'm not looking forward to that."

"Are you gonna be all right with this?" Eddie asked.

Jacob shoved his phone into his pocket. "Two days ago, we were responsible for escorting a murdering dictator—sorry, a member head of state—safely from the U.N. to his five-star hotel and back, and I did it without so much as looking cross-eyed at him. It's a job, Eddie."

"Yeah, but it's also personal this time, Jake."

A gust of wind sent some dead oak leaves skittering across the sidewalk. That, and the now-driving rain, soaking his bare head, seemed to slam into him personally.

"Why don't you come in and finish dinner with us," Eddie said. "We'll talk about it. Sherry's not bad. She's just—"

"No," Jacob interrupted. "Thanks. But I need to prepare for this job."

He didn't stick around to discuss it with Eddie any longer. But while Jacob jogged the few short blocks uptown to his apartment building, folded newspaper over his head, service weapon and badge at his hip, he couldn't help deliberating on Eddie's question.

Are you gonna be all right with this?

Of course. He had to be.

Even if Isabel Sage was as privileged and entitled as he assumed she was—the niece of a billionaire industrialist—he would never react to anything she said or did. Guarding people was his business, and he was damn good at it. He couldn't let it matter that she was related to the family that had been involved with his father's death.

Besides, his job didn't affect him emotionally. Just as his father's death didn't.

As soon as he had the operational details for the psychologist, she would see that, and all would be well. He would soon be on his way to D.C.

JUST ONE MORE year and then you'll be happy.

Those were the words Isabel Sage had written on the corner of a notebook. Old graffiti, scribbled last winter during a study session while a sad song played on her internet radio.

Outside Isabel's window, three stories above the pavement, the city's shop windows displayed the beginnings of winter decorations. In six more weeks came the Christmas break and the end of her term.

She'd been privileged to be here—a Scottish woman from the Highlands, living in the biggest city in America and studying international finance with the savviest people on Wall Street—though, to be honest, she'd been shocked by how lonely she'd felt.

Sighing, Isabel watched a queue of yellow taxicabs snake down Broadway, toward the route she knew led to the airport. Really, she was most looking forward to that day when she could fly home.

Isabel pulled off her earphones and turned away from the window to her case still open on her bed, and tossed inside a bra, some pants—*underpants* here, she reminded herself—and then added the dress she would wear to her cousin's wedding reception.

Somehow, not even the promise of a weekend respite was raising her spirits, because at the end of the day, there was no escaping the fact that she would be attending a wedding without Alex, her longtime boyfriend. Which didn't exactly ease her loneliness.

Another part of the problem, she reflected as she

tossed in her cosmetics bag, was that the groom at the wedding was her cousin, Malcolm, her competitor for the job at home—the reason she was here, studying in New York. Malcolm—her uncle's favorite—had a leg up on her. Now he was even getting married at a pretty inn—or so they said, though she hadn't the heart to look it up online—in Vermont.

Like Bing Crosby's *White Christmas,* she supposed. Her late father had enjoyed that old romantic film very much. But her father had died long ago. Her boyfriend was thousands of miles away in Scotland, on assignment as part of his lawyer duties, and he wouldn't be available to accompany her, either.

Feeling gloomy, Isabel added her flatiron and comb to the case. Tossed a pair of shoes on top. She had better cover her disappointment soon, though she supposed it was the "attending solo" part that was truly bothering her.

All she knew was that she would give anything to have someone to go with. Just someone who knew her as she really was—someone she didn't have to pretend with.

She heard a commotion outside in the corridor, near the lifts. Isabel straightened. Before she could investigate, her mobile phone rang. For a moment her heart skipped. Alex? But no, he was too busy to contact her on weekdays. And he was five time zones away, besides.

She checked the caller ID. It was the driver service her uncle used in New York. Her spirits sank lower, but she stuffed the disappointment down. *Smile.* If she put a smile on her face, then a smile would sound in her voice. A pleasant voice covered all manner of sins.

"Yes," she said lightly into the phone. "This is Isabel."

"Ms. Sage?" the dispatcher said. "I'm calling to confirm your one o'clock pickup."

She forced herself to smile so hard, her lips hurt. "I was told it was a two o'clock pickup."

"That explains it, then. Your assigned security agent buzzed you on the intercom but received no response."

Isabel groaned. She'd been wearing a headset. Obviously, she'd been playing her music so loudly, she hadn't heard the bell. "I'll go down to the lobby and escort him upstairs myself. Is this the same driver who met me at the airport last September?"

"No. It's not." There was a pause. "You've been assigned to Jake Ross."

A good Scots name. A *Highland* Scots name. That lifted her mood. Even if the man himself wasn't Scottish, the name was a nice reminder of home. "Brilliant. I'll go straight down and look for Mr. Ross."

She piled everything still on her bed into her case and then zipped it up quickly. Made one last check of her face in the mirror: fine. She looked presentable.

As she opened her door, she bumped into Rajesh, his fist lifted to knock. He blinked at her. Rajesh was her suite mate, an engineering PhD candidate, with a dark moustache and snow-white turban.

"Braveheart," he said. "There's a man looking for you in the hallway."

She didn't react when he said *Braveheart,* though she felt a bit like cringing. So hard she'd worked to stay low-key amongst the members of her residence hall. For security purposes, she'd been taught since childhood never to let people know she was a member of the wealthy Sage family from Scotland.

Still, she smiled at him. "Thank you, Rajesh. I appreciate it."

"Did you know he's a Secret Service agent?" Rajesh asked. "Why would a Secret Service agent be looking for you?" He peered at her. "Did you do something wrong?"

"What? No. Of course not." Isabel never so much as dropped a wrapper on the street. Shaking her head, she marched past him, into the living area of their four-person suite.

"Freedom," Rajesh whispered as she brushed past, and he made that signal with his fist from the movie *Braveheart.*

Usually, she smiled congenially when he did that, but today she just couldn't. He walked off, back to his group of engineer friends. She couldn't see what they were doing in his room, but she could smell the pizza and hear the adverts on his television set.

Sighing, she headed off to staunch the much bigger problem before it escalated, like the good future CEO she hoped she'd be.

She skipped out to the hallway that ran the length of the residence hall, hearing her neighbors before she saw them. They were four older graduate students who lived in the nearby suites, thirty-somethings, most of them midcareer, and they rented their miniapartments directly from the university. Usually the building was quiet, save for the occasional homeless person who set up camp in their lobby before being chased out by the superintendent.

She found her driver trapped beside the lift doors, being quizzed by Courtney and Philip, the two most vocal of the group who also happened to be journalists. Isabel groaned. Her driver—Jake—did indeed dress like an active U.S. Secret Service agent. She understood their confusion.

He had close-cropped hair. Dark sunglasses that screamed *policeman!* He wore a dark suit with a white collared shirt. At his waist, he definitely carried a gun.

For a split second, Isabel froze. She'd been around security agents for most of her life, but they were never *her* security agents. They usually belonged to someone else—her famous uncle John, or her cousin Malcolm, who was lately becoming equally famous for his new startup venture in Vermont, at least in business circles and the financial press.

But her? She'd never been assigned her own bodyguard before. Until now, apparently. And for the sake of the job she hoped for in the future, she had better show that she could handle it.

"Isabel," Courtney asked her outright, "why is a Secret Service agent asking for you? Are you threatening the president?"

"Are you counterfeiting money in your room?" Philip asked, winking slyly.

It took Isabel a moment to realize that they were mostly joking. Secret Service agents did in fact investigate both presidential threats and counterfeit money schemes, though this man her uncle had hired was no doubt a former agent, not current.

She felt like shaking her head—why on earth would this Jake Ross telegraph who he was?—but she ran a hand through her hair and smiled at Mr. Ross as best she could.

"I only counterfeit on the weekends," she said lightly to Philip. But he was still staring suspiciously at Mr. Ross, so she tried another tactic. She didn't want her suite mates to know she needed a bodyguard, or security of any sort. "Actually, Jake and I are old friends."

"Oh," Philip said. "I see." Courtney nodded as if she understood perfectly, too.

Exhaling, Isabel glanced to Jake and found him

staring so hard at her that there were two pinched lines between his eyes.

She swallowed. "Jake," she managed to say calmly. And then, because it needed to be done—she'd uttered her white lie and now it needed to be followed up—she hooked her arm around his. "Sorry I didn't hear you—I had my headphones on. Come into my room. I've been waiting for you all day."

Deeper lines appeared on his forehead, and he glanced at her hand—clutched around the thin, fine wool of his dark suit jacket—as if she'd shocked him.

Well, she'd shocked herself, too. She was definitely not in the habit of groping strange men. And really, it was his fault as well as hers. He shouldn't be so obvious—he was a terrible actor.

She would have to explain to him that if he wanted to drive her and be her security agent, then he could not go around looking and acting like a paid bodyguard, no matter how true it might be.

She smiled harder and gently dug her fingers into his arm to spur him into movement.

His biceps tensed beneath her fingertips. She heard a slight intake of breath.

But luckily, her neighbors were looking at her reaction—silly and grinning—and not his.

"Isabel, I didn't know you had a boyfriend," a familiar voice said loudly behind her.

Isabel gritted her teeth, but smiled broadly at Charles, unfortunately the team lead on her group economics project. Charles was wearing his favorite Che Guevara T-shirt and a beard styled like his icon.

Jake glared at Charles and his shirt. If two people were ever polar opposites, it had to be these two.

"Let's go, Jake." Isabel tugged on his arm as she escorted him down the corridor and through the doors to her suite. Touching him so familiarly seemed strange, much too intimate and close. But her heart was beating so quickly, she didn't pause to think. She just wanted him out of the way, out of the line of scrutiny.

This time, she managed to get him into her bedroom and safely behind a closed door.

Alone with him, she stepped back, catching her breath. Yes, Jake had probably been a real Secret Service agent at one point—that was all her uncle tended to hire—but there was something else about him, something that she couldn't quite put her finger on.

"What are you *doing?*" he asked in a low voice.

She swallowed, trying to calm her racing pulse. His expression was stone-faced. The dark sunglasses still covered his eyes, not giving her any hint as to his thoughts, but she had the impression of anger.

This just made her determined to change his mind. "I should ask the same of you," she said lightly. "What I'm doing is behaving in a low-key manner. It's what people in my family are required to do. Didn't my uncle explain this?"

"Your uncle is John Sage?" he asked in a gruff voice. It was a wholly appealing voice. Strong. That was the first word she thought of. His arms were crossed over his chest. His lips were set. Kind of full, actually. He had a crease in his chin and lines on his forehead. His hair was cut so short as to be practically shaved off. It gave him a sexy, naked look. And she, with all her long hair—well, he was such a contrast to her.

"Yes, I'm Isabel Sage." She snapped out of her distraction and gave him her winsome smile. People usually responded favorably to it.

He, however, did not. He just scowled harder at her. "We need to get going. Friday traffic is brutal."

Brutal? Were people going to jump out at them with knives and swords drawn?

She laughed at the image, and then exhaled, letting her smile relax into a normal expression. It felt good, for a change.

"May I check your credentials, please, Mr. Ross?" she asked calmly. "If I'm to get in a car with you, then I need to be sure I'm safe."

His expression stilled. Well, she didn't move, either, because her request was perfectly valid. He reached into a front coat pocket and pulled out a badge for her.

It appeared he really did currently work for the U.S. Secret Service. She stared at the star on his badge, amazed.

"May I see your driver's license as well, please?" she asked.

He seemed to stare her down. She felt a catch in her throat, but no, she had a stony business face she could give him, as well. She was a master at pretending—the more so since her stay in America.

"I always check credentials," she murmured.

With a slight exhale, he reached for his wallet, removing a card, which he handed to her.

She took it. The plastic was still warm from being in his back pocket, close to his, well… She willed herself not to blush. He was a good-looking man, beneath all his gruffness. And anger, too—there was definitely an undercurrent of anger in there.

She glanced up at him from beneath her eyelashes, but he was looking away from her. Checking in all directions, like a working bodyguard.

She studied his identification card, which was a New York State driver's license. Jacob Ross. New York City. A West Side address. A November birthday. He was two years older than her—early thirties—and he was five feet eleven inches tall.

"Everything copacetic?" he said in a somewhat testy voice.

"Lovely, Jacob." She smiled tersely and passed him back his identification card. She was used to "testy" men—the trait seemed to run in her family. He didn't scare her one bit. "Please don't take it personally. I'm trained to be careful."

"Any other questions?" he asked. It was…interesting how everything he was feeling showed in his face, his voice, his posture. He hid nothing from her. He had a smoldering intensity that was completely unnerving, like she had never seen before.

And right now, it was very clear that he didn't approve of her. She felt a twinge just realizing it.

Ah, well, she would work to change his opinion. But first, the most important thing was to help him understand that she needed him to accompany her to the street discreetly, as if he was a friend here to visit her, rather than a paid bodyguard.

"If you don't mind, I'd prefer that when we go out there again, you take care not to appear to be my driver," she said as pleasantly as she could. "And I'd prefer to sit up front in your car, in case anyone is watching us out the window."

"That isn't protocol," he snapped.

"It's *my* protocol." She smiled at him. "I'm sure you won't mind."

"I do mind, actually."

She didn't know what to say. His response was just rude.

They were silent for a moment, sizing each other up. He had the advantage with his dark sunglasses. But she was no lightweight either—she could handle anything.

"Look," he said finally, "it's not personal. I'm

trained not to talk to or be familiar with my protectees. But I've got to say something."

She folded her arms over her chest. "Yes, I'm listening."

He glanced around her room. "Why are they letting you live here? This place is a security nightmare. I would never let my protectees stay here. See that window?" He pointed. "It's sniper bait. And this building only has one way in and one way out. With your money and your profile, you should be living in the Ritz-Carlton. Has anyone ever told you that?"

"That would go over well in my study groups, Mr. Ross," she said calmly. "I'm surprised you don't see the danger in your suggestion."

Jacob's mouth opened and then closed.

She stood patiently. Waiting. From this position, she could see the corners of his eyes behind those dark glasses. He was gazing at her warily. His expressive eyes were a clear blue, as intense as he was. As if he had a hidden banked fire, burning within.

He expelled a breath. "Like I said, it's my training." He placed his hands on her shoulders and gingerly moved her away from the open window. "It's what I do."

Then he walked over and lowered the blinds. "I get people door to door safely. That's what you can expect from me this weekend. Nothing more. Nothing less."

This was an interesting situation for her. Maybe she should consider it another of her tests, the steps she'd been taking in working toward becoming the leader of her family's personal-care products business.

At least she didn't have to *pretend* with him.

"Can you do so and still act low-key?" she asked, rubbing her arms. "You know, not broadcast that the person you're with—me—finds it necessary to hire a bodyguard just to drive a few hours, the way most people do every day as a matter of course?"

"You're not most people, Ms. Sage," he said between his teeth. "You know this, don't you?"

He *could* be a big problem to her. Rajesh was right—Jacob, in his intensity, stuck out. He also didn't care that he stuck out.

She cleared her throat. "What *I* do is stay low-key, Mr. Ross. You've heard the phrase 'fly beneath the radar'?"

His frown intensified.

"*That's* what we need to do today."

He didn't seem convinced. "You don't know all the bad things that can happen to a person," he said in a low voice.

She didn't like to hear this kind of talk. "Do you feel uncomfortable with this job the way I'm describing it?" she asked bluntly.

He nodded. "Yes, I have to admit that I do. Your

safety is my highest concern. We can't just waltz out there and—"

"Would you feel better if we canceled altogether?"

His brows flew up. "No, not at all."

Still looking flustered, he removed his sunglasses. Held them out to her, and then placed them on her dresser. "Okay, fine. Against my better judgment, we'll do it your way. Here, look…"

He took off his suit jacket, shook it out and folded it. "I'm not a Secret Service agent anymore. I'm just your friendly limo driver. Satisfied?"

But that only accentuated the gun and the handcuffs at his waist. He looked so flustered at the realization that she had to smile.

She placed her hand to her mouth to cover it, but it didn't stop her feeling from coming out.

He gazed helplessly at her. Without the glasses on, his eyes were so blue…a naked blue, with naked, desperate emotion shining within.

"It isn't funny," he said.

"No, I suppose it isn't. I was just wondering what you're like when you're not on the job. Though I suppose you're never *not* on the job, are you?"

Wordlessly, he shook his head. Beneath his gruff surface, he seemed…barren and bleak and out of his element.

Maybe she had completely misread him.

"This is what we'll do," she decided. "I'll walk

downstairs with you to the car. I won't touch your arm—your gun hand will be free. It's all right, you can put your jacket on if you'd like. But I really would be more comfortable without the sunglasses. Can you live with that?"

"Sounds reasonable." Sheepishly, he shrugged his arms into the jacket. "You're lucky. Usually we carry a radio, too. Sometimes an earpiece."

"Then I'm glad I'm a CEO-in-the-making, and not a head of state under your protection."

He smiled the barest hint of a smile, and then glanced at her again. He seemed to be seeing her through a new perspective.

It pleased her. She wanted him to know that she had big dreams she was acting on. It was the reason she put herself through this loneliness in New York. To her, her goals were important, even if she sometimes needed to play down who she was in order to succeed with the people she lived and worked amongst.

"I behave discreetly," she explained, "because I need to make a good impression on my classmates. I need this degree in order to be successful in my uncle's—in my family's—company and this is the simplest way to achieve it. If I walked about telling people who I am, open about the fact of who we are, it could be a problem. People react to my family in strange ways, Mr. Ross. Some are angry or envious.

Some think about the favors they might gain if they befriend us. It's akin to winning the lottery, you see. You can only really trust the people you knew before you hit it big, and even then, money changes people."

It was the most she'd ever spoken on the topic, the most honest she'd been since she'd arrived in New York.

She bit her lip, surprised at herself. Jacob was outwardly staring, saying nothing.

"Are you sure you want to make this trip with me?" she asked. "It might be a long three days."

"Let's get you there," he said quickly, as if he was afraid she'd change her mind. "Let *me* get you there."

She felt a surprising tug of warmth. "All right." She gestured to her bed. "Let me just get my case."

"Your case?" he asked, even though he was plainly looking at her case lying shut on the coverlet.

She sighed. She was forever making mistakes—it was the small things that tripped her up most, betraying what she tried to keep hidden. She just couldn't let people know who she was, not really.

Then again, Jacob had a pretty good idea already, just by virtue of the job he was assigned. She wouldn't have to be on guard quite so much with him. It was a relief, actually.

She picked up the case. "Sorry, I meant to say *suitcase*." She put it down on the floor, extending the handle. "Are you ready for our weekend adventure, Mr. Ross?"

He looked at her as if he wasn't quite sure.

CHAPTER TWO

SHE HAD SURPRISED HIM.

Isabel Sage wasn't anything like Jacob had expected. Oh, on the surface she looked just like the photo Lee had sent him. Poised and put together. With her long blond hair, her list of accomplishments and that smiling expression, she appeared the consummate Golden Girl. Until he'd actually met her, he would have thought her a spokesmodel. Or a newscaster. Maybe a television personality.

Even a fresh-faced, though privileged, girl next door.

But beneath the surface, she was something else. An heiress to an industrialist's fortune? Nope, he never would have guessed that. He interacted with people from that background every day, and Ms. Sage was unique because she didn't display an entitled attitude.

Instead, she was accommodating. Pleasing. Appealing.

He couldn't let her too close to him—though he understood why she was asking him to treat her the way she was. He was starting to respect that she had a legitimate strategy, flying under the radar as she was. Maybe he could handle her sitting up front with him, at least until they left Manhattan.

"We'll switch out the seating arrangement once we're out of the city," he said to her, taking the handle of her suitcase. "When no one can see us, you can go back to sitting behind the partition."

Ms. Sage said nothing. Her expression was set in that accommodating smile again, that really said very little.

He just couldn't stop staring at her. He knew he should move faster, but he was stuck, one hand resting on the doorknob, the other gripping her suitcase.

And then a call came in to her cell phone.

She looked blankly at him.

He shook his head slightly. *Don't. Don't pick up,* he willed her. *We need to get going.*

But she was already glancing at the screen. Not much passed her face in terms of emotion. This woman would make a great poker player.

"Excuse me." She turned her back to Jacob. Spoke in low tones into the cell phone. No longer the American accent she probably used to blend in but a sweet lilt to her words that he clearly recognized as Scottish.

Her voice struck a chord in him, deep inside. Made him feel centered in a way he hadn't expected to feel in her presence.

Mentally shaking himself, he focused on what

she was saying. Obviously, she knew the caller. Her voice had risen in surprise.

"Where are you?" she asked the caller. "Don't worry, I know it's confusing. Please stay put, I'll come to you instead."

Oh, no. *Walkabout,* he automatically thought. His Secret Service team's expression for dignitaries who suddenly went off script, necessitating a massive operational response to accommodate the protectee's whims.

As Jacob went rigid, his hand automatically moving to a radio at his belt that wasn't there because this was an unofficial operation, she was fumbling at her desk for a pen, holding the cheap plastic cap between her teeth as she scribbled.

"No, it's not a problem about being lost," she said. "Yes, I can find you." Laughter seemed to flutter from her lips. "Actually, I'm just thankful that you're here. You have no idea. God, how I've missed you."

What the hell?

She turned to look at Jacob, but he just gripped her suitcase handle tighter.

"Change of plans," she said lightly to him as she pocketed her cell phone. "It was a pleasure to meet you, Jacob, but...er, we won't be needing your services after all."

We? Who'd been on the phone? A boyfriend?

"Ma'am," Jacob said by rote, and then stopped, remembering. This wasn't a regular assignment. All his training was out the window as far as Ms. Sage was concerned.

He sighed, swiping his hand over his forehead. She was going through the clothes in her closet, shuffling through hangers.

"Ah, Isabel, why don't you tell me what's going on so that I can help, too."

"That was my boyfriend." Her cheeks were flushed and rosy. "I'm sorry, Jacob. I know this is unexpected and I'm as surprised as you are, but we really don't need you to drive us to Vermont."

"What? What are you talking about? What's changed?"

"Alex dislikes security. He…especially dislikes guns…." She glanced at Jacob's midriff, letting the sentence fade away.

Instinctively he covered his service weapon. There was no way he could lose this assignment. "Where is this Alex?" he barked. Jacob disliked the guy already.

At the tone of his voice, Ms. Sage froze, kneeling, a dress in her hand, in the midst of unzipping the upright suitcase he still held so she could stuff it inside.

"I'm sorry," he said, unhanding her suitcase and stepping back. *Watch the intensity.* He couldn't just order this woman around. He had no authority over her. She could fire him at any time, and it appeared she just had.

And oh, cripes, he needed this assignment. The

simple truth was he needed her more than she needed him. She had little use for him, in fact.

He eyed the clothing she was adding to her luggage. "Are you still going to Vermont?" he asked in a calmer voice.

"Yes," she said, zipping the suitcase again. "I realized I forgot an outfit. In any event, Alex and I will handle the logistics of getting there, thank you."

"At least let me drive you to him," he said. Wherever this Alex was, they could all discuss it there. Jacob would prevail. He had to.

One advantage was that Alex apparently didn't know enough to get himself a cab. And it appeared he was calling Isabel on a borrowed cell phone.

He looked at Isabel, but she was shaking her head. "No, really, I'll call a taxi and—"

A knock sounded on her door. Inwardly, Jacob groaned again—nothing about this day was going right—but he did his job and opened the door before she could.

The short young man—mid to late twenties—with horn-rimmed glasses and spiked hair stood in her doorway. The one with the Che Guevara T-shirt.

Really? Really? Jacob thought.

"I didn't get to say hello to your boyfriend," Che Guevara said to Isabel. He peered at Jacob and stuck out his hand.

"And you are?" Jacob said, squeezing Che's hand hard, playing this for all it was worth. If he got Ms.

Sage tangled up in her own lies, then she couldn't dismiss him so easily.

"I'm Charles. I'm Isabel's economics partner." He winced and shook out his hand.

Isabel hastened to intervene. This time she just looked confused about her backfired plans. "Charles, thanks for stopping by. I, ah, sent the document to your email already."

Jacob noted that her voice once again held no trace of a Scottish accent.

"I got it," Charles said. "Have a good weekend." He left them.

"How is it that he's a business student and yet is wearing a Che Guevara shirt?" Jacob asked her. "Doesn't he know Che was a Communist?"

A terrorist, too, if you asked him, but he wouldn't scare Isabel by using that word.

Isabel closed the door and smiled tightly at him. "Charles is a genius at economics. His father is an investment banker, and Charles will probably work with his firm, too, someday. Think of it as him trying to express his rebel side while he still can."

Everybody was fooling somebody, it seemed. Without asking, Jacob picked up her suitcase. The good thing about Charles's visit was that Isabel had dropped all talk about not needing him to drive her across the city to pick up her boyfriend.

As he held the door for her, Isabel smiled tremulously. He gave her a halfhearted smile of his own. Already he'd ratcheted down his intensity.

His intensity. He didn't know why he'd thought of that.

Just…damn. What was happening to him?

OH, WHAT A tangled web we weave.…

Isabel's head was reeling. Never in a million years had she expected Alex to show up for the wedding. This changed everything. Now, she looked forward to the weekend—she'd added a dress because maybe they could go out to a romantic dinner alone.

His presence also solved her immediate problem of needing to make a good impression on her uncle. Malcolm had the advantage this weekend because it was his wedding, but Isabel couldn't sit back, either.

Unfortunately, Jacob needed to leave.

She glanced at him. His brows were knit as he searched the storefronts for the Starbucks where Alex waited. Poor Alex. He'd asked the taxi driver at Kennedy airport to take him to her university, but the driver had dropped him at the wrong one. There were so many in Manhattan.

Jacob pulled the black SUV alongside the storefront with its familiar green logo. He didn't seem too concerned, however. She unbuckled her seat belt as he turned to her.

"I'll wait here for you." He gave her an earnest look she hadn't seen in his expression before.

"No, please, we're fine. Thank you for the ride."

"I'm not leaving you, Isabel."

He had that steadfast look to his gaze, the one she was starting to recognize. It was refreshing, actually. Nice to think there was someone in this big, foreign city that she could count on.

However, she had Alex to pick up the slack from here. And Alex was waiting inside the coffee shop.

She opened the door and stepped onto the city street. Huddling beneath her jacket collar, she wrapped her scarf around her neck and went to the boot of his car. With her knuckles, she rapped on it.

Jacob rolled down his window.

"My suitcase, please," she said.

There was only the slightest hesitation, but Jacob got out of the SUV and walked round to the back, too. With a click of his key ring the back hatch popped open. He retrieved her small case, extended the handle and placed it on the pavement.

She reached for it but his low voice stopped her. "I'll wait here for you until I know that you're safe."

She made the mistake of looking up into his eyes. So intense, they seemed to burn, but not in a frightening way—in a way that she'd always yearned for.

Her breath sucked in, and for that split second,

her fingers shook on the handle. But it wasn't real, it was silly, and she broke eye contact.

Inside the coffee shop was Alex. Her true boy-friend.

Her heart gave a small leap. Alex had been with her from the beginning. He'd known her before the craziness with her family had happened. He'd been her wee mate, the boy next door. He'd been her first kiss. Her first love. Her only lover. This separation—her time in New York and Alex's time in Scotland—was only short-term. They'd made an agreement—a logical pact—no matter how temporarily lonely and painful it had been for her. But he'd been showing her respect by yielding to her desires and letting her know that she was important, too. It wasn't only his goals that mattered—hers did, too.

And so they'd had their months physically apart. Four consecutive terms—semesters, the Americans called them—for her, and for Alex, his intense training assignment. Their separation was almost over.... Next month was Christmas and then she would be home.

He'd surprised her with his phone call. Though, if anyone knew how important, how fraught with emotion Malcolm's wedding was to her, it was Alex.

She stopped in the doorway of the coffee shop, searching him out. When she saw his familiar face across the room, she felt tears spring to her eyes. She hurried to him, the suitcase trolley wheels bouncing across the tiled floor.

Alex seemed gaunt. Thinner than usual. Three months since she'd physically seen him, and he looked…

When he saw her his mouth twisted in a frown.

She paused, confused. "Alex, I…"

He stood awkwardly, scraping the floor with his chair. It sounded like claws on a blackboard.

And then he looked at her suitcase, and then at her. He was genuinely bewildered. "Why do you have a case with you?"

Her heart sank, which should have told her something, but she didn't want to listen to it. "It's Malcolm's wedding. You're coming with me to Malcolm's wedding this weekend. That's why you surprised me…?"

His face had fallen.

Her voice wavered. "Isn't it?"

After a long moment of him standing, staring at his shoes, and her trying to breathe through the lump of emotion that had lodged in her chest, he finally said, "Sit down, Bell. We need to talk."

JACOB MANAGED THE miracle of finding a place to park the black SUV on the street. He slammed the door and headed for the coffee shop Isabel had entered.

Somehow, he had to convince these two to let him drive them both to Vermont. If Jacob didn't have a legitimate reason to get to Vermont, then he wouldn't have an opportunity to meet John Sage. That was unacceptable.

Inside, the familiar aroma of coffee hit him. Expensive coffee, five-bucks-a-cup coffee, the kind he couldn't really afford but still found himself wanting anyway.

About a dozen patrons sat alone at tables, staring into screens. Two attendants were behind the counter—one at the register and one loudly frothing milk at an espresso machine. Jacob noted that the bathrooms were in the rear of the shop. There was just one exit that he could see. And Isabel was...

His heart softened. She stood with her side to him, one of the ends of her long wool scarf brushing the floor. She seemed to be...drooping.

He knew her enough by now to know that something was wrong.

Oh, hell. He didn't want to feel sorry for her. She was just a means to an end.

Moving silently, he slid into a seat at the table near her, close enough to see and hear her conversation. He took out his smartphone, put on a headset and pretended to be inside the cocoon of his own digital world, like most people. But he wasn't. He was listening to Isabel and her boyfriend.

Jacob had already pegged the guy. Slouching. Nervous. Didn't meet her eye. Maybe Jacob would check into him later. For now, Jacob was just watching them. Doing what he was trained to do.

He sat with his back to the wall, keeping track of the situation. Who came into the shop, who went out. Checking for anyone obviously carrying weapons. Yes, it was New York, and certain things were illegal here, but that didn't stop tragedies from happening.

"I haven't talked with someone from home in so long, you've no idea how brilliant it is to see you," Isabel Sage was saying to the boyfriend. *Alex.* She had that faint, alert smile on her face, her protective mask.

Jacob was beginning to understand this about her. Whatever thoughts or emotions she felt, she rarely showed them. What he'd first mistaken for privilege—and he should know better than to underestimate anyone—may just have been a damn good survival mechanism.

"Bell, I've come all this way to see you…because, er, it's better to say certain things in person," Alex was stuttering.

Jacob watched without moving his head so as not to alert them. "Of course it's been a difficult separation for us," Isabel said. Her mask was on tight.

"Please sit. You're making me nervous." Alex leaned back in his chair. The guy hadn't gotten her a coffee. Hadn't even pulled the chair out for her. Jacob had to keep from snorting his disgust.

Jacob wasn't sure what Isabel was thinking, but

he could imagine. She seated herself in a graceful motion and quietly folded her hands.

Alex coughed. "You've been quite busy in New York these months."

"Yes, and when I return to Scotland for Christmas, we'll have more time for each other," she said brightly.

"I've been quite busy in Edinburgh, as well…" Alex's cheeks flushed. He let his voice trail off.

Isabel licked her lips and smiled even harder. "I'm pleased to see you, Alex. I'm glad you're here, really. You have no idea how much I've missed—"

"I've come because I'm breaking up with you, Bell," Alex said abruptly.

Jacob's heart slowed. *Damn.* He'd been dreading this even though the conversation had been taking this direction and he wasn't surprised at the outcome. He glanced at Isabel.

Still with her composed mask. Wow, she was disciplined. "Pardon me?" she asked Alex. Her voice quivered slightly.

"I can't live in this state of affairs any longer," Alex muttered.

A small line appeared in Isabel's forehead. "I see. Well, my schooling here is temporary. I'll be home soon."

"Yes, I know. And then you'll be running your uncle's company. You won't need me anymore."

"It's…not guaranteed yet," Isabel said. "He required that I come here—that's why I'm in New York studying finance, why I have to be away from home." She lowered her voice. "You know this. You alone know the stress and the pressure I'm under. Like no other person on earth, you *know* me."

Jacob saw the tiny fissure in her mask. The signs of tension breaking through. He leaned closer. He'd given up the pretense of paying attention to the phone in his hand.

"Bell," Alex said, "the point is there are brighter pastures for you out there. This…friendship between us…isn't meant to be any longer."

"Of course it is! And don't you believe we have more than a friendship?"

Alex sat back. "I want out," he said flatly.

Her face pale, Isabel pressed forward. "What if we…gave ourselves a break for now? After I'm home, we'll start fresh with a conversation then."

"I want to be friends with you," Alex said. "Just friends. That's all that I want."

She took a deep breath. Jacob wasn't sure she was getting what the guy was telling her. "I understand you're angry with me," she said to Alex.

"I'm not angry, Bell."

"You…want more of my attention."

"No. I'm ending it with you."

"But that's…daft," she said, her voice getting even softer. "We've been together since we were children."

"We were never together. Not truly. I don't expect

you to understand. I didn't understand myself until recently. But…oh, bollocks. I didn't want to tell you this way, but…I'll just say it. I've met somebody, all right?"

"You…met somebody?" she repeated. Jacob waited for light to dawn. Or maybe she was just controlling her emotions as best she could.

"I'm seeing this woman," Alex said. He spoke softly, his head down, staring at the table. Jacob felt himself heating inside. "I tried, Bell. I tried to make this work with us. But you're meant for other things."

"Alex, let's go back to my flat. I'll introduce you to my mates. You'll…be part of my life here."

"See. Look at you. Any other woman who'd just been told that her man was seeing someone else would be furious. Or perhaps hurt. But you don't *feel* like other women, Bell. It's not natural."

Isabel crossed her arms. "I assure you, I feel. Very much. And right now I feel…I feel that we can fix this temporary rift." She smiled bravely. "If we both want to."

Alex glanced at his watch. "I have to go. I flew all the way here just so I could tell you in person. I'm not a bad bloke. I'm not breaking up by text message."

"Alex—"

"Do I have to say it, Bell? Fine, you've made me say it." Alex stared hard at the table. "I'm in love with her."

Isabel's mask split then. Wide open. Her look of anguish hit Jacob with a jolt.

"I didn't mean for it to happen, but it did," Alex said. "I asked her to marry me and she said yes. We're planning a small wedding in June, at home."

The pain on Isabel's face touched Jacob. Her lips quivered. Her eyes watered. She seemed to be struggling to breathe.

But Jacob gave her credit. Because with a grit of her teeth and a fierce blink of her eyes, she controlled herself again. He could see the effort it took her to swallow the hurt, but she did. Bravely, she found her mask and put it on again.

By the time Alex—now Alex the ex—glanced up from his escape into checking his phone messages, Isabel was composed again. Her slip had been brief, and Jacob was sure he was the only person who'd seen it. Alex the ex certainly hadn't.

"You're handling this well." Alex gave her a relieved smile. Unlike Isabel, he showed all his emotions on his face, in his vocal inflection, in his posture. "I knew you would, Bell. You handle everything like a champ."

Alex coughed and stood. "Well, that's sorted then. The meter's running on my taxi. I have to go. But you'll do well, I know you." He had the temerity to smile at her in relief. "Look at you. Not a tear. Never a worry with you. That's why I'm sure you'll run your uncle's company someday. Isabel Sage, CEO of Sage Family Products. No doubt you'll be the one chosen."

And then Alex leaned in and gave Isabel a bloke's awkward fake-hug. Alex wasn't even looking at her, not really. She kept her composure, and Jacob gave her credit for that. In her shoes, Jacob would have wound up and slugged the guy.

No, he wouldn't have.

When it had happened to him, Jacob hadn't slugged anybody. He'd stood stoically by while his ex had given him much the same kind of speech as Alex.

You know what your problem is, Jacob? You're too intense. No one could live with that level of intensity every day.

Jacob got up from the table and shoved his phone into his pocket. He hadn't thought about this stuff in years and years. And he wasn't going to think about it again.

Isabel. Now that Alex was out the door and on the sidewalk, about to be whisked away by his cab with the running meter, Isabel was left alone. Thinking that no one was watching, she put her hand to her mouth. Jacob knew that no one—not one human on earth—could fake their feelings for too long, and Isabel Sage was definitely human. Her mask had crumpled, her face was turning green and she looked as if she was going to lose it.

Thinking fast, Jacob grabbed a pile of napkins from the counter and followed her.

She was running—stumbling, really—for the ladies' room. This being New York City, no one seemed to notice. She could have stripped naked and belted out a breakup song at the top of her lungs with a full orchestra supporting her, and no one would have given her a second look.

He really needed to get the hell out of New York someday. God, he was trying. If not for that damn psychologist, he'd be in Washington, D.C., already, doing what he was meant to do.

But for now, it just made him angry, seeing people hurt unnecessarily—especially a kind person like Isabel.

She vomited all over the floor. With a mortified cry, she covered her mouth and ran into the bathroom. Jacob watched the door swing shut behind her.

The place was buzzing now. A typical midtown Manhattan coffee shop—short on space, long on people. But nobody was looking at him, or at Isabel. Most people had bent heads, staring at screens. Big screens, small screens, it didn't matter. They walked while staring at screens, the thumb that held the phone swiping away. It was amazing what most people missed in their daily lives.

Jacob didn't miss anything. Life came at him, smacking him square in the face. Emotions were his gut instincts, the way he made his decisions in the world. And what he felt for her was empathy.

The bathroom was tucked in a back corner. A yellow plastic bucket filled with water and a ragged mop was leaning against the wall nearby. Jacob quietly took the mop and cleaned up the floor. He also saw a yellow plastic tent, used by the cleaners, to block off foot traffic over wet floors, so he took that closed sign and unobtrusively placed it in front of the ladies' room where Isabel had disappeared.

He stood back and waited. Minutes passed. A woman came around the corner to use the facilities. She walked right past his closed sign. She addressed Jacob, still blocking the door, as if he worked there. "Is someone in there?" she asked.

"Sorry," Jacob said. "My girlfriend is sick inside." He gestured to the men's room. "No one is using that one. I'll watch the door for you if you want."

She smiled at him. "Thanks." She went inside.

He crossed his arms and stood sentinel for Isabel. He would stand there all day if he had to.

It was a long time before she came out of that bathroom. From where he stood, she seemed miserable and stunned, not altogether aware of her surroundings. Her eyes were red, as if she'd been crying her heart out, and she had nothing left but limp muscles to carry her home. As she walked past a table, she bumped it.

She'd forgotten her suitcase, so he backtracked to

retrieve it. Then he hurried ahead and clasped her by the elbow, steering her safely outside.

Once on the sidewalk, she tripped along, into the stiff wind that was whipping down Fifth Avenue. Her arms were folded over her chest, her too-high heels making her falter.

Jacob felt for her, he really did. Whereas before she'd seemed strong and confident, now she showed her inner fragility. Alex was long gone, back to his carefree life without her, no doubt.

Jacob pressed his hands into fists. Still, he did his job—head swiveling, aware of every person who moved into their zone—front, back, left, right, up on the building roofs, down below the subway grates, a cab that rolled past too slowly.

This woman he guarded was a Sage, a niece of the richest man in Scotland—one of the richest men in the world—so what was she doing, alone in a foreign city like this? Especially given her family history with a kidnapping, had she never considered her vulnerability?

Isabel stopped at the street corner, her bag dropping from her shoulder. Jacob stayed within arm's length of her elbow, one eye on her and one eye on a man who was nosing too close to her. With a shake of his head, Jacob put his hand on his gun and shifted his jacket aside to display it. The man saw the service revolver and took a step sideways, then kept on walking.

Jacob glanced to Isabel, saw the pain on her face. Maybe since nobody was watching her, to her mind, she could let her feelings out. He alone saw this.

He sucked in his breath. What the hell was happening to him? A crush, on a protectee? For the past half hour, he'd entirely forgotten his true mission.

The most important thing he needed to do was to get Isabel Sage to that Vermont inn. Feeling anything for her—even empathy—wasn't on the agenda.

Time to toughen up. Time to switch up his tactics.

CHAPTER THREE

ALL ISABEL WANTED was to lie curled up on her bed and sob. She hadn't seen this breakup coming.

Alex and she had always had an understanding between them. Perhaps she didn't express her feelings the way other people did, as he had just accused her of, but Alex had always been like that, too.

Like *her.* For their entire lives, he'd not only understood her when she'd perhaps put their relationship on the back burner because she'd needed to work on her career goals, but he'd shared these rules of living, too.

Above all, you never want to give away your power. Show the world your strength, never your weakness. If people cannot see your true emotions, then they cannot see how you really feel, and thus they cannot hurt you.

Her dad had taught her that, when she was still a wee girl. And Alex—such a frequent visitor to her house that, to her dad, he was like one of Isabel's brothers—had grown up believing it, as well.

So what had just happened?

She didn't understand. Maybe she never would. All she knew was that Alex's betrayal had *hurt*.

She wiped her wet eyes with the heel of her hand. She'd cleaned herself up as best she could in that WC—had washed her face and had reapplied all her makeup—but despite her best efforts, the tears kept leaking.

She reached for a tissue in her handbag, sitting in the foot well of the vehicle. Somehow, in the fog of her shock and confusion, Jacob had managed to lead her back across busy city streets to where he'd parked the ridiculously big, black SUV.

Even now, the motor was running. His dark shades once again covered his eyes and his face was expressionless.

Good. That told her he hadn't heard what Alex had just said. Jacob was simply doing his job as her bodyguard, and quite capably minding his own business.

For once, she was grateful he had come.

Determined to behave in as composed a manner as he did, she returned the tissue to her handbag, unused. She would not conduct herself like her cousin Rhiannon. Poor, weak, gentle, delicate Rhiannon. Everybody in their family tiptoed around her. She was the opposite of Isabel.

Her uncle, her mother, her brothers and her cousins, they all expected Isabel to be perfectly capable—cheery, pleasant, put together, in charge, competent. She was reasonable, the one whom people looked to for direction. At the wedding, they would expect her to organize the disparate factions of the family into harmony. It was what she did.

It was what her father had loved and admired so much about her. The main reason he'd praised her and depended upon her the way he had.

Her tears started leaking again. She blinked them away. The pain was just too fresh. Too soon to get over and stuff inside her, the way she always did. She couldn't lie to everyone else about how she truly felt, not just yet.

She turned to Jacob. "Please take me back to my room."

Jacob sat, unmoving. The SUV remained in place.

"Please," Isabel said more forcefully than she'd intended.

Jacob's hand rested on the gearshift beside her. A large hand. Masculine. The opposite of Alex's lawyer hands, manicured and soft. Jacob's skin was rough, the nails bitten low. She sensed that he fought with these hands. He held weapons with these hands.

"Isabel, be reasonable," he said in a low voice. "You need to go to Vermont. You're expected there."

She held herself tighter around her midsection. He was right, but for some reason his words made her angry. The rough corduroy barn coat she'd worn for her adventure to New England was suddenly too much—she felt hot and suffocated. She couldn't fake a good mood or be reasonable right now.

"Take me to my room," she said, her voice rising.

"Isabel…" Jacob's voice turned gentler, the gruffness softened. It didn't match those rough hands.

She wiped a tear that had escaped. "Drive, I said!"

He obeyed. No words or excuses, he just checked the side window and then carefully pulled into the street.

Of course, a traffic light changed to red and they had to wait. A long, painful, silent wait. She stared at her hands clutched in her lap. Her mind was racing, and she couldn't stop it.

What if she *did* go to the wedding and she couldn't control her emotions? What if she cried or raged in front of everybody? Her uncle? Malcolm? Her cousins? What if they blamed her for him leaving? What if she'd made a mistake in coming forward to ask her uncle to be named CEO after him, instead of her cousin Malcolm, who, until now, had always been thought of as the heir apparent?

Scenarios flashed of her uncle shaking his head at her, while everyone else was happy and paired up, celebrating committed love, except her. Her mind was running ahead, wanting to think through everything all at once, needing to process the best way to salvage this situation. She just didn't see one.

Stay in New York for the weekend and compose herself, or go to Vermont and risk exposing herself? They were both potentially bad decisions for her, each with their downsides and risks. And if Jacob showed pity for her over this predicament she found herself in—that she'd made for herself—then she didn't know what she would do.

She might have to jump out of the SUV and walk back to her room on her own.

JACOB COULD NOT let Isabel go back to her room. No matter how bad he felt about making her attend that wedding, he needed to remain hard and professional. He needed Isabel to stay in the SUV so that he could drive her to Vermont and meet John Sage.

He glanced at her, pale and trembling in the seat beside him. This was killing him. She was upset, and she'd proven herself to be a woman who didn't normally get upset. She was mortified about losing her composure in front of him. He didn't like it, either. But in two minutes, they would be in front of her residence hall, and if he didn't do something fast, she would be out the door and gone before he had the chance to help himself.

He looked at her, one hand on the door. She *was* getting ready to bolt. He needed to convince her to stay. But he wasn't used to talking with those he protected. He was trained for the opposite, in fact.

He'd gently put her in the front seat with him rather than the rear seat, and that was bad enough.

His hand tightened on the wheel. He felt for her, he really did. He'd been in her shoes once. But he wasn't going to breathe a word of that.

At the next light, he drummed his fingers on the steering wheel. Now what? What could make her want to go to that wedding? If he could just get her to trust him to take her there. To trust that the best thing for her would be to stand tall. Screw the boyfriend.

"You're better off," he said abruptly.

She looked startled. "What?"

Damn. He hadn't meant to say that aloud. "Nothing."

"You *listened* to us back there?"

Damn again. Jacob scrubbed his hand over his head. "I had to be sure you were safe."

She looked even more upset with that explanation, so he changed course, even taking off his sunglasses in hopes of making the situation better. "I'll never say a word to anyone about what you say or do in my presence. Not even to the people who hired me."

He glanced at her. She was listening. She was open to him.

"Do you promise?" she asked in a low voice.

"Yes. Absolutely." He nodded. Here was a key to Isabel Sage—she didn't want anybody to know her private business. He got that.

He ran a hand across his mouth. What was it that Alex had said to her? *You'll run your uncle's company someday. No doubt you'll be the one chosen.* If Jacob had to bet, Isabel was in competition with her cousin. Malcolm, the groom. Her goal to be chosen as leader obviously meant a great deal to her.

"Here's what my instructions are," Jacob said. "The only thing I *have* to report to my dispatcher is if our plans change. In that case, I'll need to call in the updated itinerary." He stared steadily at her. "So if you decide not to go north, then I'll have to call and tell them you're not coming. From there, that information will immediately be reported to the employer—your uncle."

"Can you *please* not do that?" she whispered.

The plea seemed to pierce him directly in the breastbone.

"I'd just…rather make the phone calls myself," she said. Tears were leaking again.

This was horrible. He hated to see her cry.

"He's not worth it," Jacob snapped.

She blinked. His words had come out harsher than he'd intended. She turned in her seat, her expression telling him she was obviously going to stick up for the bastard ex-boyfriend.

"You don't understand!" she said with more passion than he'd given her credit for.

"I think I do understand. Your boyfriend showed up unannounced as if he were doing you a favor. He got you all happy to see him, and then he dumped you, right before you're scheduled to go and do something that's clearly important to your future, so now he's affected your ability to perform the way you need to. But he trots off anyway, feeling not only satisfied with himself, but as if he's a hero, when in reality he's the exact damn opposite."

Her mouth dropped open. "What planet do you come from? How can you assume all that?"

"I can assume it because it's true. Isn't it?"

"It's *not* all his fault."

"*You* feel guilty?" he demanded. *"You?"* Jacob's voice shook with anger he hadn't expected.

He was going to make this worse if he didn't calm down.

ISABEL DIDN'T KNOW *what* she was feeling. All she knew was that Jacob seemed furious on her behalf. It was…shocking.

And a wee bit flattering.

She bit her lip and stared at the red light—yet another one, Jacob seemed to be attracting each and every stop along their route—and tried not to look at him.

"How long were you two a couple?" His voice was so low she had to strain to hear him. "Were you engaged?"

Should she answer? He seemed as if he was on her side. He seemed…to intrinsically believe in her.

"Sort of," she whispered. "I mean…" She glanced at him. His eyes were warm and understanding. She really felt as though she could trust him.

But this was madness. She'd only just met him and

she was a Sage—she couldn't trust outsiders. This fact had been hammered into her head growing up.

"Please take me home, Jacob."

His jaw tightened. He stared harder at her.

"Take. Me. Home," she repeated.

He reached over and picked up his mobile phone from the console. "Right after I make the call to my dispatcher," he said, opening his contact list and scrolling through numbers.

No, he couldn't! She covered his phone with her hand. "Please!"

If he made that call to his boss, then his boss would call her uncle's people. She wouldn't be able to control how the problem was presented, or what the solution might be. She couldn't have that.

Jacob closed his eyes for a moment. He didn't seem to be enjoying this standoff between them, either.

She had to convince him to be her ally. God knew, she was tired of fighting all on her own. She needed *someone* to understand her and what she was going through. But she needed to proceed in a way that didn't tell him too much about herself. She had to be careful what she shared.

"I have a hard time because…I really can't trust anyone, Jacob. I'm not allowed to have confidants. New York is not my home. I have to watch myself… all the time."

"Most of the people that I work with and protect

feel the same way," he said gently. "Isabel, I drove a guy last month… Let's just say he's from a nation hostile to this country. But he's in town speaking to the United Nations, so my job was to protect him while he was visiting here. He doesn't trust anyone he meets, but he trusts us."

She chewed her lip. She wanted to believe him.

"You know why he trusts us?" Jacob asked. "Because we—people like me—we're discreet. We don't even tell agents from our other government bureaus if they ask. We can't, and we don't. Because if we did, we'd never be trusted by other protectees. I won't betray you, Isabel. I won't tell anyone what I heard or saw today. No matter who was to torture me, I would die with your secret."

It was so tempting to trust him. Oh, how she wanted to believe!

He waited, looking at her.

"I need to call my uncle first." She reached for her phone. "Then you may call your office."

Jacob closed his eyes. A horn sounded behind them—the light had changed, and they'd both been too occupied to notice. Jacob roared the SUV forward and pulled into an open spot before the curb, right in front of a fire hydrant. He set the gear into Park.

"May I," he started to ask, turning in his seat to face her, his voice shaking. "May I tell you what I think? About…*him?*" With an intense look, he leaned toward her. "My professional opinion of your ex-boyfriend?"

She was immensely curious about the intense feeling he had. The anger over what Alex had done.

It was *so* tempting. She dared to look into his eyes and nod.

"People don't just fall in love out of the blue," Jacob said. "They put themselves into situations. Over there, in Scotland, he put himself into a mindset where he was open to another woman."

She hadn't thought of it that way.

Jacob gazed into her eyes. It was like the heat of the sun, warming and comforting to her. "It *isn't* your fault, Isabel. It wasn't your fault that he strayed."

Jacob thought all that?

"But…that's not how it will look to other people," she said.

"Other people don't know the truth."

"Well…how does it look to you?"

"I see that you're incredibly strong." Jacob nodded to the university buildings beside them. "Look where you live, far from your home, in this big city, in a foreign country."

"It's not like I have a choice. Of course I have to be strong. I'm expected to be strong, and I am what I'm supposed to be. It's what I need to do."

He was silent, listening to her, so she continued explaining, sorting it out in her head as she talked. "I cannot fail here, Jacob. When we heard my uncle was getting ready to name a successor, I went to him and asked him to consider me. Even though I've worked in positions of responsibility throughout our different divisions, he replied that I wasn't qualified because I didn't have an advanced business degree or experience in international finance, like my cousin Malcolm.

"So I found the best, most prestigious program that I could, and I applied. They accepted me, and now I'm here, working as hard as I can with my end goal in mind. I have to be successful. If not, I'll never be chosen to run my family's company if I seem to fail in anything I do. And that includes managing my relationships. That's the way he looks at it. Cold and clinical. But I don't want to be that way, and—"

Wait a minute. She put her hand over her mouth. Was this even true?

And worse, why was she saying it aloud to him? She hadn't meant to tell Jacob anything private about her or her family. If Uncle John found out, he would be quite displeased.

JACOB HADN'T WANTED to like her or feel sympathy for her. This was the opposite of what he'd intended. He hadn't really wanted to get her talking and to understand her.

He knew her world was shattered. In his mind, she could never be a failure. Or cold, or clinical. But he could imagine how she felt now, after her breakup…

unanchored, mortified, upset. He understood why she wanted to go home and lick her wounds, but he couldn't let her. He needed to get her to go to Vermont with him. The only way he knew how to convince her was to continue to talk to her, which felt strange to him.

Secret Service agents were taught never to confide with their protectees. His training was working against him.

He rubbed his face with his hands, cold with sweat. He was so close to John Sage. Maybe if he'd had his backup team with him, including some female agents, it wouldn't be so difficult. Jacob wasn't used to working alone, especially with an attractive woman.

She was just so beautiful. That blond hair, those big blue eyes that brimmed with tears. So expressive, but only here with him. She hadn't cried in front of the boyfriend, and Jacob took some satisfaction from that.

Jacob flexed his hands on the wheel. He had no template to work with in this situation, so he was winging it. So far, nothing had worked in getting her to really trust him, and he knew why, because he remembered this feeling. Slammed upside the head by a lover's betrayal. Crushed in the heart, and in the most public of places.

"What are you thinking?" she asked, darting a glance at him nervously.

It had started to rain, so he'd turned on the wipers. They *thump-thump-thumped* against the window at regular intervals. He glanced in the mirror and saw his own expression. No poker face here. That's what she was reacting to—what *he* felt about her situation, not what she felt.

He got the impression that she was usually more in tune with what other people thought of her than with what she thought. To some extent, she was a people pleaser.

Maybe Rachel had been that way, too.

He leaned back and closed his eyes. "I was in your shoes once," he remarked. "I was just thinking about that."

He felt a change in her energy. The leather seat made a squeaking noise as she sat up straighter. Her eyes were boring into him; he could sense that, too.

"*You* were dumped?" she asked in a low voice. Anticipating. Wanting to hear more about it.

He inhaled deeply. *Danger zone.* He'd never even discussed this with Eddie. Not really. "That's not the point."

"Oh-ho!" She sat up straighter. "So it's okay for me to be crushed and for you to know every detail about it, but it's not okay for you?"

"Hey, I'm just your driver."

"Really? I don't see you driving me home the last few blocks like I asked."

He opened his eyes. "Is that what you want? To

give up? A successful woman like you? You don't think it will make it seem like you're hiding because you failed?"

She winced, defeated, as if he'd just kicked her to the curb. Honestly—he didn't know how to deal with her. She was actually pretty brave. From what he could see, she had big plans and was making a courageous, bold and disciplined journey to reach them, much like he was.

"Look," he said, "your main concern is that I not pass on what just happened to your uncle, right? Because you don't want him to think less of you for it. Am I close to the truth?"

"You're avoiding my question," she said softly.

"What question?"

"I want to know how *you* were dumped."

"What does that have to do with anything?"

"Everything. It's a power issue, Jacob."

"A…what?"

"If you know my deep dark secrets and I don't know yours, then we're not on equal footing. I never should have spoken so loudly inside that coffee shop."

"So…you're more concerned about being vulnerable than about losing the so-called love of your life? Interesting."

Her lip quivered.

Damn. "I'm sorry. I shouldn't have said that." Cripes, he was handling this all wrong.

He laid his head back and looked at the skylight. Watched the rain come down. The truth was, he just couldn't give anyone any more of himself. What was private with him, he kept locked away. He had to solve this standoff with Isabel some other way.

Abruptly, she opened the door and stepped out into the rain.

"Isabel?" he called. "Where are you going?"

"My luggage, please," she said, leaning into the open door. "I'm going to phone for another driver. You and I obviously can't work together any longer."

He threw open his door and got out of the SUV, then jogged around the front until he was beside her on the wet sidewalk. The rain was cold on his head and face. "You want me to talk? You want to know *how* I've been in your shoes?"

She nodded, gazing into his eyes. "I do."

They were both getting wet. Fat raindrops were spilling onto her cheeks. He wanted to brush them away.

"I…was supposed to get married," he said. "Instead, on our wedding day…she arrived late and made this little speech to everyone as if she were doing me a favor to have shown up to the altar at all."

"You were left at the altar?" she asked.

He focused on the raindrops running down her cheeks. One on her nose. Her top lip.

"Were people there?" she asked gently. Her tone was the musical Scottish voice he'd heard in the coffee shop. Her true accent. The voice she'd shown for Alex, and he hadn't cared about it.

"Jacob?"

"All of my friends were sitting in the church. My colleagues from the NYPD, their wives and girl-friends. My mother. My stepfather. My half siblings. My stepgrandmother and stepaunts."

She put her hand to her mouth. "How did you ever face them all afterward?"

He let out a breath, remembering. "For a long time, I didn't. I focused on getting into the Secret Service. I worked long hours so I could stay away."

Which probably wasn't helping him much now, but he didn't want to go into that.

"Bottom line, Isabel, don't let the bastards get you down. Don't give Alex the satisfaction of hav-ing the power to damage you. Because you're not damaged. You're strong and you're independent and you're doing the right thing with your life. Things don't happen by accident—he put himself into that situation where he was open, just as Rach—just as my ex did. And then blamed it on fate. On me. On whomever. On everybody but her…"

He caught himself. *Whoa.* Where was this com-ing from?

But Isabel's eyes were bright. And now her hand was on his arm. Just lightly. Not the way she'd hooked him back in her residence hall, but as though she were giving him comfort.

What was happening?

"I'm fine," he said. It seemed he was saying that so much lately, what with the psychologist at work and the—

"When did she leave you?" Isabel asked.

Because she was sincere, quiet and respectful, he let out a breath and answered her. "Five years ago."

"Have you been alone since then?"

Fix-ups didn't count, not really. He nodded. "I have goals. You have your goals, well, so do I."

She nodded, too, her eyes even brighter. "The thing that hurts most is that Alex knew what my goals were. We'd made an agreement. He was going to wait for me to come home." She fell silent.

"How long were you and Alex together?"

"He…was the boy next door," she said simply. "He knew me since…before everything. Before our family business took off, I mean. Before my father died…"

"It hit you out of left field, didn't it?"

"If that means it flummoxed me, then yes—yes, it did." She blinked rapidly.

"You don't have to put on a brave face for me," he said. "If you want to scream, go ahead."

"I never scream." She smiled brightly. "I don't believe in drama."

He did. Sometimes it was necessary.

"What did you do at that church with everyone looking at you?" she asked.

"Another story for another time."

"Did you vomit all over the floor in public?" Her lips twitched. She was going to laugh, and that was a good sign.

He smiled, too, sort of. "Let's just say that like you, I was in no good shape."

"What did you do to *get* in good shape?"

What she really was asking was, how could *she* get in good shape?

For purposes of getting her on the road to Vermont, he told her a partial truth. "I stopped by a liquor store, got a whole bunch of empty boxes and then drove back to our—to my apartment, and packed up everything she had. Clothes, makeup, cooking stuff—whatever, and I left it out in the hall. Then I had the locks changed."

Her eyes widened. "Did you ever hear from her again?"

In Jacob's experience, when people left him, they really left him. He felt cold for a moment, but shook it off. "Nope."

"She didn't come back to you? Tell you she'd made a mistake?"

"No." He looked at her. "Is that what you're hoping for?"

"Me?" She shook her head fiercely. "I have very few real friends, Jacob. Few people I can trust." She sighed. "You were right. He showed me his true colors."

She folded into herself. But Jacob knew that her heart was broken.

Jacob's heart had been broken, too. Worse than the embarrassment. Worse than the jealousy or the anger or the betrayal—it was the secret inner sadness, the empty pit of abandonment that nobody ever talked about. It was the stark reality at the end of the day, when you came back to your apartment and you were alone. Because the only people you'd trusted had taken your heart and tossed it away.

"Don't feel sad for me," Isabel said. "I've just decided I am going to this wedding. I'm going to show Malcolm that he still has a competitor for this job. He's not the shoe-in that everybody thinks he is."

She leaned over and kissed Jacob on the cheek. "Let's get back in the car and drive to Vermont, please." She smiled. "But I'm not sitting in the back. There's no need for that anymore."

As she turned and climbed inside, Jacob stood there in the rain, touching his cheek where she'd kissed him.

He should be happy. He'd gotten what he wanted from her—they were going north—but at the same time he'd lost something in the process, too. Some level of protection that she'd just stripped from him.

He wondered if he could get it back before it was too late.

CHAPTER FOUR

FLIPPING HER SEAT warmer to the highest setting, Isabel enjoyed the warmth that seeped into her bum. She sighed, wriggling her thighs and stretching her toes.

Thirty minutes outside New York City, past the congestion and stops, the drive was more freeing to her than she'd expected.

She felt mostly awe as the SUV hugged the curves of one of the massive motorways she'd read about. They passed the hugest lorries she'd ever seen, most of them left in their dust. Jacob roared at a steady clip in the left lane, usually the slow lane for her—but everything was flipped backward for her, with the driver on the left-hand side of the car.

This was a five-hour drive away from the rut, the loneliness, the stalled disappointment that her life had become.

She gazed through the sparkling clean glass. *Welcome, success.* From now on, everything would be new again, including her.

They threaded through some pretty parkways that would connect to another major route, Route 91 in

Connecticut, and then all the way north to Vermont. For too long, Isabel had been cooped up in the city, bound to her work. She had barely left her campus or residence hall, unless as part of her studies.

Two years ago, during student orientation, she'd been part of a group that had toured the stock market and watched the famous ringing of the bell, and another week, had walked through Central Park. She'd even toured the museums one rare Sunday.

But since classes had started, she'd never veered from the work it took to earn her degree. This was a fresh way to start over with a renewed attitude.

"How is it that you know your way around the countryside so easily?" she asked Jacob.

"This is Connecticut." He shrugged. "I have family here."

"You grew up here?"

He gave a tight nod. "I did."

Such a different world. A different life. They shared a common language, but the States seemed so much more complicated and larger than what she was used to.

Louder, faster, more crowded. Their course through Jacob's home territory changed to a gently rolling two-lane motorway with no lorries, only cars, and then again to a larger motorway. Jacob stayed in the left lane most of the drive north. He used a GPS, as she liked, though he kept the radio off. He drove carefully, not recklessly, but he didn't fear speed traps.

They saw several pulled-over motorists with police officers in cars, issuing tickets.

"Yeah, that's Connecticut," Jacob mentioned with a smile.

"We tend to follow the rules in Scotland. Nobody likes to get fined."

"That's not a problem I have very often, being in law enforcement," he replied.

She'd almost forgotten his profession. With each passing mile, rather than feeling anxious over going someplace new, someplace she was unsure how to act in, she felt calmer in his presence.

"There's a rest stop up ahead," he said. "I'm going to pull in. There are facilities and vending machines, but if you'd rather sit down to eat, there's a better place about an hour up the road."

"You know this route to Vermont well. Do you drive it often?"

He smiled slightly, as if to himself. "I haven't been in Vermont since college, on a ski weekend."

"We have skiing in Scotland, too," she remarked.

He glanced at her. Those two frown lines were between his eyes again. "Do you live in Edinburgh?"

Was he asking if she was a city girl? She did live in the city, but during this drive through Connecticut, seeing all the trees again and the rolling hills, she was getting a bit homesick for the country.

"I have a flat in Edinburgh. I work in the corporate headquarters for my family's company. But I grew up in the Highlands."

Near Inverness. She felt a stab of nostalgia for the deep blue lochs, the glens, the relative ease with which one could drive past castles from east to west, North Sea to Irish Sea.

Jacob was staring at her.

"How much longer until Vermont?" she asked politely.

He laughed. "We're not even in Massachusetts yet. We have two more state lines to cross."

She took it to mean they had a lot more time to spend together in their cocooned, rolling world. That made her smile. And she didn't have to fake it.

JACOB HAD PLANNED out the route already, days ago. He knew where each stop was that they would make. Nothing would be left to chance. This was how he worked, how he was trained.

And yet, he'd never had a protectee like Isabel.

She'd thrown him off balance yet again.

For one thing, she sat up front with him. For the past hour, she'd been toying with the satellite radio. She was putting on music that messed with his head. '70s on 7, the station was called.

All kinds of old pop music that had played in their apartment back when he was a kid—just him and his mom, together in New York City. Sometimes even years later, alone in the new house in Connecticut with Daniel—Jacob's stepdad—she would cry silently over those old songs when Daniel wasn't around. She never told Jacob why, but he didn't need to ask.

There were some things he wasn't ever supposed to ask. They only caused sadness and silence. Daniel was a calm, levelheaded guy. He hated conflict in the home, and Jacob's mom shared that aversion.

Jacob ran his hand through his hair. He was thinking all these things just because they were driving through the state where he'd lived in his teens. He'd learned every inch of this place like the back of his hand, but especially the tristate area: southern Connecticut, New York City metro and northern New Jersey.

They were traveling away from what he knew and toward the unknown—Isabel's family wedding.

There was still so much he didn't know about the Sage family. Normally, he would take the opportunity to quiz Isabel about her uncle, her cousins, the kidnapping—everything he needed to know for his job. Somehow, though, she had a tendency to answer him in such a way that *he* ended up being the one in emotional danger.

Just when he thought he had her figured out, she shocked him into realizing he was in completely new territory.

He glanced over at her. The woman was…well,

she was obviously beautiful, but it was her vulnerability that he found most interesting—the real Isabel, not the one who was so poised on the surface. He didn't know much about how most women thought—he'd only lived with Rachel for those few weeks—but watching Isabel in action, he'd been reminded of that bathroom drawer of makeup that he'd emptied once Rachel had decided to take up with her investment banker.

Isabel had fixed her smeared mascara back at their first rest stop. Brought in that huge bag of hers and had reemerged, poised again as if nothing had happened.

There was a lot she kept hidden behind the polite smile she showed the world. The crazy part was that he really did want to protect her. He wanted to keep her safe from ever crying again, especially over that idiot who'd flown in from Scotland just to dump her.

But at the same time, it would be reckless to forget she was the enemy of sorts.

She was part of the family he meant to discover more about, and without their knowing he was doing it or why. That would bring complications. He had to be careful. The only reason Isabel hadn't ditched him so far was that he'd been on his best behavior.

He scowled to himself. He wasn't usually so friendly and open to people, not by a long shot. He did his job with a minimum of words. Silent protection. And he did it well; nobody got hurt or killed on

his watch. He didn't accomplish that by being buddies with the VIPs.

But Isabel wanted Jacob to be pleasant, right along
with her.

"Will we be seeing some of that famous New England foliage?" she asked him as they passed north
into Massachusetts.

"No. I think we're too late for that."

"A pity. I regret that I never made time to see it.
It's supposed to be brilliant."

"Ah…" Jacob rarely made time, either. "The
leaves turn red and yellow in the city, as well, but
you're right, there's nothing like the vividness of the
mountains in Vermont and New Hampshire."

"Then I'll have to make plans for another year,
maybe." She smiled sleepily at him. "I'll have to
come back and do it right the next time I'm here."

He doubted she'd ever be back.

He let out a breath. She had a scent that filled his
SUV. Shampoo, or soap, or some kind of shower gel
that just…smelled good.

Made him want to move closer to her, though he
would never actually do it.

She had long limbs, too, long legs that filled the
bucket seat, crossed at the ankle of her tall leather
boots. She had slender fingers, the nails clipped
short, unpainted. He liked that.

As he glanced over at her, she toyed with a pen-
dant on a thin chain that hung over her turtleneck,

her eyes drifting closed. Long lashes lay against her cheek. She'd tied back her hair in a ponytail, and it rested against her shoulder, making her look relaxed and untroubled.

"Jacob?"

"Yeah?" He snapped back to reality. The road was lulling him. She was lulling him. Building a rapport with Isabel Sage wasn't on the agenda any longer, and it was time he shook that off.

All he needed was to get her safely to the inn and pass her to the bosom of her family. Then he could start phase two of his operation: arrange his meeting with John Sage.

"We're almost there," he mumbled.

"Could we please stop and eat dinner together first?" she asked. "I'm getting rather hungry."

He sighed. A reasonable request. "Yeah, sure, there's a good place just ahead."

A few minutes later, an hour away from their destination, he pulled the SUV into the dirt parking lot of a roadside restaurant.

Once inside, he ordered from the counter and brought back hamburgers, French fries, a root beer for him and bottled water for her—all to their booth in the back.

He was starving; the tantalizing smell of prime Angus beef and salty, deep-fried potatoes made his mouth water. He settled himself into the seat across from her and then bent his head and concentrated on the meal.

"Thanks for taking care of me today," she said softly, that gentle hint of Scotland back in her voice.

"Yeah, no problem," he said between bites.

"I've been thinking." She ran a finger around the edge of her French-fry carton, not meeting his gaze.

Please don't think.

"Are you being nice to me just because you're being paid to?" she asked.

Oh, hell. He put down his burger and wiped his mouth. "I'm not actually being paid, so…no, I don't think so."

She tilted her head at him. "*Why* aren't you being paid?"

He couldn't spook her. Had to maintain his cover. "Ah, because I'm doing a favor for my friend. Lee. He, ah, owns the security company."

"And *how* do you know this Lee?"

Great. He'd just opened Pandora's box.

Jacob crossed his arms and stared behind Isabel at the paneled wall and the old Orange Crush soda clock. "Lee was the team lead for my first few jobs in the Secret Service."

"And…?" she prodded. She could really be a sharp cookie when she wanted to be. "What do you owe him?"

"Nothing. We're friends—isn't that enough?" Jacob concentrated on pounding the bottom of the glass ketchup bottle. "If I like somebody, I'll do them a favor. No big deal."

"Do you find that you ever get hurt that way?"

"You know, I'm trying not to take this whole line of questioning personally because I know you just got burned pretty badly," he pointed out.

"Don't show *me* any favors. Do something because you want to, or don't do it at all. That's my new philosophy."

Where was this going? He raised an eyebrow at her. Maybe the breakup had affected her more than he realized. "Sure," Jacob said. "Will do."

"And I'll do the same. With you, I mean. Nothing phony or pretend between us."

He darted a gaze at her, but she was already staring at him. They both looked away. Then back again.

"Was Lee at your wedding?" she asked finally.

Whoa. He went very still.

But she didn't move, either. She just waited patiently. Jacob carefully ran a French fry through the pool of ketchup he'd managed to coax onto his plate. Her question surprised him, but he didn't feel so bad about answering. "I'm pretty sure Lee is the one who stayed and told everybody in the church to go home afterward."

"That's a good friend," she said admiringly.

"Yeah. He is." The details were kind of hazy at this point, though. "He did come back to my apartment later. I, ah, needed help with the bandages."

"The bandages?"

"I'd punched a few walls. One of them turned out to be brick."

She put her hand over her mouth. Her chest was moving up and down.

"Are you laughing at me?" he asked.

"Sorry." She giggled once, and it made her seem young. She giggled again and it was…well, it was the most interesting sound he'd heard in a while. He even felt his face splitting into a grin.

"This is so inappropriate, I know," she said between chortles. "But suddenly, I don't feel as bad about losing my breakfast in a coffee shop in midtown Manhattan."

"Are you going to eat that hamburger?" he asked, pointing at her plate. "Because if you don't, I will."

She broke into another fit of giggles, and then suddenly he was laughing, too.

Just…damn.

Back in the SUV, facing the road again, Jacob sobered. He couldn't forget that he was walking a fine line, so many fine lines.

Maybe that part about Lee had slipped out because of where they were headed. He and Isabel each had damn good reasons not to be keen on wedding celebrations.

He just felt gentle with her. In a sense, she was a kindred spirit, phase two of his operation or not.

"Thank you for telling me that story," she said

softly as she buckled her seat belt. "And thank you for being kind today."

"You think I'm kind?"

"You *are* kind," she said. And then she went back to fiddling with the radio.

Jacob was more often accused of being insensitive. Or aloof. *Intense* was Eddie's word. Jacob was pretty sure he got that from Rachel, who, now that he thought of it, had coined the term first. Eddie's wife, Donna, was the one who'd really latched on to it of late, though.

She hadn't been at Jacob's wedding—*almost* wedding—but Jacob was pretty sure that Eddie had told her the lurid details. Hence her obsession with fixing Jacob up.

Isabel had seemed to respond to his intensity. Maybe she had some natural intensity of her own deep inside her, dying to come out. Maybe it had taken the shock of Alex dumping her for it to escape through that protective surface of hers.

And Rachel… Until today, he hadn't thought of her in years. At this point, she was nothing to him. The thought of her stirred no feelings, one way or another. She'd been a drama queen—open and direct, the opposite of his mom. He'd mistaken *that* for intensity, and at the time, he'd craved it because it had been such a novelty to him—someone who wanted to pick everything apart and react expressively to it. After being brought up in a mostly silent home, where people tended to withdraw above all, it had been intensely appealing to find someone who thrived on emotion.

Jacob squinted to find the turnoff he needed. They were almost there.

Isabel stirred next to him. Stretched like a cat, totally not conscious of him. Comfortable in his presence.

And something about that just grabbed him and held on.

Don't, he told himself. *Let her be just a job.*

He reminded himself of that over and over during the rest of the drive.

THERE WAS SOMETHING wonderfully freeing about sitting next to a man whom she didn't need to give one fig about impressing. Isabel could put her head back on the seat. Let her hair down. Not worry that it was dark outside and the SUV's engine was lulling her to sleep.

She'd forgotten how freeing it was to be on the road for a long drive. In her fantasies she could get in a car and drive all day, just get away from her life.

It felt like being in a fairy tale with him, nothing close to her everyday reality.

"Knowing Me, Knowing You" by Abba was playing on the radio. She found herself singing along about breaking up never being easy. She put her hand over her mouth and broke into laughter again. That had sounded terrible.

"I don't care," she said aloud. She felt tired of needing to put on a good front. Tired of living for tomorrow. She just wanted to laugh and sing and feel better now. "Do you mind if I turn up the volume?" she asked Jacob.

"Go for it," he said.

She reached for the dial on the radio and bumped hands with him in the dark. Both of them gasped, sophisticated city dwellers that they were. "I bet you never had a client who sat in your front seat and sang Abba to you."

That earned her a smile. Lights from a passing car illuminated his face.

"Nope," he said to her, his gaze sliding sideways. "You're my first, that's for sure."

She could grow addicted to his smile. There was something special about earning one from a gruff man. He didn't give his smiles away like candy. He guarded and kept them. To earn one was a gift.

Jacob had really nice thighs. Maybe that was an odd thing to notice. But he had strength. Sometimes he turned his head, as if his neck felt stiff. It must be exhausting to be ever-vigilant. She was good at studying people—she'd always been aware of others more than most people she knew. Jacob also had a habit of watching all around them. His gaze moved from front to rear mirror to each side of the vehicle, probably checking to see that they weren't being followed. Like in an American gangster movie.

He smelled good, too. The gum he chewed was minty. He'd offered her a piece, and she'd accepted it. She hadn't chewed gum in ages.

Mostly, she liked watching the muscles in his cheek move as he subtly chewed. It was as though he set a rhythm for himself in his careful watching of the road.

An idle thought crossed her mind.... What if he took her in his arms and held her tight?

His arms were strong. Quite sexy. He was a protector, after all. She'd watched him put his gun in the glove compartment and lock it before they'd set out on the drive. She'd never had a bodyguard of her own before.

"We're here," Jacob said, steering the SUV into the circular driveway of an elegant residence with New England clapboards and irregularly set gables. "This is it. Your Vermont inn."

In the moonlit evening, the renovated hotel set into the side of a large mountain was absolutely stunning. Light spilled from great windows onto the car park where they had stopped.

All that the place needed was a blanket of fresh-fallen snow, and the picture-perfect postcard would have been complete.

Jacob reached for the key but left the engine

idling. "Why isn't there any security?" he asked. "Where's the perimeter setup?"

"My uncle comes with his own security force. The rest of the family does not."

He looked at her quizzically. "Isn't your uncle here yet?"

She shook her head. "He doesn't arrive until the wedding tomorrow. He's flying over from Edinburgh on his private jet. Knowing him, he'll stay just long enough to hear the vows, then to toast the bride and groom and dance one short reel before he returns to his plane to work."

Jacob seemed aghast. "So he comes for only a few minutes?"

"Maybe a couple of hours, but it *is* a big to-do. His security team will block off the inn and check IDs at the entrance. No one will be able to get into the inn's reception area or the church tomorrow unless they're a guest on Malcolm's official list."

He nodded slowly and shut off the engine. She supposed Jacob was used to this, escorting diplomats as he did.

Before they got out, she pointed to the small white-steepled church beside the inn. "That, I believe, is where the wedding is taking place."

Just then, a shuttle van pulled up in the car park beside them. Isabel's mum stepped out from the sliding door in the side. Then her two older brothers, followed by their wives and kids. They didn't notice her and Jacob sitting inside the parked SUV beside them.

Isabel felt herself sinking lower into the seat. She didn't want them to see her, not yet.

She glanced over to find Jacob staring at her, a funny look on his face. Did he think badly of her for hiding from them?

Abruptly she sat up. "Sorry, I'm not quite ready to reenter the world." And she certainly wasn't keen about facing any "innocuous" questions about Alex.

"What exactly do you expect from me tomorrow?" Jacob asked, his voice tight.

She wasn't sure. No idea, really—unlike her usual self, she hadn't thought any further ahead than the next moment in the car with Jacob.

She glanced at him, and he was openly scowling at her. The mood was ruined, and she didn't want it to be ruined. She'd been enjoying herself too much.

JACOB WAS WORKING hard to stuff down his frustration. He had a much smaller window for cornering John Sage than he'd realized.

"We had a good drive together, didn't we?" Isabel asked him.

That lovely, aching Scottish accent sounded like musical bells. Isabel's smile—the real smile, the vulnerable her, not the successful cipher—flashed and then disappeared, melting away.

"Yes, we did," Jacob allowed.

"As for tomorrow...well, I don't know. I do know we'll drive home together on Sunday...." She waited expectantly, her head tilted, hoping that he would chime in. She wasn't treating him like an employee. It appeared they were on equal footing now. And why not? They knew too much about each other.

"I'll be at the inn tomorrow," he said. He had to be. If he was caught outside the security perimeter, he might never catch Sage.

From here on in he was present only to meet John Sage. That was his reason.

Maybe he'd veered a bit, tangled in Isabel's spell. But it had been a tactical mistake, because here he was at the destination, with no solid footwork completed yet as to his real agenda.

"Right, then." She licked her lips. "I'll go check us in." She opened the door, and in the dome light, he saw that her face had flushed. "Two rooms," she specified. Needlessly, in his opinion.

"I'll bring in the suitcases," he said quietly.

She nodded, and with her bottom lip between her teeth, paused in the doorway. Her jeans hugged her hips in a way that made his groin ache. Her sweater clung to her stomach, to her breasts. Her warm breath seemed to puff and then hang in the air, as if there was a question...something else that hung in the air between them, too.

If he spoke, if he moved with the spell, he could take charge and continue this...physical attraction, or whatever it was, upstairs, in a room with a bed and a door. He could play the music she liked all night with her. She was barely breathing now, her breath coming in a whisper. Her eyes bright. Her lips slightly parted.

He was half-transfixed himself.

But then, that would be too much, too far, on the first night they'd known each other. It would be the wine stain ruining a beautiful tablecloth. And furthermore, once she woke from her dream tomorrow—if they made it that far—she would roll over in bed and look at him and instantly regret everything. Whatever gold they might have found would be turned to ashes. There was alchemy to love and relationships, and whatever that was, Jacob didn't know the answer. He was just a guy with a badge and a gun and a mission to take bullets for diplomats.

He shook his head. "Good night, Isabel." Formal words that covered all manner of sins. But she was polished and put together and great at recovery. In the end, she just nodded pleasantly at him as if nothing had happened, as if he hadn't just turned her down and they'd really only been exchanging pleasantries.

"Go check in to your room," Jacob said. "I'll be behind you checking in to mine."

WITH JACOB NO longer beside her, Isabel felt as if something was missing. By now she was used to

him, the way he walked beside her, but slightly behind. The way he shined his torch on the path in
front of her. Looked all around them with sharp
eagle eyes as if he were searching for snipers.

Her intense, ever-vigilant protector was gone. She
felt as if she needed to put her own cloak back on,
her demeanor of poise and invulnerability and great
care.

Centering herself, she turned to touch her fingers
lightly to the polished wooden counter.

Inside the lobby, the air was warm and bright.
She collected her room key, listening with polite-
ness to the innkeeper's standard spiel about breakfast hours and the location of the ice machine. He
was all smiles and chatter, like a professional marketing manager. Everybody was professional these
days. If she'd expected a cold, taciturn New England
atmosphere, she wasn't getting it. It would have to
be enough to enjoy the green Vermont hills and the
fresh air and the cows.... Oh, the cows. She'd noticed them on the drive up, spotted and white, with
short horns. Nothing like her long-horned, hairy
Highland cows.

A very bold idea was occurring to her. Something
she had never done before. The idea, like a secret,
was lighting a flame within her.

In the bustling great room across the lobby, a
huge, roaring fire blazed in a stone fireplace. All
her many boisterous cousins were surrounding it.

Drinking wine. Joking with one another. Catching up. She wasn't part of that—not truly, not like this. She was usually set apart and above, but set apart and above with Alex, who was customarily bored by the whole thing in his lawyerly way.

What would it be like to dance with her earthy cousins, dance the reels with Jacob, letting herself cut loose? She'd seen his hands tap on the steering wheel when she'd played her music. She'd sensed he wanted to cut loose, too. Yes, it was necessary to have a certain decorum around her family just because of the role she aspired to, the leader of their clan of sorts, but something else was awakening inside her.

She wanted to dance. She wanted to loosen up. She wanted to chase away the rawness that Alex's breakup had left inside her.

It wasn't a matter of healing—of going back to the way she'd been before Alex had called today. In some respects, she would never be the same again, nor did she want to be.

She gathered her keys. Sidestepped her family by hiding for a moment beside a rack of tourism brochures. All the various sightseeing venues: Jay Peak! Skiing in Canada! Ben & Jerry's Ice Cream!

When the way was clear, she hastened back outside to Jacob, still inside his SUV, securing his weapon, it looked like. Rubbing her cold arms, she waited, her breath dancing in a jerky pattern, so unlike her usual manner.

She had never asked a man to go out with *her* before. But why not? Straightening her shoulders, she rapped on the cold glass lightly with her knuckles.

Jacob pressed the button to lower the window. His face was blank except for those two lines on his forehead, concentrating intently.

He wasn't going to help her along or make it easy for her. She swallowed the lump in her throat.

"Er…I was wondering. Would you like to go to the wedding with me tomorrow?"

He stared at her. "As your bodyguard?"

"No, Jacob. As my date."

JACOB HADN'T EXPECTED this *at all*. She was giving him an opportunity on a golden platter, and she didn't even know it.

But he just stared at her shuffling from foot to foot in the empty parking lot. *Why?* he wanted to ask her.

"In the morning I have the Sage Family quarterly meeting." She seemed to be babbling, making up for his silence. "Then the wedding is at four o'clock, with the reception immediately afterward."

He continued to stare. She was offering him the perfect way to access John Sage. And yet…

"We wouldn't owe each other anything," she said. "I just…enjoyed your company today. I thought we could continue that. And I really don't want to be alone tomorrow...."

"What will you tell your family about me?" he asked quietly.

"Why...of course I need to tell them that Alex and I broke up." Her smile seemed to falter. "But as for you and I, I'll tell them that you're my friend." She tilted her head, looking worried. "Are you my friend, Jacob?"

What did that even *mean*—her friend? "And your uncle," Jacob said carefully, "what about him?"

"I'll...introduce you to him, of course. I know you prefer to be alone, but you're the one who encouraged me to be strong and start anew." She sighed. "Please, Jacob. Do me this favor."

The way she said it touched him. *Dammit.* He'd never wanted to attend a wedding again, not for anybody.

But he couldn't say no to her, either. He didn't have the heart to see her rejected again.

He nodded gruffly, then opened the door and got out. "Yes, I'll go."

"Oh, thank you." She seemed so relieved. "Great," she said quickly, helping him as he removed their two suitcases from the back of the vehicle and placed them on the black asphalt. "So we'll meet at half past three, in front of the fireplace?" She lifted her finger. "Oh, and would you like to wear a kilt? I mean, we're all Scots. The men wear kilts at weddings. I'm told that even the Americans—Malcolm's bride's family—have arranged to wear them. It's a theme," she finished helplessly.

"You want me to wear a *kilt?*"

"Yes." She licked her lips nervously. "Actually, I would like you to, if you want to. I know you're American and not Scottish, but since your last name is Ross, I'll look for that tartan."

He just stared at her. She had no idea what she was saying.

"Let me make some calls, and if I can reach a kilt hire, then I'll arrange it for you. Have you ever worn a kilt, Jacob?"

He dug his nails into his palms. Clenched and un-clenched his fists.

"It really isn't that big a deal," she murmured.

It was a huge deal to him. The only photo he'd ever seen of his real father had been his wedding photo with Jacob's mother. And in that photo, Jacob's father had been wearing a kilt.

The photo was gone now. After he'd found it, tucked away in a box in their New York City apartment, it had disappeared.

Isabel mistook his anger for something else. "It won't be that bad," she consoled him. "Is your name originally Ross? I ask because I've learned that the name Ross is sometimes a shortened version of Rossi. Are you of Scottish descent?"

Again, she had no idea. He nodded abruptly.

She smiled brilliantly. "I knew it. Then wearing a kilt should come naturally to you."

If Jacob didn't wear the damn thing, then he'd not only stand out like a sore thumb, but he might seem insulting, too. Just…*dammit*.

"Are you okay with that, Jacob?"

"Fine."

"Good, then." She nodded.

He watched her walk away. But after about five steps she stopped, then abruptly turned back to him. "It will be okay," she said. "I'll help you through it."

It was as if she *knew* what he was thinking. But she didn't. "I'm *fine*."

"I know," she said simply. "I am, too."

CHAPTER FIVE

ISABEL SANK INTO a chair at an empty luncheon table in the corner and took a deep, cleansing breath. The quarterly Sage family meeting was over. Even though she'd been disappointed that Malcolm had been asked to run it, she'd survived with composure intact.

That had been Jacob's influence. Just knowing he was at the inn with her had gotten her through the morning.

For the past three hours she'd put on a good front. She'd answered every agenda question that had been directed at her. She'd been "on"—smiling so hard her cheeks and lips were stiff from the effort.

She'd made sure to greet each cousin, laugh at their jokes, play with their children, hug their wives, air-kiss their husbands—but not too close. Some, she'd had to dance on her feet to back away from. Some had been tippling since breakfast.

She sat facing her own "wee dram." This wasn't a habit for her but a special occasion. A drop to raise her desperately flagging spirits.

From the corner of her eye she saw her mother

floating over, already dressed in her wedding frock. Mum had been one of the crew sipping since break- fast, a habit Isabel had never noticed before. Not since Dad had passed on.

"Isabel, why so glum?" Mum said, pulling out the chair and settling in beside her.

Glum? Isabel looked glum? She sat up straighter and smiled harder again. Back on, just like that. "I was resting, Mum."

"You're almost done with New York and coming home again, aren't you?" Her mum moved the box that Isabel had set on the table. "I'll be happy when you're back in Edinburgh."

"So will I, Mum," Isabel said. She couldn't help smiling as one of her nephews—her brother Archie's youngest—hopped onto his gram's lap and ran his finger through the blackberry jam that Isabel had left on her bread plate. He smeared his chubby fin- ger into his mouth and gazed at her angelically. She really had missed her family.

Across the dining room, her other brother, Hugh, caught her eye and strode over to greet her. She'd seen him earlier at the meeting, but hadn't had the opportunity to say hello. Isabel felt herself grin, and he caught her up in a bear hug.

"You did beautifully in there," Hugh murmured. "Dad would have been proud of you."

Tears prickled Isabel's eyes. Hugh knew how much that meant to her. "Thank you," she whispered.

"Of all of us, you were the one he pinned his hopes on," Hugh said, taking the seat on her other side. "Dad would be happy to see you bringing forward his dream."

Isabel nodded, her eyes downcast. Her father had been the chemist and entrepreneur who'd created the first formulations for Sage Family Products. His creations—shampoos, body creams and bath salts—were still distributed in stores all over Europe.

Her mum spoke up. "It didn't sit right with your father that he never received proper credit for his inventions."

"A great wrong was done him," Hugh agreed. "I'm sure the stress of that contributed to his death."

Isabel twisted her hands. Their dad—Dougal Sage—had been too young, only sixty, when he'd passed. That day had been the worst of her life. Her dad had been her biggest champion and the person who most believed in her.

She glanced at Hugh. He'd been in the hospital room with her that day, too. He'd heard the promise she'd made to their dad. Hugh knew how hard she was working to someday become the CEO of Sage Family Products.

"I'll still be CEO," she murmured to Hugh. "That hasn't changed for me."

Hugh nodded as their brother, Archie, joined them, along with his wife, Ava. Each had plates filled from the buffet line. Isabel was struck anew by how much both Archie and Hugh looked like their dad—round-faced and scholarly, wearing similar glasses. They both worked as university professors—Hugh in the chemistry department and Archie in biology.

Hugh leaned toward Isabel. "It's a good thing you're coming home," he said in a low voice. "There's talk that Uncle John is getting ready to name a successor sooner than we'd thought."

Her hands stilled in her lap. "Why, what's happened?"

"He's not getting any younger. And sometimes I wonder if he isn't ill. When you see him this afternoon, tell me if you think he looks drawn."

Her heartbeat picked up. "I'm sorry to hear this." She didn't want anyone to be unwell.

"Isabel, you really need to step up your agenda," he continued. "Everyone knows it will be either you or Malcolm chosen. You're the only two Sages who are even working for the company at a serious level."

This was true. And not everyone in their extended family worked or earned a paycheck. Some preferred to live on the funds that came to them through their trusts set up by the family corporation. But Dougal Sage would never have accepted that from his children. Everyone was expected to be productive. He'd never understood why those who didn't work should share in the profits.

"I'm doing everything I can," she said, as patiently as she could.

"Have you talked with Uncle John lately?" Archie asked from across the table. "Because it looks like Malcolm has the better of you. Uncle John's preference for him is obvious."

Isabel dipped her head. She didn't need her brothers to fan the old resentment she felt for her cousin. During the meeting it had flared anew, especially when she'd realized that while she'd been tied down in New York with work and responsibility, Malcolm had been allowed to flit between Vermont and Scotland whenever he pleased. These past few months he'd been nurturing the company that he'd developed separately for himself in Vermont and putting his happiness above everyone else's, in Isabel's opinion.

"How can I compete with him?" she asked quietly. "Is there anything I can give Uncle that Malcolm can't?"

"From what I've observed," Hugh said, "Uncle John cares most about business acumen and loyalty. In the loyalty department, you have the advantage."

Yes, since I jump through hoops and do everything he says without question, she thought wryly.

"And my business skills? How do those appear to you?" she asked her brother.

Archie speared some salad with his fork. "Well, you've worked at the company longer, in more varying aspects than Malcolm has. You have the range and depth of experience, and the connections with the family members, as well. Malcolm spent too many years at boarding school in America. He doesn't have the relationships you have. He's also confined himself to finance and acquisitions. I don't think he's ever worked so much as an internship in the marketing or sales groups."

He was right, the connections and knowledge she'd built were strengths for her.

She sighed. "Honestly, I think my problem is familiarity. Malcolm is vice president of acquisitions, so he works directly with Uncle John. He's in the inner circle. Just by being there, Malcolm has already proved his loyalty to him. My positions haven't reported directly to him yet. I'd planned to work on that next, but…"

"You need face time," Hugh advised. "Remind Uncle that you're coming home soon."

Yes, she did need to build a closer relationship with Uncle John. And to start with, he would be arriving this afternoon. To talk at length with him, she'd have to get through his level of bodyguards and his advisor, Murphy.

She sighed. "It's not easy getting close to him, what with his security detail and his rushed schedule."

"I know you can manage it."

Because that was what she did. She succeeded. She did not fail.

Mum picked up Stewart from her lap and placed him on the floor. "So when *are* you coming home, dear?"

"In six more weeks."

"Lovely. Can we expect Alex home for Christmas, as well?"

Here it came. Isabel carefully pushed back her seat. She'd avoided saying so thus far, but she couldn't shun the topic any longer.

She focused on Hugh and smiled gently because he and Alex had always been friends. It was obvious that Alex hadn't said anything to her brother, or else this would have been Hugh's first topic of conversation with her. "Alex and I broke up," she said.

Hugh looked shocked.

"I know you're upset," she murmured. He'd been Alex's wee mate, after all. Alex was older than her, Hugh's age.

"Why did you let that happen?" Hugh blurted.

She gasped, stunned. But everyone just stared at her, waiting for her explanation.

Here it was, the truth about what they really expected from her. She was supposed to be a success in *everything*. They didn't even recognize the tension she faced between going to school in New York and maintaining a personal life in Scotland.

Hugh took one look at her distraught expression and backpedaled. "Bell, I'm sorry. I didn't mean…"

"Alex is engaged to somebody else," she said quietly.

Shocked silence met her announcement.

"You also should know," she said, her voice shaking slightly, "that I'm bringing a date to the wedding. If you'll excuse me, I need to go and tell the bride and groom to expect him."

"You're bringing a date?" her mum asked. "What's his name? Can we meet him?"

Isabel turned to her. "Of course. I love you all and I will introduce you to him. But for now, I want us to be left alone. See me at the reception after the wedding. I'll introduce you to him then."

She stood, her hands shaking. The words had just blurted out of her—it was the most surprising thing she'd ever said to them, and it was the truth. Jacob was her secret weapon. His hidden presence had been a small comfort all morning.

But now her secret was public. Before she lost her nerve, she marched over to Malcolm to inform him, too.

Her cousin stood in the center of a ring of people, holding court. They had to be his soon-to-be wife's people, the Hart family, the Vermonters Isabel hadn't met yet because they hadn't been invited to the Sage family meeting.

Malcolm had a wide grin. He was relaxed and appeared utterly happy.

Isabel took in another deep, cleansing breath. She faced the man she so rarely interacted with and yet had so much influence in her life. "Malcolm, may I speak with you for a moment, please?"

"Aye," Malcolm said. Isabel noticed that Malcolm's Scottish accent had become more pronounced since she'd last seen him.

He stepped aside, past a man in a wheelchair, three other men holding beer bottles, a short woman with dark hair and a little red-haired girl wearing a kilt.

Isabel thought of the box she'd left on the table back where her mother sat, and made a mental note to go back and fetch it when she was done.

"What is it?" Malcolm asked her.

Just then, his bride sailed over. Kristin Hart. Isabel had observed her once at work. She was an industrial engineer in their Byrne Glennie plant.

"Isabel?" Kristin Hart, soon to be Kristin Mac-Dowall, smiled at her. "I've wanted to meet you in person for so long."

"As have I," Isabel murmured. She held out her hand to shake Kristin's, but Kristin just hugged her.

She smelled nice, like lavender and country flowers—the formulation for one of Sage's newly acquired, organically sourced shower-gel lines. Malcolm's baby, of course, since he was Sage's current vice president of acquisitions. Isabel didn't have a job title yet.

As Isabel stood stiffly, Kristin stepped back and shyly slid her gaze to Malcolm. Rarely did a minute go by when the two of them were not in deep eye contact with one another. They were so obviously in love it was all Isabel could do not to throw up again.

She pressed her nails into her palms. She didn't *want* to feel angry or sorry for herself. Malcolm's happiness did not threaten her. Intellectually, she understood this. It was just her heart that was acting like a three-year-old.

"We have something to ask you," Kristin gushed. "It's...sort of a thing between us." She glanced at Malcolm and blushed. "Would you mind giving a reading for us at the ceremony? I'm sorry it's a last-minute request, but we made a mistake in the planning. I thought Malcolm had asked you, and he thought that I had, and...well, your name is already printed in the program. I'm sorry we messed up and didn't give you more warning, but we're hoping you'll say yes anyway. Please, Isabel, we would appreciate it. Malcolm says you perform so beautifully, and you're the only person we would consider asking."

Kristin glanced at Malcolm again. They were holding hands and sharing a connection that Isabel could only dream about.

But she did it because she had to. Because it was expected of her.

She politely took the small book from Kristin— Burns, it said on the spine, with a photo on the front cover of the famous eighteenth-century poet. Inside the book was a folded photocopy, presumably of the poem they wanted her to read.

Isabel kept her expression neutral as she answered, "I'm honored you thought of me. Yes, I'll read it for you."

Inside, she was screaming. She didn't feel honored, she felt misunderstood and maybe even taken for granted.

She turned to Malcolm. "When is Uncle John arriving?" The sooner she had a frank conversation with him, the better she would feel.

"He called, and he's running late," Malcolm said. "There was a problem with landing the jet at Logan airport. They were diverted to a regional airport, and Uncle doesn't expect to get here until after the reception is over, unfortunately."

"Do you think that's bad luck?" Kristin asked Malcolm.

"I think it's good luck," Malcolm said, and kissed her. "I want this celebration to be all about us. Not about him and his doings."

That was easy for Malcolm to say, with his "most favored" status. Isabel took a breath. She felt tired and drained. Sage Family Products was and would always be family-owned. Any change in officers was voted on by her family, and that was why Isabel had done her glad-handing all morning long. But if Uncle John didn't recommend her appointment, it wouldn't happen. Hugh was right—she needed every chance she could get to impress him.

Since Uncle John wouldn't be here for a while, she would go upstairs and have a rest.

"I'll see you at the ceremony," she said to the embracing couple, and then turned to leave.

"Wait, weren't you going to ask me something?" Malcolm called.

She squared her shoulders and faced him. "I'm bringing a date to the ceremony. His name is Jacob Ross."

Malcolm's eyes widened somewhat, but he said nothing.

"I'm looking forward to meeting him," Kristin said.

WHILE HER FAMILY was waiting in line for the dessert buffet, Isabel grabbed the box she'd left on the table, and with the Burns book plopped on top of it, she headed upstairs to Jacob's room.

She paused outside his door. Inside, she could hear music playing. One of the pop songs the two of them had listened to last night. She felt a smile—a real smile—cross her face and fill her heart. She tightened her grip on the box and knocked.

"Come in," Jacob called.

Pushing the door open, she didn't know what to expect. She only knew that she was glad to have Jacob to talk to and be herself with. Even though it might be daft of her, it was a comforting sort of daft. A daft that would make her feel less lonely. And nobody would know she was in his room with him.

She walked through the sleeping area, ignoring the unmade bed and the pleasurable seeds it planted in her imagination, and instead headed through the small glass slider that led to a deck.

Jacob's veranda was over the hotel's main entrance, and from here he could see every vehicle and person who came and went. With Jacob nothing was accidental; he would have requested this room specifically.

He sat dressed in jeans and a T-shirt with a navy blue jacket zipped over it. He was reading a book. Beside him on a small table was the bottle of Highland whiskey that all guests had received in their room at turndown service last night.

She sat without asking. It felt a relief to relax with someone she didn't need to impress. That the weather had cooperated—balmy, sunny and nice—was a bonus.

"I didn't know you liked whiskey," she remarked.

He glanced up and smiled at her. "I didn't either."

"You don't drink alcohol?"

"Off duty, I'll have a beer. And you?"

She smirked. "I had two wee drams of whiskey downstairs."

"Liquid courage?" he asked.

"No," she admitted. "A sedative." She sank back

in the wooden chair. It was surprisingly comfort-able. The seat was sloped so her bum was lower than her knees.

"It's called an Adirondack chair," Jacob said, read-ing her inquisitiveness. "Named for a region in up-state New York."

"Is it usually so warm in Vermont this time of year?"

"No." He closed his book. "This is an Indian sum-mer. That's the old name for a day in October or No-vember that's warm and sunny like this."

"I like it. What are you reading?"

He held out the spine. "Spy fiction. It was on the bookshelf beside my bed."

There was that word *bed* again. She sat back and inhaled a breath of pine needles. Vermont reminded her of home, her original home, the Highlands.

Below them, a lone police car was positioned in the entrance, blocking the property. A uniformed of-ficer leaned in the window of a car that had stopped by. The gray car pulled out and drove away. Jacob observed the situation with interest.

"You requested this room on purpose, didn't you?" she asked.

Jacob just smiled. A few moments later he said, "What time does your uncle arrive?"

She stretched out her legs. "His plane was delayed."

"Is he still coming?"

"Yes, but very late, they expect, well after the

dancing. Likely, he'll stay for an hour, then head straight back home. That's his usual schedule for family weddings."

Jacob frowned. Looking sideways at her, he said, "It would be a security nightmare if he were to stay overnight in this rural inn."

She gazed down at the local police officer and the blocked-off roadway. "I suppose so."

"Do your other cousins have bodyguards?" Jacob asked.

"No. Most of them flew in together from Scotland on the same flight. A hired bus was arranged for them. Just one driver to share between all."

He grinned. "Why are you special that you got me?"

He was teasing, and yet he wasn't. She closed her eyes, suddenly tired. Why shouldn't she be allowed to be happy?

Maybe she should just skip the wedding and have dinner with Jacob. She had done her duty already for the family. But she glanced at the Burns book in her lap and knew that she couldn't. She had promised.

Jacob noticed her mood and followed her gaze. The man missed nothing.

"The box on the table is for you," she said. "You don't have to wear it if you don't want to."

BEFORE ISABEL HAD come in, Jacob had had the clear understanding that he was in the enemy's den. She was right—he had requested this guest room on purpose. He'd been watching for John Sage's arrival.

Jacob had been rehearsing the conversation in his mind—what he would say to Sage, how he would approach him. It had felt overwhelming all of a sudden to realize that the father he'd never known had interacted with Sage, and possibly some of the others here.

Who and how, Jacob didn't yet know. But he would before he left.

He pulled the box she'd brought him onto his lap, mildly curious. Thanks to her asking him to the wedding, he would be well positioned to greet John Sage and speak with him privately.

He opened the lid, touching the soft wool of the garment inside. "You found a kilt for me."

"More than that, I found a Ross tartan. It's actually a major clan in Scotland. Have you ever visited?"

She had no idea. Very few people knew that he'd been born there. He'd thought of flying to Edinburgh many times.

He put down the box. "No."

"You should come to Scotland and drive to the northwest. That's traditional Clan Ross territory. There are major castles you can see, all with so much history."

"How did you know my kilt size?"

"I guessed." She looked down, obviously checking out his groin region. She stared for longer than was seemly, and he felt himself grinning.

"You're observant," he said drily.

She blew out a little puff of breath. Got up and paced. "Sometimes I wish I wasn't part of my clan at all. I wish there was a place for me where I didn't have to fight so hard to claim what's mine."

She glanced at him sideways. "Ah, look at me, running on, telling you my woeful story."

He laughed. "You're saying that to the wrong person."

"No, you're the right person. I know you can't be keen on attending a wedding, either."

"With you, sure I am. As long as it's not my own," he joked.

"That's good that you can laugh. Have you been to many since it happened?"

"Not a single one."

"Really?" This seemed to make her feel better. Which was the only reason he'd answered the question honestly, he supposed.

They were so careful with one another. For some reason that struck him. He liked it. "We'll be fine, Isabel."

She inhaled deeply. "I'll come pick you up in an hour, then," she murmured.

"No. Meet me downstairs, by the fireplace, remember?" He would escort her inside from there, in style.

She nodded. "Very well." Then, "Oh, wait. I forgot my book."

A poetry book, by Robert Burns. Interesting.

She shook her head. "This is torture. I've been asked to recite a love poem and do it beautifully for the bride and groom, as if nothing affects me."

"Here." He dragged out two shot glasses, fussy little ones that came in the room on a filigree tray. He poured them each a dram. "I don't normally do this. But nothing about this job is normal to me."

She smiled wanly. *"Slainte mhath."*

"What does that mean?"

"To your health."

"Interesting. I'd been about to toast to shared pain."

DOWNSTAIRS, THE MASSIVE stone fireplace had been set with a roaring blaze. Jacob warmed his back as he waited for Isabel to descend the flight of stairs and join him.

Already, the colonial-era inn milled with her family's half of the wedding guests—Scots, the men wearing kilts like his father must have worn, plaids in varying colors and designs, with more accessory items than Jacob ever had guessed, from knee socks with a jeweled dagger tucked under the right side, to black shoes, and hanging from the waist, a leather pouch big enough to carry a pistol, if the wearer was so inclined.

Jacob passed his hands over his eyes. He still hadn't seen the groom—Malcolm—the nephew who'd been kidnapped as a boy. Jacob needed to do something about that. He was feeling itchy, needing to step up this operation. It frustrated him that John Sage wouldn't be present for hours yet.

Just as the clock showed three-thirty, Isabel came down the stairs.

Jacob snapped up his head. She'd put up her hair and wore a low-cut, clingy dress that showed her skin for the first time—her long neck and a hint of cleavage.

His mouth was open and he was probably drooling. His gaze slid up and down her body, appreciating her. She wore a long, dark green dress. Though not out of place for the occasion, it clung in just the right places and slid over her hips when she moved, drawing his attention.

Blinking, he dragged his gaze back up. She had stilled and was looking *him* up and down, from his skirt—er, kilt—with the sporran buckled over his crotch, up his jacket, to his face.

He raised an eyebrow at her, and her cheeks flushed.

It's just a job, he told himself. *Don't take this seriously. It doesn't mean anything.*

But their gazes were locked together, and he couldn't break away. Across that crowded room, she stood still on the bottom stair, only her chest rising and falling. She held on to her end of their stared connection.

Don't, he told himself. He broke their link. But when he looked up next, she was strolling toward him, her lips twitching. On the way over, she shook out a thin plaid shawl and draped it over that gorgeous skin on her shoulders, clipping the material together with a brooch, some kind of Celtic design with blue stones against silver. The blue matched her eyes exactly.

"Hello, Isabel."

She stopped just outside his comfort zone, gazing up at him. Tiny, heart-shaped crystals dangled from her earlobes, distracting him.

"And to think I was considering not coming down," she murmured in a low, musical voice that he had to lean forward to hear.

"What made you decide to come?"

She shrugged at him playfully. "I remembered I had a handsome American in a kilt waiting to watch me recite a love poem."

Handsome, huh? "I thought the poem was for the bride and groom."

"It is." She winked at him. "But the reading of this particular poem is also a family tradition, and I've been practicing to perform it in my own unique way. You'll have to wait and see my skills."

"You've got my attention, Isabel."

"Yes, I saw that on the stairs."

He blew out a breath and looked away. The crowd was moving, heading en masse in the direction of the church next door. Someone bumped her, causing her to sway for a moment, and in quick reflex, he caught her elbow.

She smelled good and her skin was soft, as if she'd just showered and moisturized. He let his fingers subtly caress the spot.

She leaned slightly closer, her eyes twinkling. "So. Shall we walk to the church together and begin our torture session?"

"Shared pain," he said, remembering the whiskey toast back in his room.

"You don't like weddings. I don't like reading love poems. If we watch out for each other, maybe we can change our fates today."

He led her away from the main crowd and through the open doors, not knowing what to think, except that it seemed they had a shared plan. He didn't mind that at all.

She smiled and tilted her face to the sky. Outside, the balmy wind had picked up, which sent the pleats of his woolen kilt slapping against his bare knees. An interesting sensation. Underneath the kilt, he'd worn a pair of shorts he usually jogged in, even though he knew it was tradition not to wear anything beneath. And maybe, with a pretty woman on his arm, he was starting to understand why.

He hid his smile.

"What are you thinking?" she asked.

Strange how they were getting to know each other's moods. "Anticipating your poetry, is all," he said.

"'My Love is Like a Red, Red Rose.' Do you know that one?"

"No. Are you joking—that's really the title?"

"No, I'm not joking, and it's a pity. I'd thought I'd recite the whole thing directly to you, and we could both laugh at it in secret."

He saw what she was doing, distracting them both from the fact that they were walking into a church. For a wedding.

"How is *everyone* not going to laugh out loud?" he asked, playing along.

"Because as I read it to you, I'm going to pretend that I'm already CEO of Sage Family Products, and delivering a dramatic enactment for the purpose of a very clever internet advertisement." She leaned into him and whispered, "And only you will know that I'm doing this."

He burst out laughing. He was enjoying this woman.

And yet, she was reminding him of his purpose, too.

All these members of the Sage family surrounded him, and there was intel to be gathered. Now was the time to pay attention to that task.

He studied the crowd around them as he and Isabel

strolled the fifty or so yards across the grass. They followed closely behind a group who were laughing, too. They genuinely seemed to like and take comfort in each other's company.

"Who are these people?" he asked Isabel, gesturing before them.

"Who, my cousin Gerry and his wife?"

"No." Jacob didn't need to know names, specifically. He'd never remember them all anyway—there were so many cousins. He was more interested in the groom and John Sage. "I mean, what's the big picture as to how you fit in with the wedding party as a whole?"

"Well, my father had four siblings—three younger brothers and a sister, the youngest of all. The groom—Malcolm MacDowall—is his sister's only son. John Sage is my father's—*was* my father's—next oldest brother, and he's the only one of my uncles who never married."

Jacob nodded, filing away the information. There was one more person he needed to know about. He noticed she hadn't mentioned the groom's sister, the niece who'd been kidnapped.

Bridesmaids in autumn-red-and-gold dresses were lined up, chatting on the landing of the church entrance. "Who are they?" he asked Isabel, pointing to the women as he escorted her up the steps.

"Friends or relatives of the bride, I suppose.

They're definitely not siblings, because Kristin is an only sister with lots of brothers. She has four."

So…none of the bridesmaids were the kidnapped niece. "Does Malcolm have any siblings?" he asked carefully. The niece had to be here somewhere in the crowd.

They were filing into the back of a chapel with one long aisle down the middle. The fact that he was inside a church came up on Jacob so suddenly, he only had time to blink.

"Interesting that you should ask," Isabel said, and drew him aside from the main crowd, waiting two by two to be escorted into wooden pews by three groomsmen dressed in kilts with black tuxedo-type jackets. Wedding music played from an organ in the loft of the church. Jacob recognized those strains.

"Look behind you," Isabel whispered into his ear, and pointed.

"Behind me?" And he was usually so situationally aware. *Dammit*. It had to be the location's effect on him. Irritated with himself, he turned.

"That's Malcolm, the groom," she whispered.

Malcolm's attention was on a table beside him. He didn't look nervous, but then again, Jacob hadn't been nervous, either, right up until his bride had shown up and made her dramatic announcement.

Jacob couldn't help it, he glanced at his watch. The bride had a few more minutes. She wasn't late.

He glanced back at Malcolm, and then noticed

the laptop Malcolm was fiddling with. There was a hazy shadow on the screen.

"Who's that on the laptop?" he murmured.

"Rhiannon. My cousin."

Jacob squinted. There was, indeed, a woman with long dark hair on the screen, and she was speaking quietly to Malcolm over a video connection.

Isabel moved closer to speak directly into Jacob's ear. Close enough that he smelled her perfume and felt her breath. He moved closer to her, his nose practically in her hair.

"Rhiannon is Malcolm's younger sister," she said, her lips just brushing his skin.

Jacob stepped back and stared at Isabel. Her expression was inscrutable, but she seemed tense. They *had* to be speaking of the woman who'd been kidnapped as a young girl.

"Why isn't she here today?"

"Rhiannon is agoraphobic. She doesn't leave the grounds of their family's estate in the Highlands."

"Why?"

Isabel gave him a distressful look. He supposed he already knew why—Rhiannon didn't leave the safety of her home because she'd been traumatized. He'd heard of it before, in his training, especially in his reading of histories and case studies regarding the survivors of violent situations.

Agoraphobia was an anxiety disorder. It could very well be Rhiannon's coping mechanism. Likely, she had seen something deeply upsetting. Possibly involving Jacob's father.

Jacob put his hand to his head. All these years, he'd assumed he and his family had been the only ones affected by his father's murder. Obviously, he'd been wrong.

Jacob moved closer to the laptop screen behind Malcolm. On it, he could see that Rhiannon's eyes were darting—taking in the chaos of the church scene before her—which reminded Jacob that the cameras went both ways.

She could hear and see them, just as they could see and hear her. She noticed Jacob staring at her, and a look of panic crossed her eyes.

Jacob then quickly moved with Isabel at his elbow, gently guiding him along. Jacob realized that Malcolm was standing in front of the screen not just to speak with Rhiannon, but also as a deterrent, a guard so that other people couldn't speak to her or upset her as they filed past to their pews.

Every cousin in the family seemed to reverently pause and quiet down as they passed her on the laptop screen. Some nodded. Some looked down, reflective. It seemed to Jacob like a quiet, sad respect they paid her by not pointing out her hidden presence.

It spooked him, and he was a guy who carried a firearm, a badge and a radio every day of his working life. He was trained to run toward gunfire, not look away from it. He dropped threatening perpetrators with a knee to the neck. He jumped in the way of an attack, without a second thought.

This situation was different. And he saw...in a sickening epiphany that kicked him hard, that maybe the department psychologist had been right to single him out. This—his father's murder—had left its mark. It wasn't just something horrible that had happened a long time ago and was over and done with. It was an event that wasn't finished, that didn't finish, that still had rippling effects in many people's lives—more than he had ever realized.

"What exactly happened to her?" he asked Isabel. "Why does Malcolm have to protect his sister like this?"

He needed to know what Isabel knew—everything that she knew, and he needed to know here and now. The bride hadn't yet arrived and the ceremony hadn't yet started, so it wasn't unreasonable of Jacob to ask questions. Just having that laptop set up in the back of the church was likely a distressing reminder on what should have been a wholly happy day for the bride and groom. "*Why* does Malcolm's sister have agoraphobia?"

"We're...not supposed to talk about it."

He stared at her, dumbfounded.

"It's...a bit of a family secret," she said.

Well, it was time she told him, because here he

was, dressed in a kilt, attending her cousin's wedding at her request.

"I told you I won't betray you, Isabel."

"I know." She smiled slightly. "You're still here with me despite everything." She licked her lips. "You're standing in a church at a wedding ceremony, you realize."

It was crazy, but at this moment, he really did feel they had more in common than they had differences. "That doesn't bother me anymore."

She hooked his arm and murmured into his ear. "It doesn't bother me, either."

"Good." He nodded.

"All right." She drew in a breath. "I'll tell you because you're a professional bodyguard, and you'll understand how difficult this is. Most people don't understand, but you're…different." She cleared her throat. "My cousins Rhiannon and Malcolm were kidnapped and held for ransom when they were children. Malcolm was ten, and Rhiannon was just eight years old."

Holy crap. Eight years old? He stared at Isabel. For some reason, he'd assumed that Rhiannon and Malcolm had been older than that, closer to his age at the time.

"What happened after the ransom note went out?"

"I…don't actually know." Isabel looked helplessly at him. "None of us know any details. At the time, we weren't told what was happening until it was already over, and they were held for eleven days. I was young myself, and it… Well, the whole thing was absolutely forbidden from being discussed."

"But they *were* rescued unharmed?"

"I…don't know. My uncle John worked with the police, I believe. I don't know exactly what happened, either during the rescue or before, just that Rhiannon had a difficult time recovering from it emotionally. Malcolm was held separately from her, and…I don't think even he knows all that went on."

She looked down. "Rhiannon doesn't discuss it, and everybody is just…protective of her."

Jacob studied Isabel's face. Showing pain was out of character for her, but she was plainly uncomfortable with the case. There was no guile in what she was telling him, and he believed her. He believed that she knew as little about the details of the kidnapping rescue that had killed his father as he did. Yet, all these years later, the botched operation affected her, too.

It definitely affected her family. Jacob watched Malcolm, protecting his sister even as he watched the entrance for signs of his bride's arrival.

Everybody—on the Scottish side of the church, at least—accepted Malcolm's actions as normal. No one batted an eye at Rhiannon watching silently from the screen, thousands of miles away.

They accepted and moved on. What was hurt

was covered up and not discussed. So similar to Jacob's family.

"I have to ask you this, Isabel. I'm a professional bodyguard—it's what I do for a living. Why…don't you all talk about it? Wouldn't that help for the future?"

"We don't talk because of the media. And the television companies and movie people. My uncle quashed it at the time, Jacob, but there were a lot of people interested in salacious details they could use to entertain the public, and to hurt us. This is what has to be done. We need to be silent. We're Sages. It's for our survival."

"You don't like that, do you?" he asked quietly. "Tell me the truth."

She looked up at him. "I plan to be CEO of Sage Family Products someday. I suppose I'll have to act as my uncle has acted."

"But you don't *like* it."

He waited for her response. He sensed that she wanted so desperately to be normal, and yet assumed she never would be. She thought she always would have to be different. Careful and protective.

She didn't answer him. Before he could say anything else, one of the groomsmen approached.

"Hello," the man said. "We're asking everyone to move to their seats. The bride is outside, and we're set to begin."

Jacob gestured for him to lead the way. The usher

brought them to a pew with two empty seats by the center aisle, on the groom's side.

Music started playing—a lone bagpiper. A rousing, soul-stirring drone so hauntingly unique to the Scots' homeland—his parents' homeland—that it made Jacob's hair stand on end. Inexplicably, he had a feeling of déjà vu, of being in a place he'd never been before, at least not in this life. It was the queerest, spookiest sensation. And yet, it was *true*.

He looked down at the kilt he was wearing. Felt the roughness of the wool against his thighs. The pleats, the muted plaid. The short, black military-cut jacket with the brass buttons. This was borne from a military uniform worn by proud people with a long tradition. He wasn't part of it, and he knew little about it, yet he sensed its greatness.

At heart, he probably did want to know more about it. His ambition of being a federal agent today was surely related as a reaction to what had happened twenty years ago to his father.

It made sense to him in a way that it never had before.

The usher finished seating Isabel, then nodded to Jacob and handed him two copies of the wedding program before heading toward the altar with the groom and the other waiting groomsmen.

Jacob sat in the aisle seat and passed Isabel a program.

"Here comes the bride," she murmured.

Everyone rose, all at once, craning their necks to the rear of the church and getting ready to catch the first glimpse of the bride.

Isabel stood, too, gritting her teeth somewhat. He understood completely. It was hard to be at a wedding, at a place where everybody else was in love when you weren't and yet wanted to be.

He leaned toward her. "It won't be so bad," he promised.

"I'm just glad you're here," she murmured. As she shifted, a strand of her hair touched his lip and clung there.

He froze. Such a longing filled him. He wanted this woman. Maybe it was the air in the room circulating beneath his kilt. Maybe it was the bagpipes bleeding that soulful wail. Maybe it was the innocent vision of the young flower girl with her wild red hair and basket of rosebuds, skipping to drop them in the aisle in front of the bride.

It was primal, this anticipation.

"Jacob?" Isabel's voice was raspy. He stared at her lips. At the bare, flushed skin by her throat. If he had her, if she was his woman, he would be hard pressed not to worship her, to mess up her hair in the sheets of their bed every day.

He gave a guttural groan of his own. Dragged his hand over his hair and clenched his fists.

Her hand curled into the crook of his arm. "I...

almost forgot about the reading," she whispered. "Don't you think I should switch places with you?"

She was right about the logistics, but as a professional bodyguard, the aisle seat was his place. He'd be negligent if he gave it up. "Sorry, no. I can't."

"Do you want me to climb over you?" she whispered, raising her eyebrow.

"Yes, I do." He winked at her.

Her lips twitched. "Then how will I ever stay composed?"

"You said it's a love poem," he murmured. "Nobody's supposed to be composed during a love poem."

She gazed at him, just as the bride passed by. But he was really only aware of Isabel, inches from him on the hard seat. He was only vaguely aware of a ceremony starting, of verses read and songs sung. The only thing he waited for was Isabel's poem.

When her name was finally called, she rose, dignified. Like a crown, she put on her original, elegant persona. Then, as a private gesture to him, she arched one eyebrow, and he stood aside, blank-faced, for her to pass. He was laughing inside, though.

She proceeded to the lectern as if it was the most natural place in the world for her to stand. She'd taken no notes or photocopies with her.

But she wasn't fazed. Leaning into the microphone, she gazed out over her audience. "'A Red,

Red Rose.' A love poem by Robert Burns." Staring straight at him, she recited from memory in a soft, gentle voice, filled with meaning:

"My love is like a red, red rose,
That's newly sprung in June.
My love is like the melody,
That's sweetly played in tune.

"As fair art thou, my bonnie lad,
So deep in love am I,
And I will love thee still, my dear,
Till a' the seas go dry."

She was utterly beautiful. There was a line—a connection—directly from her to him. And though he wasn't familiar with the poem, the Sages were. Isabel lifted her hands, appealing to the audience to join in. Her family's side of the church *sang* the next stanza all together in a mixture of boisterous voices:

"Till a' the seas gang dry, my dear,
And the rocks melt wi' the sun!
I will luve thee still, my dear,
While the sands o' life shall run."

The next section, she sang by herself, to his everlasting shock:

"And fare thee well, my only luve!
And fare thee well, a while!
And I will come again, my luve,
Though it were ten thousand mile!"

For the last two lines, she looked only at Jacob.
Her voice was clear and beautiful. Maybe he was the
only one who noticed, but it seemed to Jacob that
on the last line—and especially the last word—her
voice faltered.

When she returned to her seat, he did what he'd
been expressly avoiding. He took her hand and
moved it under the edges of his kilt so that nobody
else could see.

There, he gave her hand a solid squeeze.

She didn't remove her hand, as he'd expected. She
kept her fingers clasped tightly around his, inter-
twined until the bagpiper finally played the bride
and groom's walk down the aisle together, and everyone in the church rose to cheer.

ISABEL FELT LIKE jumping out of her own skin.

When Jacob had clasped her hand, she'd felt the
strength of his regard for her. Her journey to this
point of feeling hope for her future had been difficult, and Jacob had been good for her.

She would miss him when they both returned to
the city.

The rest of the ceremony was a blur. She concentrated on the warmth of Jacob's body beside hers. She was aware of every small movement he made, from the shift of his shoulders to the rise and fall of his chest as he breathed.

Once, his tongue came out to lick dry lips, and it seemed her heart almost stopped.

His glance caught hers, and she gazed into the deep blue of his eyes. Like a storm of hidden feelings and emotion. Always, that sense of smoldering within him.

When at last the wedding vows were over, and Lily, the red-headed flower girl, skipped ahead dropping rose petals from a wicker basket for the bride and groom, everybody stood. Isabel and Jacob stood, too.

Jacob abruptly dropped her hand.

Saddened by the movement, she pressed her palm to her stomach.

Their eyes met. He seemed to be struggling with what to say. "You did a good job, Isabel."

"Thank you," she murmured. "That poem is… well, it's also a song, and a tradition at Sage weddings."

"You've sung it before?"

"No. Not alone like that. Not in front of…everybody."

She had left the obvious unsaid, that she had sung it to him. It must have been apparent to everyone in the church. She hadn't made eye contact with anyone in her family, but of course they would have seen.

Jacob glanced away. "You'll make a good head of your family," he murmured.

"You think so?"

He nodded, a thoughtful nod, involving teeth, tongue and lips, as if literally tasting the feeling he swallowed. "I know so."

"Thank you for coming here with me," she said. "You made it…"

"Easier?" he asked.

"I was going to say 'good.'"

They walked out of the church, through the cooler evening air, toward the inn where the reception would be held. From past Sage weddings, Isabel knew there would be reels and dancing and whiskey drinking long into the night.

She and Jacob were silent, listening to the chatter and laughter of everyone else around them.

Inside the warmth of the inn, Jacob turned to her. They weren't touching, but she had such a physical awareness of him.

"I'd hug you," he said, "but I don't think it's a good idea for me."

"Of course," she answered with dignity. "That would be…unwise. Instead, we should talk about tomorrow, and what happens then."

"Right." He seemed to think for a minute, and

then forced a smile. "We'll meet after breakfast, and then, ah, we'll leave for the city sometime after that."

She forced herself to smile, too. "Sounds like a plan."

But no sooner had she said "plan" than a lone singer in the main room started singing "Red, Red Rose," the Robert Burns poem she had just read.

Perhaps Malcolm and Kristin had chosen this for their first dance. Usually, brides and grooms in her family danced a boisterous reel, but Uncle John wasn't here to start the festivities, so maybe the order had been changed.

Jacob was staring at Isabel as if he was in physical pain.

She touched his upper arm. His shoulder felt solid and warm beneath the formal Bonnie Prince Charlie kilt jacket. "I think it's a sign. We should at least dance to this one song."

He nodded, but when it came right down to it, they didn't really dance. They both sort of stood there, Isabel with her hands on his shoulders, Jacob with one hand lightly touching her hip as he stared into her eyes.

Such blazing blue eyes he had. Their faces drifted closer and closer.

If you let yourself do this with him, then you are setting yourself up for a world of pain....

Jacob was fighting the battle, too.

They were both losing.

He took her hand again. This time he led her farther from the great room with the dancing and the merriment to a quiet corner near the fireplace in the lobby, where no one else could see them.

His rough hand cupped her cheek, and he pressed his lips to hers.

She drew in her breath before hesitantly kissing him back, her heart skittering in her chest.

This was the first time she'd kissed any man besides Alex, and it was a bit of a shock that she was even doing it. A kiss was such an intimate thing.

But Jacob steadied her. He was gentle at first, and sweet. A hand to the back of her head, his fingers drifting through her hair.

But there was fire inside him, too, and their kiss inevitably deepened. She tasted mint on his tongue. She found herself making a breathless moan. Pressed against him, her breasts to his hard chest. Her mind unable to think.

She caressed the edge of his throat beneath his shirt. His skin felt so hot…

A noise sounded behind Jacob.

Isabel broke their kiss just in time to see a group of men entering the front doors.

Uncle John!

She gasped and stepped back from Jacob, her hand to her lips.

Her uncle was surrounded by an entourage, with his personal assistant and three security men. He looked travel-weary and tired in his business suit, not kilt, but he wasn't tired enough that he didn't notice her staring at him.

He paused for a moment and blinked, as if questioning what she was doing.

Just ten seconds earlier, he would have seen her kissing Jacob Ross. A stranger. A man who wasn't Alex.

She needed to be more careful in future.

Jacob turned to follow her gaze. "Is that John Sage?" he muttered.

"Yes," Isabel murmured. "I'm sorry, but I need to go talk with him now."

CHAPTER SIX

HER HEART POUNDING, Isabel strode toward the concierge desk, where her uncle conferred with his entourage. They'd already closed ranks around him, led by her uncle's quietly efficient assistant and followed by the three burly bodyguards who were trained to anticipate threats. But she needed to talk to him, not only about Jacob, but also about the fact that she was coming home to Scotland soon.

She stood before him and quietly clasped her hands. "Hello, Uncle," Isabel said. "It's good to see you."

"Hello, Isabel." Her uncle inclined his head and smiled slightly at her. A short, balding man, Uncle John was polite with her, though he never seemed particularly pleased to see her, the way he did with Malcolm or Rhiannon.

"Is there anything I can get you or help you with?" she asked. He appeared well to her, but if he was ill, he would keep it hidden. For now, he just looked tired, and for him, ruffled. Earlier, Malcolm had mentioned that his plane had been rerouted to a smaller regional airport. That had to be exhausting. "I'm sorry about the delay with your flight."

"Thank you," he murmured. He glanced at his watch as if he were on a tight schedule, which he usually was. He was a man who stayed in the background. Typically surrounded by his assistant and bodyguards, he rarely even met with people on his own staff. She knew it was unlikely that she'd be able to speak to him about anything of substance this evening.

"As a matter of fact, there is something you could do," he said. "Kindly find Malcolm and let him know I'd like to see him."

Of course he wanted Malcolm. No surprise there.

But she smiled at him with a more pleasant expression than the one he'd given her. "Yes, Uncle. I'll go find him now."

She paused for a moment. "Later, may I also talk with you, as well?" she asked, keeping a positive tone. "I'm almost finished with my studies in New York, and I'd like to set up some time with you to discuss my next steps. You know I'm interested in a leadership position."

"When Malcolm and I are finished, if there's time, then you and I will chat," he said patiently.

She nodded, holding back her disappointment. This was probably the best she could hope to receive from him, given the occasion.

Isabel pulled her shawl around her shoulders and headed for the function room, where a full Celtic band, including a bagpiper, a drummer and two electric guitarists, were playing a raucous cover version of Led Zeppelin's "Stairway to Heaven."

They were still on the slow part, and the wedding guests swayed close together as they danced in pairs.

She glanced around for Jacob, but she didn't see him. Later, she needed to find him. It had all turned so complicated on her, and so unexpectedly.

As she passed a mirror, she caught sight of her mussed hair, her smeared lipstick and her flushed cheeks.

Inwardly, she groaned. Yes, she had thoroughly enjoyed Jacob's kiss. Yes, she would gladly take another. But for the moment, she needed her uncle to think she was worthy of leading a major company and was most concerned with business, as he was.

She quickly smoothed her hair and fixed her makeup, then set about looking for Malcolm.

Jacob stood at the fringes of the lobby. No one paid any attention to him. Isabel had left, gone back to the wedding reception.

The security detail—amateurs, was Jacob's admittedly harsh assessment of the three guards who hadn't even secured the perimeter—waited for Sage.

Sage himself spoke in low murmurs to the employee behind the front desk.

Jacob shifted from one foot to the next. Now what?

He'd come to Vermont for one reason, and that was to talk with the Scottish industrialist. Isabel had made him forget that. Jacob had been distracted by his attraction to her, the only woman he'd ever met who might honestly be able to understand where he'd come from.

He'd fallen for her courage. Her sweetness. The way she made him laugh. For that little moan she'd made in her throat when he'd pulled her so tightly against him there hadn't been any doubt what his intentions were.

Just...damn.

All sorts of small things had been torturing him about her and driving him crazy since they'd met. That poem she'd performed—her voice cracking at the phrase *ten thousand miles*—had only added fuel to an already roaring fire, as had the Ross kilt, and the fact they'd teamed up to survive this wedding together.

It had been a bonfire of distractions that had crept up under Jacob's usual lone-wolf defenses.

Being "intense"—honest with her, to his mind— had made it all worse because she had responded to it. He still could push things physically with her, if he wanted to.

But if he didn't shut down his feelings for her, fast, he wouldn't be able to salvage his mission.

He couldn't *want* her any longer because he couldn't *have* her any longer.

The two of them were headed in opposite directions. She was a mistake that he couldn't let happen again.

He took out another stick of gum, covering up the taste of her. Even after she'd left, her perfume seemed to cling to him. The trouble was, he liked what she chose.

Enough. He reverted to Special Agent Ross mode. Surveyed the scene. Observed every movement Sage made and bided his time.

He listened to Sage convince the front desk clerk to relinquish the key to a small conference room located off the main lobby. Jacob knew about it because he'd done his due diligence and had scoped out all the rooms and cubbyholes and exits in the old colonial-era building.

At the last minute, though, Sage changed his mind and diverted his path to the lobby men's room, disappearing inside as one of the bodyguards planted himself before the entrance door, legs spread, hands clasped.

This was where a Secret Service badge came in handy. Jacob was in luck, too, because a men's room was the only place that guaranteed him a conversation that Isabel couldn't overhear.

Jacob headed for the men's room, too. On the way, he opened the leather man-purse thing—sporran, Isabel had called it—and grabbed his ID. He wished he had his radio and a backup team with him, but if he handled this encounter well, soon Jacob could be on his way to Washington and the Presidential Protective Division.

Sage's security guard stationed outside the door shook his head at Jacob. "Nope."

Jacob made the universal "I really have to go" look.

The security guard didn't buy it. Jacob sighed and made a show of displaying his ID. "I'm off duty. I'm a guest at the wedding."

"You're in the Secret Service?"

"I am. In the New York field office."

The guard looked impressed, maybe because Jacob actually had jurisdiction to arrest people. "Go ahead, sir. Just please don't speak to Mr. Sage. His orders."

"Right." Two steps forward and Jacob was inside. A shot of adrenaline swept through his system as he quickly scanned the room.

Sage was alone at a sink washing his hands, getting ready to leave.

Jacob knew he had little time to make his appeal. The smartest thing was to be direct. He'd rehearsed this speech in his mind many times these past few days.

"Mr. Sage," Jacob said calmly. "My name is Jacob Ross. I'm a U.S. Secret Service agent." Leaning on the power of that authority, he showed his badge again. "Sorry for interrupting you, but what I need to ask has to be kept confidential."

With slow, calm, deliberate motion, John Sage shook his hands dry. "Is everything all right?" he asked blandly. The man was cool, no doubt about that.

"I'm here," Jacob said, "because I need to understand, from an operational viewpoint, what happened to my father, Donald Ross. All I know is that he was killed in a rescue mission involving your niece and nephew twenty years ago. I've spoken to inspectors at the police department in Edinburgh, but as I understand it from them, there's very little available in the way of old files. Their advice was that I talk with you."

"Did they also tell you to approach me at my nephew's wedding?"

Jacob ignored the subtle cut. "I was given your name as someone who would be helpful to me, and this venue is the only place I had access to you. I apologize for that, but it's critical for me that we talk."

Sage finished drying his hands.

Even more so than Isabel, Sage didn't allow

emotion to show on his face. He was serious, in his suit and his tie, and not a kilt like Jacob wore. He struck Jacob as a man who ran his business and kept it very close to the vest.

Jacob waited for the reaction. The truth was that he had no formal power to force an interview.

"If you have twenty minutes available anytime before you leave, then I would appreciate it," Jacob said quietly, because what else could he do?

He didn't know how else to get what he needed. Isabel couldn't help him any more than she already had. The nephew—the groom—couldn't help, either, because he didn't know enough. Sage held all the cards.

"I've always been an admirer of those in the U.S. Secret Service," Sage said pleasantly, meeting Jacob's gaze as he did so. Jacob recognized that he was in the presence of a master diplomat. "I've done some research on my own about your mission, and I respect it very much. It's impressive."

"Thank you," Jacob murmured.

"I'm particularly intrigued by your specialized training. It's why I enjoy hiring those with your unique skills. In fact, I have a request for you. I'd like you to watch over Isabel during the next weeks, before she leaves New York City, finishing her degree and returning home to Scotland."

"I'm not looking for a job," Jacob said. "And I'm not available for hire like you're requesting."

"You misunderstand," Sage said pleasantly. Just then, the door creaked open. It was the security guard, checking on them.

Sage waved him back. "We're fine, thank you." The door closed.

He turned his attention back to Jacob. "I want you to check on Isabel discreetly for me, as a personal favor, not a formal job."

"You're right, I don't understand."

"I need to know specifically if Isabel is speaking with any American media outlets or even to someone who in turn may be leaking information regarding the company," Sage said. "There's been an internal breach, which I hope will not be devastating to us. I'm investigating all the top staff as a matter of formality."

"No. I can't do that. I can't betray her like that." He wasn't Alex.

Sage regarded him silently for a moment, that calm expression never leaving his face. "That's a shame," he murmured.

Sage turned and looked in the mirror, straightening his tie one last time.

In a moment, he would be gone. This all was part of a negotiation, Jacob realized. Sage had turned the tables on him, a clever proposal so he could keep some leverage with Jacob, as well as with Isabel.

Sage had to know that Jacob was Isabel's driver this weekend.

"Will you grant my request?" Jacob asked.

"I feel for your situation, I really do, but I simply don't have time this evening to talk with you. I'm leaving within the hour."

"*If* I'd agreed to investigate Isabel for you," Jacob asked, "were you prepared to give me what I need?"

Sage met his eyes in the mirror. He still had no expression except a bland agreeability. "As a matter of fact, I was prepared to invite you to my private home in Scotland over the holidays, where we might have more time to talk. Perhaps I could have invited some…people—" Jacob assumed he meant people who knew his father "—in order to help you find the answers you need."

It was a stunning offer—much more than Jacob had expected.

Isabel would kill for this invitation. Jacob didn't know why he'd thought of that. It wasn't fair that he'd received it so easily.

"I can't betray Isabel," he repeated aloud.

Sage looked at him. But it was true what Jacob had said—he'd told her at the beginning of this journey that he wouldn't betray her, and he would keep that promise.

"I'm sorry," Sage said smoothly, "I was mistaken. I was under the impression that you already had betrayed my niece."

"Excuse me?"

"Have you told her who you really are? I sincerely

doubt it. If she knew what you were hiding, then she wouldn't have attended the wedding with you in the first place."

Jacob stood frozen in place. How had this happened? He hadn't even realized that's what he'd been doing.

"Further," Sage continued, "I'm *not* asking you to betray Isabel. My hope is that she's innocent and has done nothing against the company. You would simply be verifying that fact for me, as someone must. A formality. If you don't do it, then someone else will. Worst case—if no one agrees, there will be a cloud of suspicion over her. I've already questioned everyone, but…"

He gave a small shrug.

Jacob knew he had a decision to make.

"I'll expect you unless I hear otherwise." Sage stared at Jacob. "If you need to communicate with me, you'll send word via your friend Lee, I presume?"

But before Jacob could answer, the door opened.

One of the bodyguards entered. And behind him…

Isabel walked in.

THIS WAS THE first time Isabel had ever followed a security agent into a men's room, but she'd learned

Jacob was inside with her uncle, and Isabel had damage control to consider.

She needed to be part of the conversation, and if the conversation was occurring in a men's room, then, well, into the men's room she must go.

The first things she saw were the urinals on the wall, reminding her she didn't belong here. But her father had always taught her that being a woman in a male-dominated business world was not for the faint of heart. She needed to remember she was just as important as they were. And if it involved following them onto a golf course, or into a smoky barroom, or even this, a men's loo at a public venue, then so be it.

She smiled as best she could and lifted her chin. "I delivered your message, Uncle, but Malcolm is busy dancing with his bride."

Yes, it was a petty dig at Malcolm, and at some level it both shamed her and made her feel guilty over the satisfaction it gave, but theirs was a complicated family with an often painful history, and this was one of those painful times.

Clearly, Malcolm was the favored one. She was not. And as Hugh had said, her dad would surely urge her to fight, if he were here.

"I see," her uncle said.

"And I see you met Jacob." She went and stood beside him. "I was going to introduce you two, but you've beaten me to it." She smiled up at Jacob. "How are you doing?"

"I'm glad to see you happy, my dear," her uncle murmured.

She paused. Actually, she *was* happy. "Thank you, Uncle."

"I was just telling Jacob that I would like to invite both you and him to my home for Christmas dinner."

Had she heard him correctly? She glanced to Jacob, but he didn't look as pleased. He'd turned kind of green.

Perhaps this was an awful lot to deal with on his part.

"I'm impressed with both of you, my dear," her uncle said smoothly. "I'd like to see you in a more private, relaxed conversation. Please let me know what you decide. You may call Murphy with your response."

"Yes!" Isabel said. The answer was, as her study-group partner Charles would say, a "no-brainer." Isabel had been trying to get an invitation from him for years. Usually only Malcolm was favored with such offerings. "Will Malcolm be there?" she couldn't help asking.

"No, just you."

"Of course," Isabel said. "Of course I'll be there."

Jacob's lips pressed together.

"I would like to see you *both*," her uncle said gently to him.

"Jacob, as well?" she clarified.

"Yes, Jacob, as well." He smiled at her. "I look forward to it."

Outside by the fireplace, alone with Jacob, Isabel turned to him. "What happened in there? I've been trying to get that invitation for years—how did you manage it in just a few minutes?"

JACOB FELT SICK to his stomach. Isabel had no clue what her uncle was really thinking about her. Jacob understood why Isabel wanted to spend time with her uncle, but Jacob also knew that he had complicated her life in ways he couldn't even begin to explain.

There was no way he was spying on her for her uncle. No way in hell. Ever.

"I don't know what just happened," he said, "and I don't like it."

"I'm sorry," she replied. "I didn't expect that. He completely surprised me."

"You mean you didn't expect him to invite me?"

"I didn't expect him to invite me, either." She stopped her pacing and glanced at him. "The difference is, *you* impressed him. *You're* the reason for this invitation."

"I didn't impress anybody."

"What did you *say* to him, Jacob?"

"Nothing."

"He didn't see us kissing," she mused. "That was probably a good thing."

Jacob sighed. "Yeah, that was definitely a good thing."

"He likes you on your merit."

"Improbable as it is," he muttered.

She shook her head, looking dazed. "I've sacrificed a lot to prove myself to him over the years. I'm just happy that things are finally starting to fall into place. Maybe I should just leave the discussion with him where it stands."

What could Jacob say that wouldn't rain on her parade? *Be discreet*—that had been his directive all along. He couldn't even tell her who he really was. Couldn't tell her that, in a sense, he had always been using her, even if that hadn't been his intention.

Even if the tables had flipped on him and he now cared about *her,* more than he wanted to.

It was clear to Jacob what he needed to do. The person he'd always thought he was—that *honest* person—needed to come out again. He needed to go back to being just a silent bodyguard where Isabel was concerned. Tomorrow morning he would take her back to Manhattan and return her to her residence hall.

He wouldn't ruin her night, however. He walked with her into the ballroom and politely endured the introductions with her mom, her brothers and her cousins. He stood with Isabel when her uncle entered the dance floor and the guests—at least on the Sage side of the family—broke into cheers.

Then they all watched her uncle dance with the bride. Along with everyone else, Jacob and Isabel lifted their glasses and toasted the happy couple.

It struck Jacob that the laptop that had allowed Rhiannon to watch the ceremony had been moved to the reception ballroom. After the toast, he saw Malcolm speaking quietly to his sister.

All three of them—he, Malcolm and Rhiannon—had been children twenty years earlier. They'd all been affected by the events of that fateful day in Edinburgh. Rhiannon was obviously damaged. Malcolm seemed to be caught balancing between his old world and his new world.

Even Isabel, on the periphery of the tragedy, seemed to be affected by her inability to compete with her uncle's sympathy for Malcolm and Rhiannon.

But Jacob wasn't hurt like these two. He'd never known his father, and his mother had remarried even before that day. Jacob had grown up a world away. Until now, learning what had happened hadn't been critical to his life. Not until a psychologist at work had decided that it made a difference.

What was he going to do?

When Isabel came back from dancing one of the reels that he didn't know the steps to, her face was glowing and her eyes were bright. She looked up at Jacob, laughing, and his heart seemed to crater.

"Are you up for a dance?" she asked. "I could teach you." But she read his face before he could speak. "Oh. Sorry. You look like you've had a long day."

"Yeah, I got a call from work." Man, the lies were flowing easily now. "I need to go upstairs and return it. Can I walk you back to your room?"

"Not just yet, I need to stay a while longer. How about we meet for breakfast tomorrow at eight?"

"That sounds fine."

"Jacob...thank you. I don't often accept help from people, or even admit that I need it most times, but I'm glad I did with you. You made this weekend good for me, and I won't forget that."

Jacob paused. He wanted to tell her that she deserved happiness. But it was too hard for him. And he still had to drive her back to New York City tomorrow.

ISABEL'S HEART ACHED to see Jacob walk away, so handsome and strong in his kilt. He'd saved her this weekend, and she would be forever grateful to him.

She stood at the edge of the boisterous scene before her. Her family, big and loud and happy. They were all paired off now, even Malcolm. The cousins she'd once played with as children were starting families of their own.

She'd never been likely to fit into that type of family life. And now that Alex had broken up with her, she knew that more than ever. So why the ache of loneliness?

Frowning, she headed for the lobby. Her uncle was gathering to leave—she'd been keeping her eye on him, waiting for her chance.

He'd spoken in depth to Malcolm, then to Malcolm and Kristin, and finally to Rhiannon, alone before the monitor. Isabel had caught a glimpse of his face, and he'd looked sad as he'd turned away from her.

With her shawl wrapped tightly around her shoulders, Isabel approached him. "Uncle, may I talk with you?"

"About business, no. That will wait until you're home for Christmas. But walk with me to the door and tell me quickly what happened to your friend Alex."

She sighed and walked beside him. Why not tell him? It really didn't matter anymore. "We broke up. He didn't like that I've dedicated myself to my goal of leading our company."

Her uncle pursed his lips. "That's unfortunate."

"No, it's not. I'd asked him to wait for me, but he showed me what I mean to him," she said softly.

"Is that when Jacob asked to accompany you to the wedding?"

"No, I asked him, actually."

"Be careful there," her uncle warned as he stopped at the threshold.

"How do you mean?" she asked.

Murphy handed her uncle his overcoat. They all paused as her uncle buttoned himself up and wrapped a scarf around his neck. The night air had turned cold. It even smelled like winter outside.

"As with anyone," her uncle advised, "be sure that you know him. Be smart before you expose yourself."

"I'm *not* exposing myself," she said.

"In a sense, you already have. You've brought him here."

He spread his arm toward the reception at the end of the hall, the music fainter but still audible. "You've exposed your cousins to him, as well."

"Then why did you invite him and me to Christmas dinner?"

He smiled slightly at her. "You've asked for the highest position of responsibility in our company, have you not? I'd like to get to know the candidate I'm considering. And her friend." He stared at her. "I want you to be happy *and* safe, Isabel. I'll send the company plane for you both next month. We'll talk more then."

She watched him leave, stunned by his words.

Upstairs, she noticed right away that Jacob had left his door open a crack. Listening until she came up, probably.

She stared at his partially open door. Should she knock?

But in the end, she didn't. Her uncle's words still echoed in her head.

In the final analysis, she was a Sage. She needed to tread carefully.

AT BREAKFAST, JACOB had circles under his eyes as if he hadn't slept. Isabel had spent the night tossing and turning, too, thinking about her uncle's comments. She still wasn't sure what she was going to do about Jacob and Christmas dinner.

Jacob, however, had seemed to figure out everything on his own. As the SUV rolled down the highway toward Manhattan, he made his big declaration. "I shouldn't have kissed you, Isabel."

He must have seen her face fall, but he kept going anyway. "We have a connection that draws us together—I won't deny that. But it's dumb for us to continue. We don't have lives that will ever mesh in the future."

"I know that," she said, feeling testy. "You don't have to worry about me, because that's not what I want from you."

His jaw moved. "Please don't want *anything* from me. Because I can't give it to you."

"You had feelings for me when you kissed me," she said. "I felt it, too."

"It's a mistake to even go there," he insisted.

Maybe, but it hurt to hear him say so aloud. She needed to understand clearly. "Are you saying you want to give up on it entirely? For us to walk away and drop everything?"

There was a long silence. "That's the way I'm leaning, yes," he said.

Leaning. That meant he wasn't entirely convinced. She was glad, because she'd be crushed if she believed he really wanted to cut her off now.

The problem was, she had enjoyed his company as much as she knew he'd enjoyed hers.

"Well, consider my input, for what it's worth," she said. "My proposal is that I would like to see you for the next few weeks, while I'm still in New York. Then, if we both decide, why *not* take my uncle up on his offer? You could visit Scotland for once. See the land of your ancestors."

Jacob just looked at her, desolate. "You've got this all figured out, don't you?"

Actually, she had just decided—influenced, no doubt, by being in his SUV with him on the long trip home. "I think it's a livable plan."

He glanced at her, not saying a word.

"If we still decide at the end of the month that it's a good idea," she said, "then my uncle said he'll send his private jet for us.

"So, yes, I would very much like to see you in Edinburgh for Christmas dinner, Jacob. That is my invitation. Think about it, and we'll be in touch."

CHAPTER SEVEN

BACK IN THE CITY, Isabel bided her time. That first week, she had an economics project to present, a paper on social responsibility in investing due and two case studies for her business law elective to read. All this work just made her that much more motivated to buckle down and concentrate on achieving her goals for the future.

The Christmas meeting at her uncle's house was key to her plans, no question, and she would never have a better opportunity to make it happen. To do so, she needed Jacob's cooperation.

Of course, she knew that too much prevented them from ever being together as a long-term couple, and she accepted that.

Ironically, though, she also needed to heed her uncle's advice. She needed to investigate Jacob. Was he, in fact, trustworthy enough to bring into her uncle's home?

Yes, the invitation was for the two of them, but if she found reason not to trust Jacob and presented those facts to her uncle, her uncle would think more highly of her than if she brought him to Christmas dinner without thought.

She was sure she would find no reason not to trust Jacob. He was a Secret Service agent, wasn't he?

She waited until her school coursework was successfully completed before she initiated her first "tail Jacob Ross" assignment—scope out where he lived.

The driver's license he'd shown her had included his address. So, four days after they'd returned from Vermont, and without hearing a single word from him, she set out on a rainy Thursday under her brolly—umbrella here, she reminded herself—to his apartment twenty blocks away.

She enjoyed the walk in the light breeze. Being Scottish, she was used to the drizzly weather. Fallen leaves from the trees lining the avenue skittered past her feet. She'd chosen early morning, just before the commuter rush. She still had an hour before her first class of the day, and the walk was also serving to clear her head.

She'd been having trouble sleeping of late. She'd been waking up after dreaming of Jacob. It was just a fantasy that made no sense. A stage for her to pass over quickly.

She fell into the rhythm of the walk. Each short block took about a minute to hike, so that meant twenty minutes total until she reached Jacob's building. She passed over a subway grate, the warm air from the trains a welcome blast on this cool day. She tightened the belt on her short raincoat. Pulled the hood over her hair, which was held back in a pony-tail. In her coat pocket were just the keys to her room and her ID. She wore flats and jeans so she could run if she needed to.

All this time she'd been living in New York, she'd been mostly confined to her campus area. This was new, this walk. Different. Even a bit exciting. She hummed to herself.

Jacob's neighborhood wasn't what she expected. Down a shaded street, he lived in a small brick walk-up with ivy winding around it. Rather like the pretty Georgian home where she owned her flat back in Edinburgh, which was currently undecorated and rented out to a marketing contractor in their cos-metics division.

She tapped her umbrella on the pavement. As she was deciding what to do, Jacob came striding out of his building, still putting on his suit jacket as he trotted down the steps. He bounded over to lean into the driver's-side window of a black SUV—a familiar-looking black SUV—idling, double-parked at the curb.

There appeared to be a man inside, to whom Jacob was talking. Curious, she crossed the street and edged closer. Jacob straightened, then headed into a nearby coffee shop.

Pulling open the shop's heavy glass door, she went inside, too. In the foyer, she closed her umbrella, shaking off the raindrops. Inhaling the enticing scent of freshly brewed coffee, she took off her hood.

"Isabel!" She should have known Jacob would spot her before she spotted him.

She turned. The shock in his eyes was almost palpable as he bounded out of the queue at the register and marched over to her. "You followed me here, didn't you?"

She sighed. Should she play coy or just banter with him to throw him off?

"I did," she finally said, deciding to take the direct route. It suited her best, anyway. She smiled at him. "Did you miss me?"

His gaze flitted up and down her body. She felt her nipples tighten as his attention brushed over her. After everything they'd been through, this man just…did something to her.

She felt a hunger, a physical attraction for him that floored her.

He touched her arm, gently guiding her behind a section of wire racks holding mugs and other merchandise—a more private alcove for them to talk. Her toes curled inside her flats.

He put his hands on his hips and opened his mouth but then said nothing. He shook his head as if he didn't know what to say. She'd shocked him that much.

"Jake, what are you doing? I've been waiting for

you outside and—" The man who'd been sitting in the SUV stopped when he saw her. "Whoa."

"Hello," she said, smiling. "I'm Isabel Sage."

The man nodded, wiping his hand on his trousers. He was shorter than Jacob, with black hair and deep brown eyes, warm like chocolate. "You're the woman from the Vermont weekend," he said.

"Jacob talked about me?"

A broad grin answered her. "As much as Jake ever talks about anything."

"Jake?" She turned to Jacob, pulled a face and then turned back to his friend.

"Damn, I love your English accent," Jacob's friend said.

In situations like this, before she'd met Jacob, she always would have let the mistake go, in favor of remaining low-key. It was a relief to be honest. "It's Scottish," she said.

"Right." He nodded.

"Did *Jake* tell you he wore a kilt last weekend?" she asked.

A laugh split his face. "Seriously? I wish I'd seen that."

"And he danced at a wedding, too."

"Enough," Jacob said, growling.

"We're friends and we work together, even though sometimes you might not know it," the man said to Isabel. He stuck out his hand. "Hi. I'm Eddie Walsh."

"Pleased to meet you, Eddie." She shook his hand. His other hand had a wedding ring on it, she noticed.

"You know," Eddie said, "a bunch of us are going out tomorrow night."

"No," Jacob said automatically. He motioned Isabel to the coffee aisle, away from Eddie. Isabel thought for a moment, and then followed Jacob behind a row of racks.

"What are you doing?" Jacob asked her when they were out of earshot from Eddie.

"Nothing, Jacob," she said in all innocence.

"This isn't your neighborhood."

"I know. But it occurred to me that you were right—I'm leaving New York in a few weeks, and I really haven't stepped out of my comfort zone. So, I decided to see what I'm missing." She picked up a bag of coffee beans from the shelf and sniffed them.

"I really wish you hadn't come here," Jacob said, groaning as Eddie came wandering toward them.

Eddie held out a business card to her. "This is for you, Isabel. Anytime you want to go out with us, give *me* a call."

She accepted Eddie's card. Jacob knocked his forehead against the metal rack, a purposeful reaction to show his displeasure. "Thank you, I just might do that," she said to Eddie.

Eddie grinned. "That's it—it's a definite. Call me tonight. I'll work on him." He shot a glance at Jacob.

"No," Jacob said flatly.

"Intensity," Eddie murmured to him. Jacob glowered.

That word was obviously a code between them, which showed Isabel that she wasn't the only recipient of Jacob's sometimes-bad attitude. She didn't see what the fuss was about, but it was making her more determined not to give up, especially now that Eddie was on her side.

Why shouldn't they all be friendly? It was only for another five weeks until she left New York. She obviously wasn't looking for a relationship.

Many people felt romantic feelings during a wedding ceremony. She and Jacob had been no different. But the weekend was over.

"Goodbye, Jacob," she said cheerfully. "I have to be getting back. Nice to meet you, Eddie. I'll talk with you later."

"You can't leave now," Jacob said to her. "Come over and get in the SUV. We'll give you a ride home."

"You're not my bodyguard anymore, Jacob."

"Jacob." Eddie snickered.

But in the end, they all climbed into the big black SUV. Once inside, she saw that it was a different vehicle from the one she had ridden in with Jacob earlier. It either belonged to Eddie or was a work vehicle. This time, Jacob sat in the backseat beside her.

To Eddie, he said, "Head uptown, I'll tell you when to stop."

Jacob didn't speak to her during the short ride. But when the SUV stopped, he stepped outside with her and escorted her the few paces to her building.

At the door, he asked, "Is this all just to get me to go to Scotland with you?"

"Maybe," she said.

"So that's the reason why you came by my neighborhood?"

She sighed. "No."

"What's the reason?"

"To see you."

He scowled at her. "Why can't you just say what you mean?"

She winked playfully, enjoying seeing him again. "Don't be so intense, Jake."

"Isabel, don't toy with me."

"Then give me your phone number so I don't have to call your partner for it."

"He isn't my partner anymore. We were partners in the NYPD. In the Secret Service we work on teams."

"Well, he said he's your friend. And he's driving the SUV like a partner."

"Because we're currently assigned to investigating a credit-card-fraud case together," he said between his teeth. "It's short-term."

"I suppose he sees you every day."

"Fine. You win." Glowering, Jacob took out a

card. Put the pen cap in his mouth and wrote his phone number using his knee as a support.

He was so intense and tortured. "It's not about winning, Jacob," she said gently.

"What do you want with me?" he asked, shoving the card forward.

"To get to know you better."

"That's not a good idea," he said flatly.

"You wrote your phone number," she said, glancing at the card but not taking it from him. "That means you're participating, too. Whatever it is that we're doing, you want it, too."

"Actually, I don't." He lowered the hand holding the card.

"You haven't had any kind of relationship with a woman in a long time, have you?" she asked softly.

"What does that have to do with anything?" he growled. "Because other than…that other guy…you haven't, either."

"Yes, just one real relationship my entire life, and his name is Alex." She closed her fingers around Jacob's card, but he wasn't releasing it to her.

She tugged it gently. "I'm not here to talk about anyone except you."

"Is that so?" He kept his grip on the card.

She struggled with his card some more. "Are all bodyguards so stubborn?"

Jacob let go of the card abruptly, and she had to

step back a pace. But he'd let her have it. She smiled at him, clutching his phone number.

He turned and walked away without a word.

"Pick up the phone when I ring you tonight, please," she called after him.

"I'm *not* taking you out," he said over his shoulder.

"I don't want you to take me out. My conditions are that we meet in a group. I need to be safe and check you out first, and that means evaluating you by your friends, in the safety of a group setting."

He stopped cold, gaping at her. His mouth was left hanging open, but she turned on her heel without reply.

Jacob had started this. He'd gone into that loo and met her uncle. Now her uncle wanted to see him in Edinburgh for Christmas dinner. She was just doing her due diligence.

JACOB GOT BACK into the SUV and held up his palm before Eddie could say a word. "Don't start."

"You didn't tell me she was smokin' hot," Eddie said.

"I forbid you to look at her."

"She's hot for you, not me. Besides, I'm not looking at anybody." Eddie put the gear into Drive.

Jacob groaned and leaned his head against the seat back.

Eddie laughed as they pulled into traffic. "You didn't tell her, did you?"

"I have no idea what you're talking about," Jacob muttered.

"Uh-huh. She has no idea why you took that job driving her to Vermont, does she?"

Jacob sighed. "Nope."

"You are an idiot, my friend."

Jacob raised his head. "If I tell her the truth, she's gone. If she's gone, then I've lost contact with John Sage, the one guy who can give me the information I need."

"Well, Jake, you won't be dating Isabel for long if you don't tell her the truth about it."

"I'm not dating her, dammit!" Jacob leaned his head back again. "She wants to go out with my friends in a group."

Eddie cracked a smile. "Perfect. I'll call Donna. She lives for this kind of thing."

"Do not make a big deal of it," Jacob insisted.

"Why are you so ruffled?"

Should he tell Eddie? "You haven't heard the worst of it." Jacob slapped his hand on the dash. "Sage wants me to investigate her in exchange for talking to me."

Eddie was silent. "You gotta tell her, man, because she's gonna find out at some point."

Yeah. Yeah, Jacob knew that. But he couldn't do

it just yet. He needed to figure out what his plan really was. There *had* to be a way out of this so that both he and Isabel each got what they wanted.

And she didn't get hurt.

IN THE OFFICE later that morning, Jacob knew he had to go and tell his grizzled, old-school manager, Tony Marshall—just a year away from retirement and therefore very interested in following protocol—that he was doing…what exactly?…with Isabel Sage.

And the reason Jacob had to report his involvement with her was because, technically, Isabel was a foreign national. Jacob's government security clearance was due to be renewed soon, and since he already had major problems with his employee file, he wanted to be sure to head off any other issues.

He was still scratching his head over exactly how to handle his dilemma with Isabel when he got back to his desk, only to find that Eddie and the gang were running Isabel's info through their litany of investigative databases.

Oh, hell, no, he was going to say to them, but then he paused. He leaned over the computer screen. This was just basic stuff they were checking into. Everyday due diligence. If done properly, it could satisfy part of what John Sage had asked, but…did Jacob really want to go down this road?

If he wanted to exchange info with John Sage— and he wasn't sure he did—it would probably be best to have something, even a basic shell of nonincriminating "evidence," to show.

For example, did Isabel even have any contacts with magazine or tabloid editors? Jacob thought back. Her suite mates were journalists, weren't they? Maybe there was a connection there.

No, Jacob did not want to investigate her suite mates, too.

He pushed his hands through his hair. While he was still contemplating his role in the whole damn thing, he got called into Tony's office.

"I talked with Diane," Tony said.

The department psychologist. Great, Jacob thought.

"She mentioned a reminder about scheduling a follow-up appointment with her. She wants you to set it up ASAP."

Jacob had been working on the paperwork she'd left him with. It had just seemed humiliating considering he was the only person he knew who was required to go through her extra scrutiny. Diane had also wanted him to meet with her every week for an "assessment," but he'd wanted to get his ducks in a row with Sage before he met with her again.

Maybe he should be worried, though. "Why ASAP? What's happened?"

Tony shook his head. He wasn't meeting Jacob's eyes, and that wasn't a good sign.

"Just get it cleared up, Jake. You need her authorization before you can go on to your next assignment. My endorsement isn't enough."

"Okay," he said carefully. "You should know that I, ah, need time off to go to Scotland over Christmas. Diane's asking me a lot of questions about, ah, people and events there."

"Good." Tony nodded. "Get it done. Go now, if you'd rather not wait."

Without Isabel? Other than getting to Sage through her, he didn't see how. What else would he do, crash a heavily fortified corporate-headquarters building in downtown Edinburgh and waylay the guy as he left Sage Family Products one evening?

Yeah, right. Even if he avoided being arrested by the local police, he'd know that Isabel would hate him forever because he would've screwed her reputation with her uncle, too.

He never should have kissed her to begin with.

As soon he was back at his desk, Jacob picked up the phone and made his appointment with Diane, dragging out the unfinished paperwork as he did so. Then, as he sat in his mental purgatory over what to do about Isabel, he fiddled with his credit-card-fraud case, which included going out with Eddie and conducting an interview.

Even then, Isabel slipped into his thoughts. He was being driven crazy. He would see a blonde walk past on the street, and he was immediately turning to check if it was her. The whole situation was nuts.

After lunch, Eddie called Jacob over to his desk. Three of the guys from the Counter Assault Team were huddled around Eddie's screen, chortling. Eddie had brought up a photo of Isabel with Alex, in evening dress. The kicker was they were accompanying some of the royal family at a charity event in London.

Jacob felt two inches high. "Turn that damn thing off," he snapped.

"These are the kinds of people she's used to socializing with. Jake, you can't be a schmuck to her."

"She must be slumming with you," one of the CAT guys said.

Jacob walked away. This sucked. It was a mess.

But nothing was as bad as the kick in the gut when Tony came out of his office to address them directly. It was the coup de grâce.

"Listen up, people. The call came in. We have some transfers to announce. I'm just gonna do it now rather than prolong the agony."

Jacob got a very bad feeling.

"Eddie, you're going to Washington, D.C."

Jacob sat and waited for his name to be announced, too, but the announcement didn't come. Jacob's longtime pal had been chosen for the Presidential Protective Division, not him.

The irony was, Eddie had only quit the NYPD and moved over to the Secret Service because of

Jacob. Presidential Protective Division hadn't been his dream the way it had been for Jacob.

Jacob felt as if a freight train had run him over. But he went through the motions, giving his congratulations to his best friend. Eddie was over the moon because Donna really wanted to move back to the Washington, D.C. area.

Afterward, Jacob sat at his desk in front of the documents for the fraud case he'd been assigned to investigate—not even a particularly interesting scam at that—and he put his head in his hands.

Eddie strolled over to his desk. "I'll do what I can to get you down there with me, pal."

"Thanks." Jacob closed his laptop and stood. "Go out and celebrate," he said, suddenly feeling tired. "You and Donna deserve it."

"Funny you should say that. Donna is planning something special for all of us to celebrate tomorrow night."

By the tone of Eddie's voice, Jacob was sure the event involved Isabel, as well. Great, he had a splitting headache already.

He leaned back and pinched the bridge of his nose. "I'll call her. That's what you want me to do, isn't it?"

"You really like her, Jacob, you know you do."

His problems were bigger than that. It was painfully apparent that Jacob needed to get serious. He couldn't stay in the New York field office, stagnant and alone. His goal always had been to work on a presidential protective detail. That's where he needed to be. That's where he needed to focus his efforts, even if it involved interacting with Isabel for the next five weeks until she left for Christmas break.

If he didn't go home with her to see her uncle, then he was left doing financial fraud investigations, or the occasional small-time diplomatic-bodyguard assignment while Eddie worked the job Jacob wanted. This standoff with Isabel had to stop.

Bottom line, it looked as if he *was* going to Scotland for Christmas with her.

And investigating the hell out of her until then.

CHAPTER EIGHT

Isabel didn't hear from Jacob, and she didn't call him, either. She did, however, receive a phone call from Donna Walsh—Eddie's wife—with an invitation to a get-together on Friday night. Isabel accepted for one reason: to check out Jacob. It would also be fun to keep him on his toes.

When the day came, Isabel wrapped up the afternoon session where she'd been playing tour guide to a visiting university speaker who was also a friend of her uncle's. She raced home from campus and took a shower, then dressed in a short blue dress with trendy tights and her favorite tall zip-up boots. She dried her hair, applied her makeup and put on some fun, artsy jewelry and a leather jacket.

"Are you *sure* you don't need me to walk with you?" Rajesh asked as she headed for the lift outside her residence suite.

"No, thank you, I'd like to walk to the subway station myself. It's only three blocks away."

"Once you're inside, remember to choose the Downtown platform," Rajesh instructed. "Not Uptown. *Downtown.* And count the stops."

"I'll remember. Thank you, Rajesh."

"You have my number in your phone. Call me if you need assistance."

Philip snickered at her. Yes, Isabel had actually been in New York City for all this time, and she'd never before ridden the busy city subway system.

Since she'd met Jacob, it seemed, she'd been stretched far out of her usual sphere of habit.

"Go, Braveheart," Rajesh whispered. "Freedom," he added with a fist pump, as the lift doors closed between them.

Rajesh's instructions were good and Isabel easily merged with the flow of the crowd to ride the rattling subway car to the station one block from the address Donna had given her.

Actually, Isabel was having fun already. She had one major purpose tonight, and that was to question the women in the group about Jacob's character.

The night was cool and the street was lit so brightly there were hardly any shadows to threaten her. Shifting her shoulder bag beneath her arm, she pushed open the doors to the venue where the party was to be held.

The impromptu celebration for Eddie's promotion was held in a private room above a midtown Manhattan bar, with brass railings and shellacked wood and mirrors with rows of bottles in front.

The jostling, talkative crowd packed inside the main floor reminded Isabel of the traditional bar haunts near Edinburgh Castle. For a moment, she felt homesick, but then remembered she only needed to last a few more weeks in New York before she would be flying home.

Inside the pub, she climbed the creaking, winding staircase to a function room with high ceilings and a smaller, separate bar area.

"You must be Isabel," said a woman with an infant in her arms. She followed Isabel's gaze to the baby's sweet face and said, "Sorry, I couldn't get my usual sitter for him."

"He's precious," Isabel cooed.

"I'm Donna, Eddie's wife. This is Alden. He's almost four months old, and he's pretty mellow. Would you like to hold him?"

Taking Isabel's smile for a yes, Donna handed the bundled-up Alden to Isabel, and then marched off to hunt down a cocktail server.

Nervous, Isabel eyed the drooling but warm and sweet-smelling cutie, his oversize head tucked inside her elbow. He smiled toothlessly at her, and she felt her nerves dissolving into wonder.

Donna was taking an awfully long time, but Alden entertained her with his baby charm. He gurgled and winked, and she tentatively rubbed her knuckle along his cheek. Such soft skin…

"Careful, there," said a familiar deep voice at her side. "You can't take him home with you."

Jacob. He'd obviously just walked in from outside. His wool jacket smelled like a cool late-fall night. His hair was damp and he seemed fresh from a shower.

He also looked rather good in a pair of jeans and a green jumper—*sweater*—that complemented the blue of his eyes.

No, don't look there. She put her attention back on baby Alden and smoothly passed him to Jacob. "Maybe you should hold him."

"Very funny, Isabel," Jacob said. But he looked down at the baby and made a silly face at him.

"Do *you* know what his name is?" she asked.

"Of course. This is Alden." Jacob smiled at him and shifted him to a more comfortable position against his chest.

Isabel's heart seemed to flutter. Well, Jacob had passed *that* small test. A man who was kind to children was a positive start.

"Have you talked with Philip and Courtney lately, your journalist roommates?" Jacob asked.

"Why?" she said, not knowing where he was going with this.

He shrugged. "No reason."

Donna returned, wagging a finger at Jacob. "You. Go over there with your friends and leave us alone with Isabel. We want to talk with her."

"Yes, Jacob," Isabel agreed, "let me talk with the women."

Jacob rolled his eyes, but he didn't argue. "Fine. I'll take Alden over with the men."

He promptly strolled over to Eddie, the baby still against his chest.

Donna hooked Isabel's arm and brought her to a table in the corner, crowded with seven or eight other women. Then she flagged down a cocktail server, a young guy dressed all in black. He walked over, looking harried.

"One good thing about not being pregnant anymore is that I can have a cocktail," Donna said. "You first, Isabel. What'll you have?"

Isabel glanced at what the other women were drinking. Wine. Cosmopolitans. One or two mixed drinks.

"I'll take a gin and tonic, please. What kind of gin do you carry?"

In a bored tone, the server mentioned a brand that Isabel hadn't heard of. "Is that okay? It's all we have upstairs."

"That's fine," she said. "What kind of tonic water do you have?"

The server shrugged and glanced at the busy table beside them.

"Well," Isabel said, knowing she was being rushed. "May I please have the bottle on the side? I prefer to mix my own drink."

He stared at her.

"The tonic water comes from the gun," Donna

explained to Isabel. "The bartender mixes it with the liquor for you. I think that's a rule or something."

"Very well." Isabel smiled at the server, who was already turning away. Yet again, she'd subtly misunderstood the customs. This wasn't how they did it at home.

Across the room, a bartender was setting down a beer bottle at Jacob's place before the bar. She smiled as he sipped his beer and contentedly bounced Alden on his lap.

"I'll be damned," Donna mused. "That has to be the first time I've ever seen Jake Ross go near a baby, never mind hold one."

"Is that so?"

"Are you kidding? Usually he acts like he's allergic to Alden."

And yet, Jacob was quietly smiling at the little one. Surely that couldn't be just to prove a point to her?

She felt an itch to join him but restrained herself.

She wished she could stop the diplomacy act for once and just blurt out to Donna, *Tell me everything I need to know about Jacob,* but that wouldn't be wise.

Instead, she followed Donna and took a place with her at the table.

"So, how did you meet Jacob?" Donna asked. "That's what we've all been dying to know. We've been trying to fix him up with our girlfriends for ages."

"Er…" Isabel paused. She hadn't expected to be

the one being quizzed. "Well, my boyfriend…my long-term boyfriend broke up with me unexpectedly…and I was upset…and Jacob was there, and he helped me."

"The damsel-in-distress thing." Donna shook her head. "Darn. I should have tried that."

Isabel's relationship to Jacob had nothing to do with that dynamic, but she kept that information to herself. To her mind, her attraction to him was private.

"Jacob works too much," the woman on the other side of her said, and Isabel turned to her. "They all work too much."

Isabel nodded politely. *Is Jacob trustworthy at work?* she needed to know. *Do his bosses like him?*

The waiter set their drinks before them. Isabel took a sip of her gin and tonic, quite different from what she was used to, and tried to think of another way to phrase her question. "Is there a reason, you suppose, that Jacob didn't get the transfer to Washington that he wanted?"

Donna ate a piece of sushi from a passing plate. "My guess?" she said, wiping her lips with a napkin. "Politics—because Jacob doesn't play them. Mind you, I'm not saying that Eddie does."

"Jacob *is* rather blunt and gruff," Isabel agreed. "If he's mad at you, you certainly know it."

Isabel liked that about him, though. A person always knew where they stood with Jacob.

Not like her uncle John. He tended to be a closed book.

Her father had been closed, too, now that she thought about it. Still, she knew how deeply his circumstances had bothered him, but that was because she was one of the few people he'd confided in.

Like Jacob. Isabel glanced over at the bar where he sat on a stool, quietly rocking Alden as Eddie relayed to him some expressive story that required the use of both hands.

Jacob *was* rather sexy.

Suddenly, he turned and stared back at her. She had the feeling he'd been watching her all along.

Isabel quickly turned away.

"My family is from Maryland, on the Eastern Shore." Donna had pulled over a plate of nachos and was talking between bites. "I'm so happy to be moving back to the area. I miss my parents. When I was in high school, I never thought I'd say that. But it's true." She waved a chip as she spoke. "Did you hear about that teenager who's in court trying to divorce her parents but she still wants them to pay for her to go to college?"

"No. That's crazy." Isabel sipped her drink.

"If that ever happened with Alden, Eddie would have a fit. End of story."

"Mmm," Isabel sympathized.

"If you're going to date Jacob, then go into it with your eyes open," the woman on the other side of Isabel warned her. "Because they travel all the time, without warning. I didn't expect that when I signed on for this."

"We're here for you, Sandy," Donna said, pressing her hand. "It will get better."

"No family event is sacred," Sandy said. "It seems like we're always sacrificing."

Donna leaned over the table and gave her a hug.

Then she turned to Isabel. "I hope we're not scaring you away. Don't get the wrong idea."

"*Why* do you suppose Jacob wants to guard the president of the United States so badly?" Isabel asked.

There was silence at the table.

"He's a protector type like Eddie." Donna shrugged. "It's what they do."

"The PPD is the most elite job in the Secret Service," another woman said. "To make it proves they're the best in their business. They all aspire to guard the president."

"Even though it can trash their personal lives," Sandy said gloomily.

There was more silence.

Donna whispered into Isabel's ear, "Sandy's husband got called out of town this weekend and he's missing their daughter's birthday. It happens a lot in this job. It's why we all stick together so much."

"SHOULDN'T YOU GO over there and intervene?" Eddie asked Jacob. "She's probably getting all the dirt on you."

Jacob rocked Alden in his arms and shrugged. "Doesn't matter. I'm not involved with her. I'm not going to get involved."

"That's not what it looks like from where I'm sitting," Eddie said drily.

Yeah, so? He and Isabel *were* glancing back and forth at one another, but so what? That was part of the setup. Spy versus spy.

"Don't worry about it," Jacob said, shifting Alden because the baby was frowning as if his neck were uncomfortable. "We're good."

"What happened between you two up in Vermont last weekend?"

Jacob held out his finger for Alden to latch on to. The little bald guy had a major grip. "Not a damn thing," he said to Eddie.

"I don't know why I hang out with you," Eddie muttered. "You're no fun."

Jacob hid his smile. Alden was making funny faces in his father's direction. Every time Eddie spoke, the kid gurgled and jerked his body toward him. Kids knew their fathers, that was for sure.

"So," Jacob said as casually as he could, struggling to get his finger back from the little guy, "what did you find out about Isabel? You ran her accounts, right? Phone records? What did they say?"

"Aha!" Eddie reached over and snatched his kid back from Jacob. "I knew it. Something is going on. I knew there had to be a reason Sage invited you to Scotland."

He laid Alden against his shoulder, rubbing his back. "He wants you to find out specific info about her, doesn't he?"

Jacob couldn't fool Eddie. Jacob hated having to ask this, but… "Were there any big lump-sum deposits in Isabel's accounts?"

Eddie danced around a bit, in a bid to help Alden stop squirming. "Not that I noticed."

"*Any* calls to any of the big newspapers or magazine reporters?"

"Nope. She doesn't call much of anyone, it seems."

"She works too damn hard," Jacob muttered. Something about that bothered him. A sweet woman like her, well…

He glanced across the room at her, just in time to see her looking back. Why was she tormenting him?

"I WANT JACOB to come to D.C. with us, too," Donna was saying to Isabel. "Did you know he's godfather to Alden?"

"I did not know that, no."

"I like you, Isabel. If you two do decide to date,

and you get serious, is there *any* chance of you moving to D.C.?" Donna asked, swaying slightly.

Isabel smiled politely. *Not even an inkling of a chance.*

"Well, on the bright side," Donna said, "at least he never painted that mural I wanted. We wouldn't have been able to take it with us anyway."

Donna was starting a fresh drink. Isabel wasn't sure what she was talking about. Had she missed something?

"What mural?" Isabel asked.

"I asked Jacob," Donna said loudly, "to paint Alden a mural for the wall over his crib, but Jacob wouldn't do it."

Isabel glanced at Jacob across the room. He was staring at her again. A muscle was ticking in his jaw. "Did he say why?"

"No."

"Excuse me," Isabel said. "I'll be right back."

Jacob's eyes were still boring a hole in her, so she walked over and sat on the empty stool beside him.

"Did you do your investigative due diligence?" Jacob asked.

"Well," she drawled, carefully crossing her legs and placing her hands over the gap on her tights where her dress drew back from her tall boots, "I've learned nothing but normal, everyday things about you, stuff that I already knew. And then, out of the blue, Donna mentions that you *paint*. Do you paint, Jacob?"

He laughed dryly. "Donna exaggerates."

"She says you refused to paint a mural for Alden." Isabel glanced over at the wee bairn, who was now being passed between his mum and his dad, each of them cooing over his whimpering cries. Actually, Eddie was now sniffing his wee bum. "Is that true, Jacob? You told them no?"

"Is that a problem if it is?" Jacob crossed his arms. "I refuse to do a lot of things that people ask me to do, as a matter of principle."

"Yes, I can see that," she said calmly.

Jacob's lips quirked, as if she was making him smile and he didn't want to smile. "Is that a deal breaker for you?"

"It depends," she said. "Don't you think that Alden might like a mural someday?"

They both glanced over at the infant. Donna had grabbed the diaper bag and was rushing him toward the toilets.

"Would *you* do it?" Jacob asked.

Was he talking about the mural or the nappy change? She was confused. "Well, truthfully, yes, *I* would paint the mural, but I would do it, er, to serve my friend and give him something comforting to look at." She smiled at Jacob. "But I think I understand why *you* won't do it."

Jacob leaned very close to her. Into her space.

"And what's that you think you understand about me?" he said in a low voice.

She wanted to fan her flushed face, but she didn't. Instead, she leaned even closer to him, her heart beating more quickly. "I've noticed you don't do something just because someone asks you. It has to mean something to you."

"And where do you get that from?"

"Well, the only reason you kept helping me at that wedding was because you saw what happened to me with Alex. And you'd been through it, too. It was meaningful to you, and that made you want to help me, in your way, in your time. Isn't it?"

"This is about a mural, Isabel."

"Yes, and you didn't paint it because you want the gift to him to be your expression, your idea, on your terms and with your meaning. Don't you?"

JACOB STARED AT HER. She'd shocked him. That was probably as close as anyone had ever come to getting him.

"And I think that's perfectly valid," she whispered.

She had cast her spell on him yet again. He couldn't keep his eyes from her. Couldn't keep from moving closer and closer into her orbit.

Isabel Sage was classy and perfect and successful. Jacob had no doubt she would fit in smoothly and completely wherever he took her, never showing discomfort.

"The truth is," Jacob said, "I don't paint murals. But I do sketches sometimes."

Isabel's gaze flicked to a piece of artwork on the wall behind him. "Like that?" She pointed.

"No, not landscapes," he said.

"People? Do you draw portraits?"

"Is this part of your investigation of me?"

She smiled slightly. "No. My uncle doesn't care about this sort of thing."

So she had been checking him out for Sage. It didn't surprise him. He took a swig of his beer, now getting warm, since he'd been playing with Alden and concentrating on her. "I want to know about you, Isabel."

But not about her phone calls and her finances. He personally didn't give a damn about those. "What do you do at home in Edinburgh? What do you like, really?"

"Besides work?" She lazily stretched her fingers against her legs.

He nodded, waiting, because there was more to her. He wanted to see deeper.

"Sometimes, on weekends, I go to the National Portrait Gallery by myself and I walk around for no reason. My uncle is a donor there. Sometimes I sit and meditate on one of the benches inside. It's peaceful."

She glanced up at him, beneath her eyelashes. "Actually, Rhiannon is the one who paints. My uncle helps her sell her landscapes. They do very well, monetarily."

He stared sharply at her.

"You remember my cousin Rhiannon?" she asked.

Yes, he remembered. The woman from the monitor, at the wedding. The one who'd been kidnapped when his father had died. "I do," he said softly.

"Well, that's what she does inside her castle, she paints landscapes. I suppose it's her therapy, her way of expressing herself and coping." Isabel looked so sad. Maybe she felt a longing to fix her family. Maybe, like him, she just couldn't do it.

"What kind of landscapes does she paint?" he asked.

"Pleasant places. Beautiful places. The countryside near the castle. She walks a lot, in the Highlands." A line appeared in her brow.

"Do you ever visit her?"

Isabel shook her head. "We were friends as children, but then, afterward…she stopped wanting to see anyone but Malcolm." She shrugged. "I have my life in the city, as I've said."

"What else do you do there?"

"I told you, I work. I love my work. My last project before I came to New York involved developing a marketing campaign for our new lipstick line. For years, I've worked small projects in just about every department in our company, but that was my favorite. Marketing is intuitive. It's less about numbers and accounting and tax rates, and I like that." She glanced at him. He had the impression she was reading his face, adjusting what she told him based on his approval. It was easy for him to smile at her—he did admire her. On many levels he was growing to understand her.

"How about after work?" he said. "At the end of the day? What do you like to do then?"

"Well," she continued, "let's see… I enjoy films. I read. I walk around the city…."

"Aren't you worried about security?"

"I stay low-key, remember?" she said playfully. "Besides, I take a yearly self-defense class." She winked at him. "I could flip you on your back if I wanted to."

He smiled, doubting that very much. "Do you use a private driver for protection?"

"At home? No, I drive myself. Here…it's the wrong side of the road for me, and you have a much bigger, more confusing system, so I'd rather not drive."

"Do you walk around Manhattan the way you walk around Edinburgh?"

"My, aren't you asking a lot of questions about me." She laughed lightly. "The answer is…no, not until very recently. It's mostly a matter of my being busy," she said quickly. "I'm taking five courses per semester, four semesters in a row without break. I'm here to gain knowledge my company can use. And then, I'm to go home and hopefully get promoted so I'm on track to be my uncle's successor. That is my plan."

"What if you don't get promoted?"

"Then I will be terribly upset." She pulled a tragic face for him. "Seriously, it's the most important thing to me. Which is why I very much would like you to agree to come to Edinburgh with me for Christmas. Think about it, Jacob."

Ah. And so she had circled back to the thing neither of them could avoid. "How, exactly, will it help you to have me there?" he asked.

"Well, my uncle obviously sees something in you that interests him. He's never seemed to see as much in me." She sighed. "Or he hasn't thus far. But I'm going to *make* him see the advantages I have over Malcolm. I'd assumed top-shelf grades would do the trick, but…"

She shrugged. "At the wedding this weekend I learned that I need to speed up my timetable. I need reasons for him to spend time with me. And that's why you have to come home with me for Christmas." She looked brightly at him.

Yes, he did need to go to Edinburgh to see her uncle. But not for the reasons she thought.

"ISABEL DIDN'T DO anything that would harm her family's company," Jacob said to Eddie later. "She didn't leak any stories or give company secrets to the media. I'd stake my life on it."

"Then why did Sage ask you to investigate her?" Eddie asked.

Jacob patted Alden's back. He was freshly diapered now, and yawning, his thumb aiming for his mouth and getting ready for a big sleep, which gave Jacob some level of satisfaction.

Jacob was getting awfully used to this little guy. The two of them were buddies now. "I'm not actually sure yet," he said in response to Eddie's question.

"Attention, everyone!" Donna clapped her hands as two servers brought in a large sheet cake, decorated with the words *Congratulations, Eddie!* and lit with a ring of candles.

Jacob felt happy for his friend, but he didn't feel so great for himself—he couldn't lie about that.

So he carried Alden to the back wall and stood by, watching from afar while their colleagues and their spouses and partners sang and made a big deal about the celebration for Eddie's promotion.

Donna came over and lifted the sleeping Alden from his arms. "Thanks for being good to my baby." And then Jacob was alone again.

"May I talk with you a minute?" Isabel asked softly beside him.

She'd crept up on him; Jacob hadn't even noticed. He nodded and then followed her as she led him out of the banquet room. They skirted the crowd of his friends, who were now passing out cards and presents to Eddie. Joke gifts, it looked like, and small things that were meaningful only to their group.

Turning away, he let Isabel lead him to the top landing on the empty stairway. The air was cooler out here. Jacob stood against the wall beside her and exhaled, leaning his head back.

She dug inside her big handbag and drew out a package. "This is for you." She held the packet out to him, wrapped up like a present, with foil wrapping paper and a red bow.

He slowly took it from her. "Why? This is Eddie's party."

"I know. Donna told me when she called there was to be a cake and gifts. I barely know Eddie or Donna, but I know you. And I know how bad it feels to be overlooked, especially when you really want something, so…"

She lowered her chin. "I just want you to know that there's somebody who appreciates you, even if you didn't get the prize that you wanted. Not yet, anyway."

He stood holding her present, feeling as if something had just exploded inside him.

"Open it," she urged.

His gaze down, away from looking at her, he peeled away the paper and opened the box.

It was a soft, woolen scarf in a green, blue and black plaid pattern. "Is this your family tartan?"

"No. This is Black Watch. It represents the most famous military regiment in my country, with a long, elite history. And it, well…it reminded me of you. What you stand for. The Secret Service, I mean. The…best and most faithful at what they do, no matter the obstacles against them."

He touched the soft wool, not able to lift his eyes, not able to look at her. This sweet, sweet woman. He took the scarf from the box and placed it around his neck. "Thanks," he said gruffly.

"Isabel!" Donna poked her head into the hallway. She noticed Jacob. "Oh, never mind. You're busy."

"That's okay." Isabel smiled at Alden in his mother's arms and made a move to follow her, but Jacob touched her arm.

"You could have your own someday," he murmured, nodding toward the baby. "You don't have to do this."

She smiled sadly at Jacob and shook her head. "No. I don't think that will be possible for me. And yes, I do have to do this."

"Right." He nodded. He could understand her because he was the same way. They both had their chosen lives. That's what they'd been telling one another all evening, in essence. It honestly wouldn't be possible for him to have children, either. Not in a dangerous job like his. He wasn't like Eddie in that respect.

But Isabel looked so sad. She was lonely in Scotland, too. He'd felt that when he'd been with her at the wedding. He was sure that she didn't get out and see people, or watch films, or read books as much as she said she did, or as much as she wanted to.

He dropped his hand, and she headed into the room with the others. He stroked the scarf around his neck. He just…wanted to do something for her. Something to make her feel less lonely. Something to let her know that she meant something to him.

On a whim, he went in and found Eddie. "Will you watch Isabel for me? Don't let her leave yet."

"Why? Where are you going?"

"Nowhere. I'll be back in twenty minutes."

LATER, AFTER JACOB dropped Isabel off in the SUV at her residence hall and insisted on walking her to the lobby, he caught her hand before she could press the button for the lift.

She wondered, briefly, if he was going to kiss her again. She'd been looking at his mouth so much during the drive home, watching it as the shadows passed over them from darkness to light.

His lips quirked when he talked sometimes. They were expressive lips. She remembered how they felt when she'd kissed them. How they tasted…

But he didn't lean in to kiss her. He hadn't come close. He just passed a piece of folded paper into her hand and muttered a quick good-night before he left her alone again.

Up in her room, with the door closed, she opened

the folded paper. To her shock, it was a pencil sketch of her, most flattering, cleverly making her appear far more attractive than she actually was.

But it was her face, no doubt about it, surrounded with flowers. Below was a stylized caption: "A Red, Red Rose."

She stared, blinking at his small gift. Her heart felt full to overflowing. Was this how he saw her—beautiful and worthy of romantic feelings? And what he thought of her—moved enough to express the truth of his heart?

She carefully pinned the small drawing on the corkboard over her desk, where she could gaze at it as she worked. It would give her pleasure.

But pinning the drawing up wasn't enough. Impulsively, she picked up her mobile phone. She'd never done anything like this. It was late to her, after midnight.

To give Jacob enough time to return home to his apartment, she waited twenty more minutes, watching the old battery-powered clock tick away the seconds on the side table beside her bed. Her nerves jumpy, she got up and washed her face, then changed out of her clothes and into warm flannel pajamas.

It was time. She climbed into bed with the pillows propped up behind her. So many evenings she'd spent studying into the night like this. Calling Jacob would be more fun.

Before she could second-guess herself, she pressed

the button. She'd already programmed his name and phone number into her phone.

"Hello?" Jacob's low, rough voice sent a thrill through her.

"It's Isabel." She had his phone number, but he didn't have hers. "I just…wanted to say thank-you for the drawing." She hesitated. "I *really* like it."

"I'm…glad." He seemed awkward, not quite himself. Then again, they were in new territory. They'd been at odds ever since they'd been back in Manhattan, and tonight was a fresh intimacy.

"Well, I just wanted to say, you have talent, Jacob. I'm lying in bed looking at the sketch over my desk."

"Yeah. I don't sleep well, either." He laughed somewhat.

"Why not?" she asked.

"I don't know." He paused. "It's always been like that." He paused again. "Sucks, really."

"I know what you mean." She slid down, deeper under the covers, shifting the phone as she lay on her side. "I hate it, too. I usually just stay up late, working, until I finally fall asleep."

"But not tonight? It's Friday."

"Doesn't matter. My coursework is difficult. I usually have to work weekends, too. But tonight… I'm just thinking, taking the night off. You have nice friends, by the way."

"Yeah, they're good. But, Isabel…" There was a pause and his voice sounded farther away, as if he was doing something in the background, moving around as he spoke.

Maybe he was taking off his clothes. She bit the side of her cheek and held back the happy giggle that wanted to come out.

"…You should see the city while you're here, too. Too much work isn't good for anybody."

"Says the man who works weekends himself," she said lightly.

"Yeah, well, did Donna also tell you that tomorrow morning I'm supposed to go out to Long Island and help her and Eddie start packing up their things for the big move?"

"Ouch," she said softly. That had to be hard since they were leaving for Washington and he wasn't.

"Yeah, I've got to be out of here by seven."

She hadn't meant that the *time* was hard, though that was true, too. "Well, don't ask me for a wake-up call, because I'm terrible. I was late so often my first semester that I made a point to schedule no more of those eight o'clock classes."

He chuckled. "Damn, I don't blame you for that."

"Thanks for the vote of confidence." She sighed, gazing across the room at her pencil sketch. "And thanks again for the drawing. Nobody has ever done that for me before, and I find I quite like it."

"It was my pleasure, Isabel," he said in that low, gruff voice.

"Kiss Alden for me tomorrow. He's a cutie, that one is."

"Will do. Good night, Isabel."

As she hung up the phone, smiling, she realized that she'd shared more in her short conversations with Jacob tonight than she'd shared with Alex these past few years. Then again, Alex hadn't shared much with her, either.

Jacob had.

CHAPTER NINE

MONDAY MORNING, JACOB headed over for his appointment with Diane, the department psychologist. The weekend spent helping Eddie move his stuff had upped the urgency for him. He needed to get this transfer rolling, to convince Diane he was on the right track with his plans for Scotland.

But when Jacob arrived at the appointed time, Diane was on the phone, so he stood in her doorway, silently observing.

Cardboard boxes were stacked on the floor. She must have brought in some personal belongings but hadn't yet unpacked them. In one box, laid on top of a row of books, were three framed diplomas.

He tilted his head to get a better look. Her name was on all of them—Diane was seriously educated. He didn't know whether to be grateful or worried.

Finally, she hung up the phone and stared up at him over the top of her reading glasses. "Thank you for coming in. Sit down, please, Jacob."

He approached the chair in front of her and sat, handing her the folder containing his paperwork. He looked her in the eye.

"I want you to know, Diane, I took some steps to get the bigger information we discussed last time we met. I've set up an appointment in Scotland, and I'm taking a week there over Christmas. I'll interview people who knew my father and his work, and I'll see about the information you requested to process my transfer. Then, I'll write a report and have it on your desk by the first of the year. How does that sound to you?"

Diane gazed across the desk at him. "A trip to Scotland is excellent. That's a good start."

A *start?* He got a sinking feeling in his chest. But he forced out a nod.

"I understand that you never met your father," she said, folding her hands and gazing directly at him across the desk. "Did anyone ever speak to you about him when you were growing up?"

"Yes," he said tersely. "Of course they did."

She waited for him to say more.

He tapped his fingers against his knee. "Aren't you going to look at my paperwork?" He gestured to the folder he'd brought. He'd gone to a lot of trouble to put it together for her—as she'd directed.

"Would you like me to?" she murmured.

"What I would really love is for you to sign my transfer papers," he cracked.

She didn't smile. She gazed at him quietly.

He pressed his hands against his pants. This wasn't going well.

"The last time we met," she said in a steady, neutral voice, "we talked about your mother moving from Scotland to New York with you when you were still a baby. Then—" she checked her notes "—she married a schoolteacher, I believe."

Jacob nodded, not seeing why this was relevant.

"How did your mother characterize your father to you, Jacob? His job as a police officer?"

"Ah…she didn't talk about him, really."

Diane waited for him to continue.

He cleared his throat. "My mom doesn't talk about him because the divorce was painful to her. And I respect that because I protect her. I've always protected her." His voice rose.

Almost imperceptibly, Diane's eyes widened.

He clamped his mouth shut. *Ratchet it down, Jake,* Eddie would say.

He didn't want to turn her against him. He didn't want to jeopardize this.

"So…" Diane continued in that neutral tone, "you're protecting your mom by being a Secret Service agent? The same sort of job that your father held when he was killed in the line of duty?"

"No," he said hotly. She was totally misunderstanding him. And she was venturing on territory that shouldn't be crossed.

He changed the subject. "My mother realizes I'm a grown man and I make my own decisions. She has three other children—my half siblings—to worry about now."

Another almost imperceptible widening of Diane's eyes. "Is that why you chose law enforcement as a career—to break away from your family?"

"No, I chose law enforcement because I'm drawn to it," he said, irritated. "It's important. It matters."

"Like your father's death mattered to you?" she said softly.

Where was she going with this?

"Can you tell me about the day you first told your mom you were joining the NYPD?" Diane asked.

That day was seared in his memory. It had been their one and only blowup argument. Daniel had jumped in, of course, warning Jacob off. Even his siblings had been present, and they'd been frightened by the harsh words exchanged.

"No, sorry, I don't remember," Jacob said. Because he wasn't tearing open that ugly wound for Diane, someone he didn't even know.

This was private. The relationship he had with his family wasn't relevant to his work.

He was a damn good special agent. He belonged in the PPD. Everybody who mattered said so.

"Jacob, what did your mom say about you joining the police force?" Diane asked gently.

It was clear she wasn't going to let this go. He could tell her the truth—that his mom had screamed at him that one time, blowing up in anger. She'd said that his father had abandoned them. That his real dad didn't care about them, and that Jacob shouldn't try to be like him.

Jacob had been stunned—scared, even—because it was the most she'd ever said about his father, and he hadn't wanted to see her so upset. He'd always tried to avoid her grief by protecting her from reminders of anything unpleasant.

"Jacob?"

Diane wasn't videotaping him. She didn't have him hooked up to a lie-detector test. Lying would be easy. To protect his mom from pain, he'd lied to her all his life about all sorts of innocuous things—grades at school, boyhood indiscretions—because he'd had to in order to keep her happy.

"My mom was proud of me," he said to Diane. "She respects what I do, and I want her to be happy, too."

Only the last part was true. He did want her to be happy. And these days, he accomplished that by not mentioning his job.

Diane stared at him for a long time. Her lips pressed together, she turned to his paperwork. She perused the pages. Took off her reading glasses and looked at him.

It appeared she believed him.

"Where is the copy of your original birth certificate that I asked for?"

It figured. She'd zeroed in on the one document

that Jacob couldn't gather. "I don't have it," he said. "And they didn't ask for it in the original security clearance, so…"

She closed the folder and looked at him. "Jacob, I know you've already been through the full security clearance for special agent status, but if you want PPD, it will take more than that to satisfy me."

Obviously—she'd made that clear. But he kept his patience.

"As I said to you the last time we met, there are red flags in your background," she continued. "The psychological effects your father's death had on you are a concern to us, and we want to dig into why you want this particular assignment, given that fact.

"But before we can begin to do that work together, I need you to complete a homework assignment for me. Going to Scotland and conducting interviews is very important, yes, but so is my request for you to bring me your birth certificate."

"It doesn't exist anymore," he protested. "I was adopted even before Donald Ross—before my father died. At my adoption, the state generated a new birth certificate for me—which is my legal certificate—and that's the certificate I continue to use today. The old certificate is no longer valid."

"Yes, I understand the law regarding adoptions and birth certificates. I am asking you for a copy of your original, Scottish birth certificate."

He just sat there. He knew damn well who he

was born as. He also knew that what she asked for was impossible.

She tapped her pen on the desk. "Jacob, you're asking for a higher level of clearance and responsibility, which I have to sign off on. You need to humor me. Trust where I'm going with this."

Her trust wasn't a matter of consideration to him. What was important was *finding* the damn thing. Where could he get this document quickly? Scotland? He didn't know what their rules or bureaucracy might be like. The lawyer in Connecticut who'd prepared the original adoption? But there were rules about a minor's adoption....

"I might need a court order to retrieve it," he mused aloud.

Diane looked at him sharply. "No one in your family has an original copy? How about your mother? Isn't she the obvious person to see?"

He remained silent.

"Perhaps you should ask her where it is," Diane pressed. "Initiate a discussion with her."

"She's in Connecticut."

"You could go there today."

"I don't think that's a good idea," he said. His real father was dead. What was the point in reopening old wounds?

Diane stared directly at him. She appeared to have a point she wanted to hammer home. "If you prefer to stay in the field office, avoiding my assignments, then I'll let it go. But I can't in good conscience recommend you for promotion to any of the presidential or vice presidential details if you don't cooperate with me."

She held up her hand. "If you want to stay as you are, that's perfectly fine, too. You just need to tell me—do you want to stay as you are, Jacob?"

He shook his head. That would mean that he was a guy who wasn't good enough. A failure to make the cut, and he wasn't a failure.

He was better than that.

His life had way more meaning than that.

"No, I want to advance." He was an elite protector. It's what he did. It's what he was drawn to do.

Diane leaned back in her chair and stared at him for a long time. He thought she was wrong for doing this. In his opinion, she was being too zealous with his case.

But Jacob had worked for the government long enough to know that the bureaucracy game must be played. And if he didn't play it, the results were to his peril.

He stood. "Fine. I'll get that information for you. But I'd like my case expedited. Can you…" He swallowed. "Can you help me with that?"

She nodded. "Yes, I can. But you need to show me you're open to what I'm exploring with you."

Brusquely he nodded.

"Go see your mother today. I'll wait for the results. We'll talk again once you have them."

She had no idea what she was asking him to do.

At least he saw what the consequences of failure to play the game were, though. Eddie had moved on to get what he wanted, and Jacob hadn't.

An hour later, Jacob had signed out for an extended lunch break and was steering his SUV up the West Side Highway. As he drove, he watched the seabirds swoop over the broad Hudson River, which was glistening in the sun. He wished he could be as carefree.

Seeing his mom about this wouldn't be easy for him. She'd never been the most stable person. She'd been brought up in foster homes, she'd married his father at eighteen, and his father had left them when she was twenty and Jacob was almost two. He didn't even remember Scotland; didn't remember the move to New York City where he and his mom had lived with her cousin—his mom cleaning houses and babysitting—until she'd met Daniel when Jacob was ten.

Jacob had spent his youth mostly concerned about taking care of and protecting his mom. A tough Brooklyn kid, often angry, sometimes confused, he'd fantasized about someday going to Scotland and telling off his father.

But then his father had been killed, and that was that. His mom had been married to Daniel by then, and Jacob's oldest half brother, Danny Jr., was just a baby.

It was the same year they'd moved from Brooklyn to Connecticut. His mom was happy, and Daniel was good for her. Jacob saw the writing on the wall— her loyalties were shifting. He wasn't the center of her life anymore.

But that was okay because the year before, he'd met Eddie. Eddie had moved to their Brooklyn neighborhood, and they'd become best friends, both wanting to be cops when they grew up.

His stepdad was teaching at a private secondary school in Manhattan that year, so Jacob had been adopted and then enrolled in his school, tuition-free. Jacob had never really had to deal too much with fitting in to his mom's new family. He'd coped by building his own life, focusing on his own dreams.

And being better at it than his father. He'd never said a word about it to anybody, not even to Eddie, and especially not to his mom.

Trying not to think too much about how he was going to bring up the question of the birth certificate to her, he headed toward rural Connecticut and the area where he'd lived for one year, until he'd transferred to boarding school permanently.

When he pulled into his mother and stepfather's driveway an hour later, he felt as if he was visiting a foreign country. He'd never been part of this cul-de-sac world.

But it was beautiful and safe, and he was glad his mother and three half siblings were part of it.

He slammed the door to the SUV, realizing he'd brought his service weapon with him by force of habit. He touched the cold steel strapped to his side. So much a part of him that he often forgot it was there.

His mom hated guns. Before he headed up the walkway to the large, new colonial home on the hill, he went back and secured the revolver inside the locked case in his vehicle, specially made for this purpose.

Two of his three younger half siblings—sixteen-year-old Emily and twelve-year-old Zach—were hanging out at the top of the driveway together, near the garage doors.

Zach was shooting baskets, while Emily typed on her phone. It seemed early in the afternoon for them to be out of school, but what did Jacob know?

They barely looked up when he passed.

"Hi," Jacob said, pausing for a moment on the driveway beside the pots of mums and arrangements of pumpkins and gourds. His mother was obsessed with domestic perfection—the place looked like a Martha Stewart catalog. "What are you two up to?"

Emily stared at her screen as she murmured, "We have a planned half day. Why are you out of work?"

Zach kept shooting baskets. The ball hit the rim,

and he grimaced, then looked at Jacob as if feeling bad that Jacob had seen him miss.

Jacob retrieved the ball and tossed it to Zach. "Try again," Jacob said.

Zach lined up his shot and then jumped, following through nicely. This time, the ball swished through the net. Zach grinned.

"Great job," Jacob said.

Emily glanced up from her phone, watching him. "I'm here to talk with Mom," he said to her.

Emily frowned and put her phone down. She looked at Jacob from side to side. "Are you wearing your gun?" she asked, staring at the spot beneath his suit jacket where he usually kept his weapon.

Jacob shifted on his feet. It was pretty obvious to him that Emily didn't share much enthusiasm for what he did for a living, either. "No. It's locked up."

Emily breathed a sigh of relief. "Mom doesn't like it when you bring your gun to the house."

Yeah, he knew that. It also appeared that Emily had maybe co-opted his old job and was acting as a gatekeeper, granting access to and protecting his mom. Jacob could have said a lot more about it, but he simply chose to nod.

Emily was just a kid. She was a good kid, from what he'd seen, but he wasn't going to be the one to bring up adult topics with her.

"Play one-on-one with me," Zach said to Emily, tossing her the basketball. She hopped up, complying. Jacob watched them for a minute, hating that he was thinking about Diane, the psychologist. As if he were seeing the scene through her eyes.

His half siblings were comfortable together. They went to a big public high school—except for Danny Jr., who, at twenty, was in community college. Danny, Emily and Zach were easy with each other; they were not easy with Jacob. He'd been ten when his mother had remarried, twelve when Danny was born.

All of them had lived through that day with the blowup after he'd announced he was going into law enforcement.

Jacob jogged up the steps, hoping that he'd catch his mom alone, knowing now that it was unlikely. Daniel now taught math—he was department head—in the same high school his children attended. If the kids were home, then chances were good that he was, too.

His mom was standing alone in the kitchen, chopping up vegetables and putting them into a stockpot. She didn't see him, so he watched her, instantly recognizing that she was making chicken soup, great for a cold, blustery late-November day.

His mom loved to cook. When she and Jacob had been living alone in a tiny Brooklyn walk-up, their kitchen had been too small for her to make much more than the basics. Here, in her domestic paradise, she had a state-of-the-art "country colonial" work space.

He was happy for her, really. Besides that, his mouth watered and his stomach growled. He hadn't eaten well in days, with missed meals and grabbed bites, always on the go, it seemed. Those root vegetables she was handling had probably come from her late-summer garden.

She blinked to see him standing there, watching her. "Jacob."

"Hi, Mom." He gave her a peck on the cheek.

"You didn't call," she said, glancing up and down at the suit he was wearing, his Secret Service clothing. "I wasn't expecting you."

"Sorry." He should've changed. "I'm just stopping by, I can't stay long."

Her shoulders seemed to relax a bit. "I'm making soup for dinner."

"I saw. It looks really good."

She wiped her hands on her jeans. "Why did you stop by?"

He couldn't tell her exactly why. He knew what he needed, but he hadn't figured out quite how to say it.

I want to grab some paperwork from the den. But that was ridiculous—Jacob had no paperwork in the den. He'd never even lived in this beautiful house. She and Daniel had planned it and overseen its new construction during his freshman year in college.

She tilted her head. "Jacob?" The musicality in her voice reminded him of Isabel's soft Scottish accent.

He looked away. He hated that he had to do this to her. "I've applied for a new job at work, and they've asked me for some extra documents. Specifically, they need my original birth certificate."

She stiffened visibly. "Didn't you tell them that Daniel is your father? That's what's important."

"Of course I told them. But...you know the government." He held up his hands. "We used to have that box—I think I saw it last in the bottom drawer of the desk in the den. How about if I just check it and see if—"

"It's not there." She licked her lips and bent over the stove again. "Maybe you should talk to your father about this."

"Mom, I'm sorry," he said. "I don't like this any more than you do."

He liked it less than she did, actually, because he hated hurting her.

She'd been through enough. He didn't want to ever see her cry again. He just wanted her to be happy.

"Please talk to Daniel." Her voice sounded somewhat shrill.

As if on cue, Daniel came into the kitchen. "Is everything all right in here? Oh, Jacob. I didn't know you were expected. Are you staying for dinner?"

"No," Jacob said.

Behind him, a door closed. His mother had left, gone into the bathroom.

Daniel sighed like the long-suffering teacher of adolescents that he was. Then he looked warily at Jacob. He crossed his arms and leaned against the kitchen island as if creating his plan of attack. Daniel was nothing but rational.

"What's going on, Jacob?" he said in a neutral voice.

"Do we have a copy of my original birth certificate anywhere?" Jacob asked point-blank.

Daniel recoiled. "After everything that's happened, I'd rather you didn't come here with topics like that. You know you'll upset your mother."

"I'm asking *you*," Jacob said quietly. "It's a simple request."

"Why? What's the point?"

"Because I need it for work."

Daniel cocked his head. "Opening a can of worms about the past does no one any good. Focus on the future. You can't live your life by watching the wake from the boat behind you."

"I am, Daniel. It's for work," he repeated. "The *government*."

Daniel nodded. "Well. Tell them that some things are unknowable. Tell them our family doesn't keep reminders of what's left in the past. I tell my students—"

"Have you ever had a kid who *needed* to know

something?" Jacob interrupted. "Because this isn't something that's a nice-to-know. It's a need-to-have."

"Dad?" Emily was standing in the doorway. She glanced sideways at Jacob as she walked in to hug her father. "Can you give me a ride to cheering practice?"

"Of course," Daniel said. He turned to Jacob. "Are you staying for dinner?"

Jacob smiled gently at Emily. He didn't like her seeing that there was tension between them. "No, sorry, I have to get back to the city," he answered Daniel cordially.

"I hope we'll see you for Thanksgiving dinner," Daniel said.

Jacob hadn't thought about it yet, or even checked his schedule. "I'm not sure if I have to travel yet, but I'll let you know."

"Yes, please do call your mother. She's planning dinner for two, after Emily's game. You know she'd like to see you for the holiday."

Jacob nodded. He was aware that they were being rational and adult, for Emily's sake. She stared between him and Daniel, listening to everything.

"I'll say goodbye to Mom and then follow you out to the car," Jacob said to Daniel. To Emily, he smiled and said, "Have a good practice."

Then he went and knocked on the bathroom door. "Mom? I'm sorry I upset you," he said through the door. "I love you and I'll try to see you on Thursday."

His mom opened the door and came out, drying her hands on a towel.

"I'm sorry, too." She met his eyes for the first time. "Stay safe," she whispered.

The guilt pierced him. It always pierced him. But he cracked a smile for her, knowing her fears were unfounded. He wasn't Donald Ross. He was *Jacob* Ross.

Still, he left, aware that he'd failed in his one small mission to get a birth certificate for his employment record.

It was a crapshoot, anyway, Jacob told himself as he headed for his SUV. Since there weren't any photos of his father in the house, it probably wasn't much of a stretch not to have Jacob's original birth certificate on hand, either.

An hour and a half later, Jacob was back at work.

He went out with a new case partner—not Eddie, who was spending the day watching training videos in preparation for his big move—and retrieved surveillance video from a convenience store in Chinatown, then came back and wrote up some paperwork for a handwriting-analysis request.

He didn't get his work finished until well after dark. Back at his apartment, there was no food in the kitchen, and he didn't feel like eating out, so Jacob ordered Thai food, and after it was delivered, he brought the bag into the living room and set it on the coffee table.

Jacob rubbed the back of his neck. His life felt as if it had twisted into noodles, as big a mess as his pad Thai lumped into its cardboard carton. The only thing he liked about his complicated situation was that it had twisted him up with Isabel.

He was really lucky to have her on his side. He reached for his phone to call her. Ever since the night of Eddie's party, they'd adopted a ritual in which one or the other of them called at night before they went to sleep.

Lately, their ritual had expanded to include mornings, as well. The excuse was that Isabel burned the midnight oil and then had trouble waking up when she was supposed to. She had a habit of sleeping through alarms, she said, which worried her that she would miss something important.

All this talk, of course, had put scenes into his head, imagining what she looked like sleeping at night. What did Isabel wear to bed, if anything? Did she tie up all that long hair, or did she leave it loose, fanning over her pillow?

Bad stuff to consider. A too-tempting place to go.

Yet it was about the only comfort and outlet he had lately.

If he were to explain to Isabel about his day—about the psychologist and Daniel and his mother—she would understand. But he couldn't tell her about it because to explain those specifics about his past would drive her away. He needed access to John Sage too much to risk that.

Still, he wanted to talk with her anyway. Even if she couldn't know everything about his day, he still wanted to hear her voice. Still wanted to talk with her about other things.

He could keep two parts of his life separate. In a sense, he'd been doing it his whole life.

Jacob was in the midst of scrolling through his phone for her number when the phone vibrated in his hand. "Isabel" read the caller ID on the screen.

He felt the smile tug on his lips as he connected the call. "What's going on?" he asked her.

"What do you think of Thanksgiving?" she asked.

Ah, it's too complicated for me, was his first reaction.

But he didn't say that aloud. He toyed with his Thai food a second before giving up on it. He sprawled back on the couch instead, feet crossed on the cushions at the other end. "Why do you ask?"

"Well, classes get out early on Wednesday, and everyone is going home for the long weekend. People are excited about traveling." She paused. "We don't have Thanksgiving in my country, so I'm curious. What *is* Thanksgiving, actually? Last year, I was new to New York and busy, so I just avoided it. But this year, I'm aware that I'm leaving soon, so I'm interested."

"It's, ah, well, you could look it up on the internet."

"Yes, but then I wouldn't get your point of view on it, would I, Mr. Ross?" she said playfully.

He smiled, then laid his arm under his head and stared at the ceiling. He didn't know why, but he grabbed his old guitar, too, and cradled it on his chest. "Tell me what you know, first."

"I know about the Pilgrims and Plymouth Rock and the *Mayflower* ship," she said. "It sailed from England, remember? I'm mainly curious about how you celebrate the holiday nowadays. What do you *do* on Thanksgiving Day?"

"It's a family holiday," he said quietly. "People, ah, go home…to people that they care about…and share a homemade meal."

He plucked on the bottom E string, tuning his guitar. "Unless you're away, that is. Last year, I was out of town for work—we were in Denver for a guard detail. We stood duty and watched our protectee eat at a restaurant."

He laughed softly at the remembrance. "The guy wasn't North American—I can't say exactly who he was, but he didn't get the concept of turkey and mashed potato and stuffing and cranberry sauce. He ordered steak instead, but…the point of the holiday isn't the food."

Jacob paused. He was in a talkative mood, which wasn't typical for him, but something that Isabel brought out. That, and he was probably overly frustrated at not being able to talk with his mom. "Are you still there?"

"Yes. I like listening to you talk."

"What are you doing?" he asked her.

"I'm taking a break from editing my thesis paper. My laptop is on the desk, my door is closed and I'm looking out the window at a pigeon on my windowsill. I named him Morris. He keeps me company."

Jacob smiled. He got lonely on the road, too. He really wished he could tell her about what had happened today with his mom and the birth certificate he needed.

"Now that I think of it," Isabel said, "at certain restaurants in Edinburgh, they do advertise elaborate Thanksgiving menus in late November." She paused. "Does anything else happen on Thanksgiving Day besides eating?"

"Well, yeah, there's football. My siblings go to their high school game—it's traditionally a day of school rivalries. We also have the Macy's Thanksgiving Day Parade in the morning. And Black Friday, the big pre–Christmas shopping day, is the day after Thanksgiving."

"Tell me about the food. What specifically do you eat?"

"In my family?" He could feel himself smiling again. He was getting hungry just thinking of the meal. He moved to tuning the A string. Pluck, pluck, pluck… "Well, the main course is turkey. On the side we have stuffing, cranberry sauce, sweet potato, mashed potato and squash. For dessert we do pies, all kinds of pies. Chocolate cream, pecan, apple. My mother, being…"

He almost said *Scottish*. Jacob cleared his throat, put the guitar aside and sat up.

Isabel didn't know that about him. He kept getting confused, forgetting that he hadn't told her certain things about himself. With Isabel, it was so easy to forget that he was keeping things from her…big things that she would hate him for if she found out.

"Do you bring presents to the dinner?" Isabel asked.

"What? No," he said with a laugh. Then he thought of his aunt. "Well, some people might bring a bottle of wine or a pie you made for the hostess. The kind of thing you'd bring to anyone's house for dinner."

"Interesting. Are you traveling this year, Jacob?"

"No." He'd checked when he'd returned to the office this afternoon, but he had no such luck. "I'll have to call my mother," he said aloud.

"What does she do for dinner?"

"My mom? It's a huge event—she really gets into it. Every dish is homemade, and it's all laid out beautifully. She invites the whole extended family— Daniel's siblings, parents, sometimes even cousins. She loves it."

"Interesting," Isabel said. "I've never experienced a real Thanksgiving like that…."

Oh, no. Had she been fishing for an invitation? He couldn't have her there.

"Isabel…" He grabbed at the first excuse he thought of. "It's my mother's affair, and she likes to keep it small."

There was a silence. "Actually, Jacob, I already have an invitation for Thanksgiving dinner. You aren't the only person here I know."

He stood up. "Whose house are you going to?" he demanded, pacing his small studio apartment.

"Charles's."

"You're going to spend Thanksgiving with Che Guevara and his family?"

"You don't need to be rude, Jacob."

"Do you even *know* anything about him?" he asked.

"As much—or more—than I know about you."

"Don't go with him," Jacob insisted. "You should go with me."

"I should?" She let the question hang there, and Jacob felt like kicking himself.

"You're right," he said quickly. "It's a bad idea."

"Why? What are you afraid of?"

"Nothing." But the whole house of cards was set to come down if he wasn't careful.

For one thing, Isabel would hear his mother speak and know that she was Scottish, and that would be mistake number one, because he'd lied to Isabel about that back at the wedding. He'd had many openings to tell her that both his mom—and he—had been born in Scotland, and yet he hadn't told her. When she found out, it would be awkward, at best.

"What is the problem for you?" she asked.

"It's…" He grasped at the first thing he thought of. "My family can be, uh, difficult to understand sometimes. I wouldn't want to put you through that."

"Why not? You've met *my* family." She laughed. "How could your family be any more difficult to understand than mine?"

Jacob sucked in his breath. *Fine, just say it. It's not the worst thing she could know.*

"My mother is Scottish. I mean, she was born in Scotland. Really."

Isabel burst out laughing. "That's a good joke."

"It's true. She divorced my real… Well, it's hard. She doesn't talk about her youth or want to be reminded of those days at all. Sometimes I forget she wasn't born here."

Isabel was silent for a moment. "What part of Scotland is she from?"

"She…" He paused. "I don't know. Just…Scotland. Glasgow, maybe?"

"That's the biggest city in the country," Isabel said. "It covers a lot of area. Do you know where in Glasgow?"

He had no idea. "She's had American citizenship for years now. Her parents died when she was young, and I think she really struggled. She just…

she doesn't talk about the past. Even now, she's not one for reminiscing. She doesn't even enjoy looking at old baby photos, or anything like that."

But how could Isabel possibly understand? Jacob had never known anyone so relentlessly positive. Isabel believed that she could fix and make a success out of anything, even a difficult past.

And especially Jacob, which was nearly impossible for him to believe.

ISABEL WAS FLOORED. Jacob's mother was Scottish? How could he not have mentioned this while they were at her cousin's wedding?

Something was off about this revelation he'd just made. Her uncle's warning came to mind.

She *had* to visit his family; it was imperative in order to better understand him.

Charles wouldn't mind if she declined his invitation—he'd invited the whole study group, not just her, so it was more an act of goodwill and generosity than anything else. Jacob was her immediate concern. If he failed her fitness test, then how could she take him home with her?

"I've scared you off," he said quietly. "Haven't I?"

She sighed, crossing her feet as she lay on her bed, gazing at the picture he'd sketched of her. That image eased so many difficult feelings…. "Jacob," she said gently, "why did you never say anything to me, especially given all the time you spent with my family?"

"I know it seems strange," he admitted. "But truthfully, my mother prefers I not talk about that part of her history. When I...when I had to go through my initial background check with the Secret Service, some of this stuff had to be dug up. My mother was...she was really upset and adamant about not discussing her life back then. To her mind, she's American through and through. Every now and then, though, her old accent comes out, and... it's like yours. Musical. That's how I thought of it when I was a kid."

"So...when I meet her I suppose it's best I not discuss Scotland?" Isabel said, turning to hug her pillow.

"Yes, please."

Isabel chewed on her lip.

"You think this is too intense, don't you?" he asked.

She loved Jacob's intensity. It was one of the things she liked best about him. "No. Keep your intensity. I'll handle it well with her, Jacob. Don't worry about me."

She could hear him exhale in relief on the other end of the line. "I'll pick you up at noon. Hopefully, you won't run away screaming when you meet them."

CHAPTER TEN

ISABEL KNEW THE moment she saw Jacob standing at the lift on Thursday morning that something had changed inside her.

She pressed her hand to her stomach. He was here in her empty residence hall with all his burning intensity focused on her.

He looked nothing like the officious and slightly irritating Secret Service agent who'd come to pick her up weeks ago.

Now he was dressed in street clothes—jeans, a collared shirt that was open just enough to see a bit of his chest and a light jacket. Plus, he'd worn her Black Watch scarf.

Her heart began to thud. She turned the key to lock her apartment door and then dropped it into her pocket. She slung her handbag over her shoulder and then freed her hair from inside her jacket.

His gaze burned at her, with all the passionate energy he carried with him. Over the phone, where she couldn't see him, he'd been so easy to talk with. Now, in person…she was just so aware of him.

Her cheeks warm, she walked to him. In one hand,

she gripped the small hostess gift she'd picked up for his mother. The other she lightly placed on his arm.

He smelled like windy New York autumn and fallen November leaves. She leaned forward to kiss his cheek because, well, that was what she did with her friends at home. But at her touch he froze, and she froze, too, filled with awareness of him.

And yet, she couldn't step back.

The lift came, its creaky doors opening with a rattle, breaking their spell. Jacob guided her inside with a hand on her lower back. He stood slightly behind her, as was his practice, but this time he left his hand where it was. She wasn't used to being touched like this, and it felt…sexual. She seemed to hum with the need to be closer to him.

She twisted her neck and gazed up at Jacob, and found that his eyes were burning into her. She licked her lips and leaned back against him.

It was wrong. She had an assignment for the day: check on his background. Was he okay for her to take him home? Could she trust him with her family's business? But she couldn't stop herself, and neither could he. She felt his solid warmth behind her and the steady movement of his breath.

His hand moved from the small of her back to her side and then up against her belly. Her coat was open and beneath it, she wore a thin jersey-knit shirt. As his palm rested on her stomach, she closed her eyes and nearly groaned with the sensation.

His low, deep voice murmured into her ear. "I'm addicted to you. Your voice is the first thing I want to hear in the morning and the last thing at night."

"I feel the same way." She turned to him, and they were pressed together, body to body. He was taller than her, so she stood on her toes. Her breasts rubbed against his chest.

She heard his groan. His hands settled over her waist, then kneaded her behind. She opened her mouth and let her tongue mingle with his. He was a great kisser. She'd been thinking about their first kiss for so long now, ever since the wedding. But this kiss was different. It was passion for the man she'd been falling for, more and more as the weeks went on.

She'd never been kissed in a lift before. The bell rang and too soon the doors rattled open. She felt the rush of the cooler lobby air. Still, neither of them moved.

The door shut again, and they were alone. She cupped his rough cheek with one of her hands, the other holding her bag.

"You still want to do this?" he asked, breaking the kiss. "You still want to go to my parents' house for dinner?"

"Yes," she answered breathlessly.

"Damn." He stared, rubbing a hand across his mouth. "You do like to play with fire, don't you?"

She did. She liked to play with *him*. But he was

right—giving in to the physical attraction wouldn't be smart. She enjoyed Jacob, but he was only for now, for easing the loneliness she felt here in New York.

She smoothed her hand over her hair, fixing it, and then adjusted her bra and her shirt again. She tried to remember what they'd been talking about.

"Don't you think that since your mum is a countrywoman of mine, it might be easier for me to talk with her?" she asked.

"You can't bring that up with her. Trust me."

"I do trust you." She straightened his crooked scarf. "But knowing that we have that in common is very appealing to me."

He squinted at her. "You think so?"

"It's brilliant." She playfully poked him in the chest. "There's no need to be worried. I can handle dinner with your people."

"Yeah," he said slowly. "You do have a talent for talking with anybody."

"Thank you, I think." She *was* curious about meeting his family. The way a person interacted with their parents and siblings told so much about them.

She felt certain she knew Jacob well enough already, and this would only be verification of what she trusted about him.

No matter what happened, though, she clearly knew her intent: she flew home in two weeks, and then, if she was focused and if Jacob helped, she could take another step toward the job she truly wanted.

"Are you parked in front?" she asked, heading for the exit.

"Yes. But first I'm curious—what's in the bag?" He touched the white paper bag with the colorful logo that she carried pressed against her chest.

"I wanted to bring your mum a small hostess gift, something for later, just for her."

He frowned at her. "Nothing Scottish, right?"

"Give me some credit! New York City has the best bagels, so I picked some up an hour ago, fresh from a market I just discovered. New York really is lovely, Jacob. If I could have been sure the cream cheese wouldn't spoil, I'd have brought that along, too."

She smiled brilliantly at him. "Any more concerns about me today?"

HE'D BEEN SIMULTANEOUSLY dreading this day and welcoming it.

Welcoming it because he got to *see* her again. Bask in the ease of her company and partake of the drug that was uniquely Isabel.

She made him smile and feel alive again. She smelled amazing, she looked fantastic and he couldn't get enough. He hadn't planned to kiss her, but she hadn't stopped him, either.

He pushed the dread back to another place and led her to the curb where he'd parked in a fire lane. He'd put an emergency light on the roof, as a signal to the meter maids. He didn't normally take advantage like this, but he'd known he wouldn't be gone long.

"This isn't the SUV you used for the wedding," Isabel noted.

"No, it's my personal car. The black SUV was Lee's vehicle."

She settled into the passenger seat and quickly found the button for the seat warmer. Wriggling her bottom, she sighed. Isabel loved those seat warmers. *Bun warmers,* she charmingly called them.

"So…" she chattered. "What is the route for today? I love our American road trips together."

He hid his smile as he pushed the buttons to program the GPS for her. "Here are the directions. I know you like to follow along."

"Brilliant," she said, squinting at the map on the screen. "And how long will this journey take?"

"About an hour without any brutal traffic." He said *brutal* because the word made her laugh.

"Lovely." She grinned at him. "And when was the last time you visited your parents?" Her fantastic hair was fanned over the headrest. He was sure she was attempting to charm him.

"Ah…this week," he said. "Before that, I don't know. Maybe a few months ago?" He felt himself frowning. "I've traveled a lot for work this year."

He glanced over at her. *Traveling.* He hated that

he'd made a reference reminding her that this was just a temporary relationship.

She smiled at him as if to buck him up. Another thing he loved about her. "Who will be there today?" she asked.

An even worse topic, but she was right, he did need to give her the lowdown.

"I have three younger siblings. They'll be there, and they sometimes have friends hanging around, in and out of the house like it's Grand Central Station. My mother is a homemaker. She loves taking care of everybody. My stepfather is the math department head at the local high school. He coaches soccer, too."

"Grandparents?"

"Yes, Daniel's parents will be there, plus his sister and brother and their spouses. Probably at least fifteen people in all."

"Impressive."

"Keep that thought in mind," Jacob said drily. He'd already phoned them to ask permission to bring a guest to dinner. "Of course," Daniel had answered. "And who is the guest?"

"Isabel," he'd simply replied. Emily had come on the line to quiz him after that. What was Isabel like? What had Jacob told her about them? It made a sad kind of sense to Jacob that his young sister, not even out of high school, would be so concerned about who came into the house. He'd once given himself that job of concerned watchkeeper, too. Maybe she was the one in the generation who'd taken up the mantle.

"She's a friend," Jacob had told her.

"A friend from where?" Emily had asked.

"She's a student in New York City by way of Scotland," he'd answered.

"Jacob, you are so unbelievable," Emily had said.

"What do you mean?"

"I don't want to see Mom upset."

"There won't be any arguing or discussion about Mom's past in Scotland, I promise."

But he knew he had a problem. He had no idea how any of them were going to react to Isabel's presence.

"That's a beautiful park," Isabel said, breaking into his thoughts. Her musical voice both calmed him and further reminded him of the upcoming ordeal.

"Sorry?"

"That park." She pointed to his left. It seemed she observed everything they passed with joy and interest. He could live with this, easily—a woman who brightened his day with just her presence. When he allowed himself to relax with her, she made him feel whole. "And is that the Hudson River?"

"Yeah." The river sparkled in the distance. "And not too far away is the spot where a jet landed on the water some years back. There's a famous photograph of the passengers standing on both wings. It was a horrible situation, but a great pilot was able to turn it into a miracle."

"I remember that story," she said. "What an uplifting ending."

The thought gave him hope. He glanced at the park beside the river, a strip of green lined with community gardens, now showing the gourds of the season. There were joggers and dog walkers and people pushing baby carriages while they enjoyed the sun, even on Thanksgiving Day.

These signs of their bustling hive were the best parts of New York. Isabel was getting ready to leave the city, but before she did, he had a few more weeks of her company here.

He drummed his fingers on the wheel, their conversation dying out. It often went like this with them at night, before they went to sleep, if one of them remembered that this…whatever they were doing… was for a practical purpose only and with an end in sight.

"You're nervous," Isabel remarked, turning from the road to look at him.

"I wish it were different."

"I told you, I'm okay with meeting new people."

"Yeah, but you don't know *these* people."

She swiveled her head toward him. After a moment, she asked, "Will it help if I promise to stick by you whatever happens?"

It would, but he wasn't that naive. "That's a big promise."

"I know." She smiled. "But you did it for me at Malcolm's wedding. There were parts of that day that were awkward for both of us."

He ran his finger around the steering wheel. "If I can show you the best of Thanksgiving, then our day will be a success. There's a reason it's a pretty good tradition that we keep going back to."

She was just looking at him, blinking, her head tilted.

Wow. How much is she changing me? She actually had him almost believing this crap.

Eddie had a theory, one of his half-baked philosophies, that women civilized men. Jacob had always scoffed at that. In his own life, women had usually served to rile him up or make him crazy or even just sadden him, like his mom. But Isabel…she calmed him. She centered him.

She also made him want to tear her clothes off and make love to her, which was another thing driving him insane.

"I've gotta be honest, Isabel. By bringing you home, they're gonna think we're dating or something. We both know…what this is we're doing." He glanced at her. But instead of being hurt or insulted, she was nodding, too.

"You can tell them that you're making me feel less lonely," she said.

"Am I?"

"Aye." She winked at him. "We're a good team that way."

But there were other, more important things that made them a lousy team, and Isabel didn't even know it.

Jacob pulled the car into a parking spot on the street, on the hill below his mom and Daniel's home. The driveway was lined three-deep with other vehicles from his visiting relatives. "Last chance. Are you *sure* you want to do this?" he asked as he shut off the engine. "There's still time to back out."

"Get on with you, then." She opened the door and stepped resolutely onto the lawn. "Escort me inside, Mr. Ross."

CHOCOLATE CREAM PIE. Pecan pie. Apple pie. Pumpkin pie.

Isabel jumped into the spirit of the event and tried a sliver of each. But her personal favorite was the apple pie, with a crispy butter crust and lots of cinnamon and nutmeg.

Fourteen people in three generations—plus a small white dog named Lulu who begged by their feet—sat at a large oval dining table set with pretty china plates, glittering silverware, crystal glasses and a centerpiece of roses.

Jacob's mum loaded the table with course after course of food. A professional-level cook, in Isabel's opinion, her grandest dish was a massive turkey that had been marched into the room by Jacob's sister, Emily, a teen still dressed in her cheerleader skirt and school jumper from their earlier "football" outing—American football, and not the "soccer" Isabel had envisioned. The turkey was carved by Jacob's stepfather.

Then, as Jacob had described to her, they passed side dishes of mashed potatoes, green beans, cranberry sauce, gravy and buttered rolls. Isabel was given to understand that Jacob's mum had prepared it all herself, refusing any help. She must have worked in the kitchen for days, Isabel decided. She hadn't had the chance to talk much alone with Jacob's mum, since Jacob had timed their arrival so precisely that as soon as they'd taken off their coats, they were hustled to their places for the meal.

Still, it was quite apparent to Isabel that Jacob was protective of his mum. He sat next to her, with Isabel on the other side of him. She sensed an undercurrent of tension in the room. Not a lot of the conversation was directed his way, but Isabel easily fielded questions and brought him into the fold where she could. It seemed sad to her, really. His family were lovely people, and she hadn't quite figured out the dynamics at play.

"Did your team win their match?" Isabel asked

Emily, who'd alternated between helping her mother ferry serving dishes to the table and ignoring the conversation in favor of silently watching the interplay between her and Jacob.

"Match," chortled Zach, the youngest brother. He was a skinny lad who'd had to be told to turn off his mobile phone at the table. Still, he kept it between his thigh and the chair, glancing down at it every now and then.

Emily elbowed him. "Don't be rude."

"It's all right." Isabel laughed at herself. "Sorry, I meant *game*."

"Emily doesn't know the difference between offense and defense," Danny, the older brother, teased.

"They lost. That's all that counts." Emily stopped pouting and gazed at Isabel. "You don't have Thanksgiving in your country, do you?"

There was a slight silence at the table. Emily seemed mortified. She put her hand over her mouth and went pale, glancing quickly at her mum.

Isabel felt sorry for Emily. She supposed that Jacob's family were aware that she was Scottish, but it seemed nobody wanted to pick at that scab. Jacob had put his fork down and was observing his mum, who said nothing. There was a sort of tug-of-war at work, but Isabel was just getting bits and pieces of what it all meant.

Isabel smiled at Emily. She had seen the frowns around the table. She could go with it, do what they wanted and brush off the question. But she looked at Emily and decided to be kind to her.

It was very odd. Emily reminded her of herself at that age. Indulged by her father. Watching him watching her.

"We have harvest festivals near Edinburgh in October and November, but not a formal holiday. Right about now, the Christmas decorations are going up. It's my favorite time of year. The New Year's holiday is big, too. We call it Hogmanay."

"Hogmanay." Zach laughed.

Isabel could feel eyes boring into her head, but she kept her gaze on Emily. "Which holiday do you like best?"

"Christmas is my favorite, too," Emily said. She glanced to her father. "Can we get a Christmas tree on Saturday?"

"Sure," he said. "We can do that."

Emily seemed to relax. "I'll take the plates out to the kitchen." She nudged Zach. "Come help me."

"I'll help you." Jacob scraped back his chair. He gave Isabel a grateful smile on his way out to the kitchen.

ISABEL WAS DOING what she did best, smoothing the way for everybody else. Jacob saw it. It made him ache for her. It made him ashamed of himself. It made him want to stop the pretense and tell her the truth.

"I like her," Emily said to Jacob as she came into the empty kitchen carrying piles of dirty plates.

He'd turned on the faucet and was rinsing the plates over the running garbage disposal. Back in the family room, he'd made sure Zach was showing Isabel how to play some computer game, and she was enthusiastically occupied.

She was curious about the world, he thought. Everything she touched turned golden and successful.

Him? He was usually reserved. Concerned about protecting other people from pain. Maybe he was tired of it.

"Jacob, did you hear me?" Emily waved her hand in front of his face.

"I like her, too," he said, putting the stopper in the sink and squeezing some dishwashing liquid under the running water. His mom didn't like to put her fine china into the dishwasher. She insisted that it be washed by hand so as not to dull the gold detail in the pattern. Idly, he flicked a finger over a flaw on the top plate.

Emily tied her frizzy blond hair into a ponytail. "I like Isabel better than Rachel, that's for sure."

He thought about keeping silent but decided he didn't want to any longer. "Ah…how much do you know about what happened?"

"I was a junior bridesmaid, remember? I was *there*. I saw it."

Ouch. He'd forgotten that. "Yeah, well, I was

kind of in shock, so I probably didn't react in the best way."

"Don't worry. I thought Rachel was the one who was the jerk."

He'd been thinking about that lately. At the time, he'd pretty obviously blamed everything on Rachel. But these past few weeks with Isabel...

All the talking they did on the phone—initiated more on Isabel's end, but he was participating, too— had opened his eyes. "Nah, she probably had her reasons for calling it off," he said.

"She shouldn't have left you. She should have stayed and fixed it."

"She didn't like that I work so much," he said.

"I don't think so. It's that you never smile or have any fun."

"*That's* what you think?" With a flick of his fingers, he playfully splashed some water at her.

She giggled and jumped away from the sink. "Did you bring your gun with you?"

"My service weapon? No, I did not."

"Good." She thought for a moment. "Does Isabel know about it?"

"She does."

"Does she know that Mom was born in Scotland?"

"Yes." He was proud to say it.

"And does she know that we're half siblings?"

He sighed, but nodded. "She sure does."

Emily sighed, too. "Good. I think it's important

you tell her the truth. That's what I would want if I were her." She cocked her head. "Will we see her again, do you think?"

He knew better than to get her hopes up. "No, unfortunately, she's going back home at the end of her classes."

Emily stopped stacking plates in the sudsy dishwater and crossed her arms. "You don't know that for sure yet."

"Yeah, I do."

"Well, if you don't tell her that you like her then you're lying to her by omission, right? And if you lie to her for too long, you'll definitely lose her. She'll run away screaming, trust me. And you don't want that, right, Jacob?"

Isabel came into the room still laughing from the game in the den. Her face was lit, her eyes bright.

"What are you two talking about?" Isabel asked, looking from Emily to Jacob.

Jacob sat on the stool his mother used to stir her sauces over the stove. It had just hit him upside the head, but the sixteen-year-old was right.

He needed to tell Isabel the truth. If he didn't, he was an even bigger jerk to her than he thought Alex had been.

So what was he going to do about it?

CHAPTER ELEVEN

JACOB RUBBED THE heels of his hands against his eyes.

"Are you okay?" Isabel asked, leaning over the kitchen island. "You look a little green."

He opened his eyes to see Emily standing beside Isabel, making faces at him that Isabel couldn't see.

Jacob slowly straightened from the stool. "No, I'm not okay. I have to tell you something. My father…my real father…was killed in action when I was young. That's what I want you to know. I don't want you to hear it from anyone else."

"Oh," Isabel said. Her eyes softened as if she was saddened by what he was saying.

"His name was Donald Ross." He waited for her to make the connection between that name and her family history, but she just looked at him with kind eyes as if she felt empathy for him.

"I'm sorry. My father died unexpectedly, too," she said, her voice gentle. "I can only imagine how that would have affected you as a young boy."

"Yeah, it ripples through everything," he agreed. "Even when you don't think it should."

He glanced at Emily, and realized he was saying

this as much to her as he was to Isabel. Emily just bit her lip and stared at him.

"So, if your father was killed in action…then he was in the military?" Isabel asked.

"No, he was in law enforcement. He was a police officer."

"Oh," Isabel said. Her eyes grew huge. "Oh." Maybe now she would understand. Jacob welcomed more questions—he was tired of silence. He looked to both her and Emily, but neither said a word.

For Emily's part, though, her crushed expression said it all. As she gazed at him with her big eyes, Jacob doubted she'd known these details. He had to fight not to turn away. Other than that one blowup about it he'd caused years ago, there had been nothing but silence on the subject since then. Too many adults flinching from questions asked. From Emily's perspective, likely all she'd known was that their mother didn't want Jacob working with guns.

Isabel glanced at Jacob's waist, where he usually kept his service weapon, his radio and his handcuffs. He was pretty sure that she still didn't entirely understand what was going on, either. She really had no idea of the scope of the secret he'd been keeping from her.

One step at a time. Isabel needed to know how he felt about her, first and foremost. He cared too much about her to "lie by omission" anymore, as Emily had put it.

"Em, I'm gonna take a walk with Isabel now. You and I will talk later. Is that okay with you?"

His sister nodded vigorously at him, still gripping a plate she'd been in the process of settling into the dishwater.

Make her stay, she mouthed, pointing to Isabel again, behind her back. Maybe she was anxious for happy endings. When he was her age, he'd wanted to make the world right, too, whatever that took.

Jacob's way had been to let his mom go to her new family, while he focused on becoming a cop. Emily seemed to hover, sensitively observing and directing what was going on. He understood, because at one time, he'd been similarly affected. His brothers didn't seem to be as sensitive.

Maybe they coped with their mom's sadness and refusal to talk in other ways. Or maybe they took it as normal.

Jacob smiled at Emily. He would call her later. Daniel and Mom might be angry at him for talking to her about it, but Jacob was simply tired. Tired of the lies. Tired of the omissions. He wasn't protecting anyone by staying away. Not any longer.

He went to the closet and handed Isabel her coat, and he put on his own, too. He'd been wearing the Black Watch scarf she'd bought him everywhere, even to work. The name—Black Watch—and the history made him feel like a professional protector.

That Isabel had been inspired to give it to him made him feel a little bit loved.

He led her out the sliding-glass door and down the stairs of the wooden deck, then past the backyard pool area. The aboveground pool was covered with a black tarp. A puddle of stagnant rainwater had settled on top. In just a few weeks it would be frozen solid.

He took Isabel's hand—cold, so he rubbed it in his—and they walked toward an old snowmobile path he'd found one Thanksgiving, years ago, when he'd felt alienated and had wanted some time to himself.

The faintly trod path wound about a hundred yards through a meadow, and then veered to a stand of trees. Both he and Isabel were silent, the sound of their footsteps kicking up dried leaves and crunching the occasional fallen twigs.

She squeezed his hand and veered closer to him, smiling in question, clearly not sure what this walk was about. He knew he needed to start talking because it was time she heard the truth.

And he would tell her, even though there was a good chance she might leave him.

There was a large, flat rock at the side of the meadow, and Isabel went to it, drawing up her feet and sitting cross-legged. She looked as though she belonged there, on a hike on a beautiful day in the country with him.

"You're easy to love, you know that?" He wished he could erase everything he'd done up until this moment and start over again. He sat beside her, looking out over the field. "Alex was an idiot."

She smiled sadly. "Maybe, but I don't care about that anymore." She rubbed his chest. "Jacob, I'm really sorry about your dad. Emily didn't know how he died until just now, did she?"

"I'm not sure what my siblings know, honestly." He sat beside her and put his chin in his hands. "I'll make things right with her later. Right now I'm more concerned about you."

He interlaced his fingers with hers. Their situation killed him. Every day was slipping by so quickly. He really did want her to stay with him longer. "We don't have much time left."

"I know." Isabel turned, sliding her arms around his waist in a sweet, sexy hug. "I've been thinking about that, too." Shyly, she nibbled at his ear. He was instantly aroused. He just wanted her so damn badly.

"When you come home with me for Christmas," she whispered, "will you be coming because you want to visit Scotland, or…because of me?" She lowered her eyes. "I mean, I just…wish you cared more about spending Christmas with *me*." She put her hand on her chest. "This isn't coming out right, is it?"

"It's coming out perfectly." His voice was hoarse. "You want me to go with you *because* of you."

She nodded. "I'd be lying if I said otherwise. It's Christmas," she whispered. "It's not a time to be… false."

"No," he said, "it isn't."

"I don't want to pretend anymore." Isabel stared at her hands, twisting them in her lap. "I know what I feel. I mean…of course I want you to go for dinner with my uncle and me, that goes without saying. But it's grown into more than that for me." She gazed up at him. "I loved meeting your friends and your family. I like feeling closer to you."

He traced her cheek with his finger. He just wanted to make love to her. Skip all this other stuff they needed to talk about.

"Say what you will about your family," Isabel said, laughing softly, "but they really do want to be together. Do you see how careful they are with each other?"

"They're careful with my mom because they don't want to upset her," he said.

She blinked at him, a questioning look on her face. *Dammit.*

There was no turning back. He'd started on this path. All he could do was hope she understood.

"Please hear me out," he said quietly. "Don't leave me until I'm finished."

"Why would I leave you?"

He took a breath. "Because me being your body-guard? That wasn't an accident."

She looked at him in disbelief.

He ran a hand through his hair and plowed on. "I asked my friend Lee to help me meet your uncle. Driving you to Vermont was the solution he came up with."

Her face seemed to pale. "Why would you want to do that?"

"Because…" This was where he had to choose his words carefully. "I needed some information about my real father that only your uncle knows."

Isabel was blinking fast, no doubt thinking back to that weekend. "Why didn't you tell me this earlier?"

"Because I hadn't fallen for you earlier, Isabel."

Her hands went to her head as if she was angry and flustered. "Tell me this isn't happening."

Which part? That he'd fallen for her? Or that he'd used a job with her to meet her uncle? "It's all true."

She pushed up from the rock and paced between two trees, rubbing her arms. "What did you need to know about your real father? What does he have to do with my uncle?"

Jacob braced himself. "The name Donald Ross doesn't mean anything to you?"

She shook her head. "No. I don't understand."

This had gone on too long. Jacob was sick and

tired of the whole charade. "Donald Ross was the policeman who was killed during your cousins' rescue."

Her hand went to her heart. She seemed to be in shock.

"Isabel, I need to know what happened to him," he said quietly.

"Does my uncle know this is why you were at the wedding?" she asked in a low voice.

"Yeah."

"Are you *sure?*"

He was all in, going for broke now. He had to be completely honest with her. "Positive. I was in the middle of talking to him about it when you walked into the men's room and he invited us for Christmas."

"You didn't!" She held her head with both hands. "You told him that? He knows why you were there at the wedding and I didn't?" She rocked, in pain, seeming to be thinking through the ramifications.

"I doubt he'll hold anything against you." He hurried to reassure her. "He realizes that you and I have something important in common. I'm sure he figured we would work it out between us."

"You and I have *nothing* in common when it comes to this!" she said, her voice shaking. "*I* didn't betray you." She thumped her chest. "*I* don't betray people I care about." Her voice cracked. "All this time, and you should have told me what was going on."

What could he say to that? She was right—he wished he could have told her.

"Why didn't you tell me when I first asked you to be my date to the wedding?" she asked.

He only had the obvious answer. "Because our trust wasn't strong enough. You wouldn't have helped me."

"No, *your* trust wasn't strong enough. My trust is fine. I would've realized the importance of what you were asking, and I would've found some way to help."

"You would have?" His wonder at her never ceased.

"Our families are connected in this, Jacob." She shook her head. "But you didn't give me a chance."

"Isabel, I just want this finished. I'm tired of the effects rippling through us. You were at dinner today—you saw how everybody clams up at the mention of Scotland. I was born there, too, by the way. And yet I can't talk—"

"*You* were born there?" Her mouth fell open. She stared at the scarf—the Black Watch scarf she'd given him—and then back to his eyes. "All this time you've let me go on and on, getting closer to you and telling you things about Scotland that you already knew, and yet you still couldn't tell me?" Her voice rose, and she stood.

"Isabel, wait..."

She turned. "Do you even have *any* idea how

you've hurt me with my uncle? I've given up *every-thing* to try to be CEO because it means that much to me. I promised my father, Jacob. My father—on his deathbed. And you, by making me look foolish, using me for my connection to my uncle, you've done me more damage than anyone else ever could have."

"Isabel, I'm sorry," he said quietly. "I really am."

"I wish I could believe you." She looked so worried and upset. Jacob had threatened everything she most cared about in herself. He saw that now.

She walked away from him, the wind blowing in her hair. His heart sank to see her leave, but after everything, he couldn't blame her.

"I wouldn't have done it," he called to her, "if I hadn't had a damn good reason."

"There is no reason good enough," she turned and shouted.

He jogged toward her. "But you haven't even asked me what my reason was. What drove me to do something so crazy and outrageous." He went to her, stood as close as he could without touching her or making her back away. They were both breathing heavily.

"I never would have done this," he said quietly, gazing into her stricken face, hoping he could convince her, "if my employer hadn't been pushing me to find out. The only place I could find the information was from your uncle. Of course I want to know what happened to my father, especially the more I get into it. But it's the Secret Service who really made me see that the only way to solve this, to get my transfer at work, is to go to Scotland and conduct my own investigation of the kidnapping and—"

"Stop!" Isabel gaped at him. "Are you saying that you told *my uncle* you need to *investigate the kidnapping of Malcolm and Rhiannon? That's* what you said to him?"

"Well, yeah, that's what I need to do, in a nutshell. What did you think we were talking about?"

She backed away from him, her face etched in pain.

He stepped forward and reached for her arm. "Isabel, wait…"

"Don't." She'd balled her fists, but in the end she just pushed him, two flat palms on his chest. She packed more of a wallop than he'd believed possible.

He stumbled backward. Off balance, he reached for a tree trunk to straighten himself.

"After all this time, you have no consideration for what's important to *me*," she said, her voice shaken. "You don't even see how you've destroyed my chances with my uncle. That's the worst of it."

"Isabel—"

"Don't *ever* talk to me again. Don't even call me."

And then she turned and strode up the hill.

He straightened, brushing his palms on his pant legs. Isabel was headed in the wrong direction, away from the house and deeper into the woods. "Where are you going?" he yelled.

She had pulled her phone out and was punching buttons as she walked. He loped after her, and in a few strides was beside her.

"Please stay away," she insisted, holding up her hand like a stop sign.

He saw that she was messing with the location app on her phone, probably trying to figure out a way home that didn't involve him. He'd ruined their relationship that badly.

But he was still on her side. He was worried about her. He *cared* about her. "I brought you here," he said. "Let me at least get you home safely."

"No," she said flatly. "I can't be with you any longer."

"Isabel, don't—"

She stopped. "This is my *life* you're messing with! You made me look like a fool, and to the one person whom I cannot look a fool to. You should *know* that you betrayed me in the worst way possible to me." She glanced at the path, reassessed where she was heading and then started speed walking back to the house.

"I'm sorry," he called to her.

She turned her head back to him. "There's nothing you can do to fix this. The damage is done."

"Let's talk it through," he reasoned.

"I need to go home." She stopped and scrolled through more information on her phone.

"Are you calling your uncle?" he asked, catching up to her.

"It's late in Scotland. Of course not."

She was probably calling a taxi.

"At least let me find someone to drive you home safely," he said.

"Who?"

"Lee Palmontari. I can ask him to send a car here."

"Right," she said sarcastically. "The man who set you up with me in the first place. He knew about the connection with my family's kidnapping, too, didn't he? And don't lie."

"Lee's a good man," Jacob said quietly. "He warned me not to screw this up, and it's not his fault that I did."

That seemed to appease her, his admission that he'd made a mistake. Well, he had. A colossal one.

"I wish you'd told me the truth *before* you met my uncle," she said again.

"Would you have helped me if I had? Honestly? If you'd had to choose between helping me and staying on your uncle's good side, which would you have done?"

"We'll never know, will we?" She turned away, looking as if she was going to cry.

Jacob felt like the world's biggest jerk. He wanted to comfort her, but he didn't know how.

He let his hands hang to his sides. "I'll call Lee," he said finally. "He lives twenty minutes away. You can trust him with your life."

She didn't argue, because really, what was she going to do? Call a taxi? Even if Isabel managed to reach a dispatcher on the holiday, they were still forty-five minutes from Metro-North, the nearest train station with service to Manhattan.

Jacob pulled out his phone and called Lee while she hugged herself, shivering.

"It's me," Jacob said when Lee picked up. "I wouldn't be calling if this wasn't an emergency."

"That's why I picked up," Lee said. "Jake, what did you do?"

"I…" He looked into Isabel's eyes. They were watering now.

He tore his hand through his hair. "I'm begging you to come to my parents' house, pick up Isabel Sage and drive her back to the city for me."

There was a long silence. Jacob knew he was asking a lot of his friend, on Thanksgiving Day, during family time.

"You're begging me?" Lee finally said. "Since when do you beg?"

Jacob bit the side of his cheek. "Since now," he said.

There was another silence. "I'll be right there."

Jacob closed his eyes. He ended the call, put the phone in his pocket and opened his eyes to face Isabel.

She was walking alone, across the meadow toward his parents' house. He followed her down the path, across the backyard.

At the house, she paused before heading up the porch steps. With a resolute grasp, she pulled back the sliding-glass door and went inside.

But it was the old Isabel inside his family's kitchen, polite and poised. Thanking his parents for inviting her. Saying goodbye to Emily and his other relatives.

And then, a few minutes later, she was outside again, this time at the end of the driveway, standing beside the mailbox. He walked over to wait with her. But he didn't have to stay long, because Lee roared up in his 4x4 pickup truck. Lee wore a sweatshirt and a New York Rangers cap.

Isabel opened the passenger door and climbed into the front seat. Jacob headed for the driver's side and leaned into the open window. "Thank you," he said quietly to Lee.

Lee shrugged. "It was a boring game anyway. Pretty much a blowout."

Jacob hadn't even thought about watching football. "You know where Isabel lives, right? Please get her home safely."

"Will do. We'll, ah, talk tomorrow, Jacob."

Jacob nodded. He stood back and gave the roof of the truck two light taps with his palm, by force of habit.

He watched them drive away. He felt numb. His brain didn't seem to process anything. He only knew that he'd screwed up.

"Jacob!" Emily hurried down the front stairs, barefoot, not wearing a jacket and shivering. She handed him a sealed envelope. "This is for you from Dad. And Isabel forgot her purse."

"Oh, hell," Jacob muttered as he took the bag from his sister. But he sucked in his breath and smiled at her as best he could, pocketing the envelope she'd handed him, too. "Hey. You want to talk about anything?"

"No! I want you to go get her!"

Jacob wanted that, too, but Isabel had made it clear she didn't want to see him. He didn't tell Emily or anyone else that, however, because he still hoped that he could fix this situation for both of them. There had to be a way. The forgotten purse, at least, gave him a reason to see her.

After he said his goodbyes, he set Isabel's purse on his front seat and drove back to the city, alone.

By now it was dark. He took the long way, with all the lights and the traffic and the extra cars and people. He didn't want to be on a lonely back road in the dark, not now.

He kept an eye on his phone, also on the seat beside him. How many times had Isabel called him over the past two weeks? Plenty. He knew she had her phone with her—he'd seen it in her hand. But she didn't call him now.

Obviously, she would need her purse—he couldn't remember if her apartment keys were inside or not. Lots more stuff was inside, as well, but no way was he risking betraying her by rummaging through her private things.

He kept waiting for his cell phone to light up—maybe even with Donna's number so that Eddie could arrange to pick up the purse for Isabel—but it never did.

Isabel wanted to avoid him that much.

CHAPTER TWELVE

THAT EVENING, ISABEL paced her apartment, hands over her ears. She'd calmed down a bit during the drive home, though she still hadn't processed everything Jacob had confessed. It had taken all her control not to quiz Jacob's friend Lee. *Did you know he was going to do this when you gave him the job of driving me?*

She thought of everything she'd gone through with Jacob that first weekend he'd shown up in her residence as her bodyguard—from Alex breaking up with her to introducing him to her family at Malcolm's wedding, and ending with Jacob kissing her.

Kissing her! And then, somehow, Jacob managing to find his way to Uncle John before she could, saying God only knew what to him.

That was the real problem she needed to concentrate on fixing. In all likelihood, Uncle John now considered her incompetent—or at least gullible, which to him was the same thing.

She'd wanted to be with Jacob at that wedding. She'd enjoyed his company, and she'd thought they had a connection. But it was also her fault for not taking charge more, for allowing him to deceive her. Yes, in a sense she could understand why Jacob wanted to talk with her uncle. She sympathized with Jacob's situation—felt sick that his father had died protecting her cousins—but he should have told her earlier, from that first day they'd met.

Maybe she really *could* have helped him. Now she was so angry and hurt, she didn't see how that was possible. That he'd messed with everything she had worked so hard to achieve during her months in New York only made the pain worse.

The buzzer in her room went off. *What if it's Jacob?* She had left her handbag on his mother's kitchen counter, and maybe he was here to return it. Isabel froze.

She went into their communal kitchen, where Rajesh was cooking something spicy over a frying pan on the stove.

Rajesh stopped stirring and peered at her. "Braveheart? Are you all right?"

She didn't feel so brave now. "I think Jacob might be downstairs, and I don't want to see him. I'm wondering…would you go down and check the lobby? If it is him, I'm fairly certain he has my handbag."

Rajesh handed her the stirring spoon. "Take over for me. I'll be right back."

Isabel sautéed the bubbling onion mixture in the pan. Her eyes stung even more, but it was a welcome trade. She didn't see how she could get past Jacob's betrayal.

Rajesh returned quickly, holding Isabel's handbag. She was relieved to see it again. Luckily, her keys had been inside her coat pocket, but her wallet and all her ID were inside her purse. If she'd lost it somehow, it would have been a hassle for her to replace everything, especially now. During the next two weeks she had final exams to prepare for, as well as writing her end-of-term papers. This was a difficult period for her even without the day's revelations.

"He looks terrible," Rajesh said.

She swallowed back a lump in her throat. This was so hard. "Thank you for getting this for me," she whispered. She swapped Rajesh's spoon for her handbag. "And thank you for not asking questions."

"Do you want to know what he said to me?" Rajesh asked.

She shook her head. "Good night, Rajesh. I'm going to sleep."

"Have you eaten?" Rajesh asked, peering at her. "I'll bring you some of my food. I have fresh rotis with ghee, and the vegetable curry I'm preparing."

"That's kind of you, but no, thanks. I'm not hungry right now."

Once in her room, she locked the door and then, still dressed, flopped onto her bed. She curled around her handbag on top of the coverlet but lay awake, unable to sleep.

A sob escaped her. She hadn't wanted to fail. But she wasn't back in Scotland yet. There was still time to fix her mistake.

She sat up, thinking. What should she do? What would her father have advised? How would Malcolm handle this?

How should *she* handle this?

Of course, she needed to talk with her uncle, especially since he already knew what Jacob had done. Nine-thirty in the morning, her uncle's time, would be the best hour to reach him. She turned and set her alarm clock for 4:30 a.m.

One alarm wouldn't be enough. Jacob had also been helping her with waking up early. Tears pricked her eyes, but she blinked them away. Instead, she set the alarm on her mobile phone and turned it to its highest volume, then slept with it under her pillow.

When the shrieking buzzer roused her, she felt groggy and dazed. It was dark outside. Isabel had only been sleeping for about an hour, but she sat at her desk, a notebook and a pen before her. She'd jotted down some talking points and a delivery strategy in the middle of the night when she couldn't sleep.

Uncle John's assistant answered his phone, measured and calm. "Yes? Isabel?"

"Hello, Murphy. May I speak with my uncle, please? It's important."

She heard a low murmur as Murphy relayed her message. She'd chosen this time because it was just after her uncle arrived at their Edinburgh offices, where he would confer with Murphy over his morning schedule. She hadn't been sure he wasn't traveling—he frequently did, but this time, she was lucky.

"Yes, Isabel?" It was Uncle John, and from his tone, he wasn't in a mood to chat.

She sat straight in her chair and smiled, as if he could see her. It also helped her remain calm.

"Good morning, Uncle," she said briskly. "I'm calling because I've discovered that Jacob Ross is not who he pretended to be at Malcolm's wedding. In actuality, he's the son of…" Her voice faltered, but she quickly recovered. "The son of the policeman who died when Rhiannon and Malcolm were kidnapped. He's…interested in information about it for his Secret Service file. He…targeted us because he thinks we can provide him with what he needs. Given that, I think it's best we not invite him to your home for Christmas. I would still like to see you, however."

She had spoken in a rush, and she took a measured breath after this last part. So much of her heart and soul had gone into preparing herself to helm the company, to be the guardian of her father's legacy. Was it still possible to convince her uncle that she was the most worthy successor?

Of course, her uncle already knew the information

that she'd just relayed to him. But this was a deliberate strategy on her part. She wanted him to know, in the best way possible for her, that *she* knew, too.

Her hands were shaking. She squeezed her eyes closed and hoped for a positive outcome. *May he please forgive me.*

"What do you think? Do you believe that Jacob is a threat to the company?" Uncle John asked quietly.

She closed her fingers over the phone. This wasn't the reaction she'd expected from him. He'd never asked her what she thought. Their relationship, slim as it was, was always about her pleasing him. "I'm not sure what you mean."

"Does Jacob pose a risk to Sage Family Products in any way? That's the most important question for us, as stewards of the family, to ask."

Being stewards of the family, to her businessman uncle, meant keeping a strong financial position above all.

"I don't see how Jacob could cost us money, if that's what you mean."

Her uncle's sigh was audible, even over their phone connection.

"Isabel," he said in his patient voice, "a determined foe could threaten us in many ways. Lawsuits, for example. Negative media attention, which would lead to brand damage and thus, a decrease in sales. Jacob is in a particular position to hurt us this way. He has a sympathetic story—his father was killed while rescuing Rhiannon and Malcolm. The press would lap it up. I don't like that he's sympathetic, and I worry that he's suddenly so motivated to meet our family. Does this worry you, as well?"

"I..." Her brain was racing. Uncle John always operated on a different level than she did. She just didn't *think* this way.

In her gut, she'd never felt that Jacob wanted to hurt them. Not purposely. But in not considering it—did this mean she wasn't cut out to be a leader? Were her instincts wrong?

"I could assess the risk for you," she said instead, resorting to action, her uncle's forte. "I have some time left in New York. I can see him—" as painful as that was to her "—and evaluate the danger to us. I could perform a risk assessment." A term she'd learned about in her business strategy class. "Will that help?"

There was a short silence. "Yes, it would, very much," he said gently. "You're learning. I'm quite pleased."

She closed her eyes and felt relief. *Finally,* he thought her valuable. "Thank you," she said.

"Very well," he replied brusquely. "For your remaining days in New York, until you come home, you'll monitor the situation for us. Watch him carefully. Stay in contact with him and perform an indepth risk assessment." Her uncle paused. "Do you feel capable of this, Isabel?"

"Of course." She would be CEO—she *had* to be capable.

"Excellent. And, Isabel?"

"Yes?"

"Don't rescind the invitation for Christmas dinner just yet, especially not for yourself. You and I will see how this goes and we'll take stock later." He disconnected.

Her heart pounding, she stared at the screen of her phone, pleased that she'd made progress with her uncle.

But what had she just agreed to do for him?

She'd assumed she would never see Jacob again. But now...

She had to. And though a part of her wanted to see him—was leaping with joy at the thought of seeing him again—she honestly didn't know what she was going to do.

ON MONDAY MORNING, still feeling lousy, Jacob was sitting in the passenger side of the SUV as Eddie drove. They were on their way home from court. The plan had been to meet with the federal prosecutor to transfer the credit-card-fraud case they'd built, but the plans had fallen through. Eddie was still fuming about it.

"So he's running late and wants to reschedule. Typical. How am I supposed to leave in two weeks?

You watch—I'll be gone before this guy gets his act together, and then he'll want me back."

"Is it two weeks?" Jacob muttered. That was about when Isabel would be leaving New York, too.

Eddie glanced at him. "You want to stop for lunch? You don't look so good."

Jacob shook his head. He did feel like garbage, though. He hadn't been sleeping well at all. He just kept thinking about Isabel. He'd fallen for her, hard, and that made no sense to him.

He should be focusing on setting up another meeting with Diane. That envelope that Emily had passed him from Daniel had contained a copy of Jacob's original birth certificate. Jacob hadn't bothered to look at it closely—he just wanted to send it quickly to Diane to prove that he was serious and working hard toward pulling this thing together.

He *wanted* to spend Christmas in Scotland with Isabel. He wanted to regain the feeling that he'd had with her. She'd wanted to be with him, too, until he'd messed up with her by not being honest with her until it was too late.

"Why don't we drive north about forty blocks instead," Jacob said to Eddie.

Eddie raised a brow. "Headed for a certain university, are we?"

Yeah, that was his point. It was late morning and the usual time when Isabel headed to campus on a Monday. "Don't judge me."

Eddie sighed. But he swung the car around.

Broadway was busy. They were already past Times Square. Eddie eased the vehicle uptown and fell into an easy groove where by some miracle they timed all the lights perfectly. Within minutes they'd made it nearly to Isabel's campus without stopping once, as close to divine intervention as Jacob was likely to see.

"Jeez, look at that," Eddie noted. "There're Christmas trees on the street corners already. It's not even the season."

"It's after Black Friday." That was the cue for the full-out commercial season to begin.

"Right. So where are you spending Christmas this year?" Eddie asked.

"Don't know," Jacob muttered. That was what he needed to fix. Since Isabel had sent Rajesh downstairs to get her purse from him, Jacob had been trying to figure out how to apologize to her. He still hadn't come up with an answer. He only knew that time was slipping away from him.

He didn't regret breaking his silence and telling her the truth. He would do it again in a heartbeat. What he regretted was not knowing how to repair their relationship. He understood why she felt angry and hurt. He wished she could understand his side of it, too. The whole thing was a mess.

"Slow down," Jacob said. They'd just sailed past a

familiar blue diner with a red neon sign. "Her building is on this block."

"What's the plan?" Eddie asked.

Specifically? Jacob had no idea. They slowly cruised past the residence hall. Jacob counted floors until he found her window, and then studied it for movement. Great; now he was a stalker.

"I'm turning around," Eddie muttered.

"We're here already, just keep driving. Go past her campus. It's two blocks north."

Eddie gave him a put-upon look, but he did as Jacob asked.

"Look. There she is." Another stroke of divine intervention—someone was really looking out for him today. Isabel was walking on the sidewalk ahead, and wearing what Jacob liked to think of as her Scottish raincoat. It was hard-core—heavy waxed cotton with a hood and lined with flannel, as if the wearer was headed for a Baltic hurricane.

Isabel, though, made the storm wear look stylish and appealing. She'd belted it tight around her waist and added a beret, plus her high-heeled boots, the ones that gave her the look of long legs that went on forever.

Eddie said nothing, simply pulled the SUV to the curb ahead of Isabel and put it in Park.

"Give me a minute," Jacob said.

"What are you going to do?"

"I don't know."

Eddie sighed. "Then you've got two seconds to do it. Move, man. I'm sick of watching you mope around."

Jacob hopped out of the SUV and was on the sidewalk in less than two seconds. He stuffed his hands in his overcoat pockets and waited for Isabel to see him.

He knew the exact moment when she did. He felt it like electricity.

Her gait slowed and her gaze darted up and down the length of him. Her jaw slackened. She stopped entirely. She had a laptop case slung over her shoulder; she adjusted it and gripped it tighter.

He jogged over to her, his heart feeling as if it was in his throat.

"Jacob?" Isabel's voice was that lightly accented song that he'd grown to count on so much.

He couldn't think of anything to say. Words couldn't express what he felt. He stood there, gazing at her, drinking her in, while she stepped closer.

Her eyes were locked on to his. Big, blue, beautiful eyes. Eyes that he wanted to look into all day.

"I…was going to call you," she said.

"Really?" That was a shock, but a good shock.

"Jacob, you look terrible."

"I… Yeah."

She gazed at him. "You shaved funny." She reached up and lightly touched his cheek. "You missed a spot here."

She seemed so sweet and awkward and tentative. Without thinking, he took her wrist. He rubbed the sliver of her warm, smooth skin that was exposed between her coat sleeve and her winter gloves.

Somehow, the two of them melted together. His hands bracketed her shoulders, then her face, flushed and warm and happy to see him. Her body moved closer to him, inside the private circle they made in the corner of a bus shelter.

He kissed her. Oh, man, did he kiss her. Like a dying man given a reprieve.

"I did *not* intend for that to happen," she whispered, breathless, pulling away from him for just a moment.

"I know you're mad at me, with good reason, and I'm sorry." He captured her mouth again. Opened her lips with his own. She was hot and breathless and she tasted like mint gum. That struck him more than anything she could ever have said or done—that she was chewing mint gum like he did.

He groaned and stroked her tongue with his. Her knees started to buckle.

"I…thought *you* might be angry with *me*." She gasped.

"Never," he growled.

"But my reaction—"

He kissed her one more time, then lifted her chin so she was gazing into his eyes. Cupped the back of her head so she could see the intensity of his feelings, of what he had felt, all last night, lying awake and thinking of her, unable to sleep. "You had every right to walk away. I kept something from you that I shouldn't have, for too long."

He sighed and started again, saying what he really meant to say, the heart of it. "That part of us is over. Okay? We're not going to do that again to each other."

ISABEL FELT DRUGGED. She was so thoroughly kissed that all she could think of was how she wanted more of Jacob.

She had a vague sense that her life was confused, that her plans had gone topsy-turvy and that the encounter with him hadn't played out the way she'd envisioned.

It was so unlike her to be losing control, to be doing something insane like kissing a man on the sidewalk on Broadway. *She* was supposed to be the inquisitor now—the one with the secret. *Cautious and careful* had to be her MO. She really had planned to phone Jacob during her dinner break, but he'd surprised her in that way he always had, of cleverly shaking her up. He was the bodyguard who walked beside her, the watcher with the intense eyes and the slow-burning fire always banked inside him, waiting to blaze. Jacob never gave up on her.

His delight in her was heady. The attention was exactly what she needed and wanted.

Maybe it was the feeling that Christmas was near. On the corner, she could smell the balsam from a tiny stand where a vendor was hawking his trees. At home there would be roasting chestnuts sold on the pavement. A warm spot to stand around on a cold December afternoon.

Without thinking or analyzing, she took what she wanted, pressing herself against Jacob's warm chest. He opened his coat around her, closing her inside with him. Gazing down at her, he reverently stroked her hair.

"Let's go somewhere," he said. "Now."

"But…? Isn't that crazy…?"

"Isabel, let's play hooky," he said with a gleam in his eye.

She wasn't sure exactly what that word meant, but she had an idea she would like it very much indeed.

She breathed in deeply, and biting her lip, she nodded quickly, before she lost her nerve. He glanced behind him, and there was the beep of a car horn. Eddie, at the wheel of their black SUV. Of course.

"Can we walk to your place?" Jacob asked.

"I…" She licked her lips. She felt daring. Going to lunch and joining her study group to prepare for next week's business law exam was suddenly out of the question. *Jacob* was lunch, and her study group could wait.

"Let's go to your flat." If she was to continue to assess him, it was the perfect place.

He didn't hesitate. "Your wish is my command."

"Just give me one moment to call my study group and cancel."

He nodded, waiting.

Charles didn't pick up the call, but Isabel quickly sent him a text message and then tossed her phone in her purse. "Let's go," she said to Jacob, feeling breathless.

She followed him to the rear passenger door of the SUV Eddie drove. He helped her up, into the seat, which wasn't easy because she wore her boots and a short pleated skirt under her raincoat. Once she was settled in, he leaned over her to address Eddie.

"We're going to my place," Jacob said.

Eddies brows rose. "Uh-huh."

With her chin on her chest, burrowed beneath her coat collar, Isabel had a split-second opportunity to collect her wits and rethink her actions before she let herself be whisked away with Jacob.

Was she certain she knew what she was doing? Was this really wise of her?

Do it, the daring part of her said. *Relax and take a look round his flat. See what's what. Talk with him. Dig deeper into his motivations.*

But that wasn't what happened at all. As soon as they reached his building, he took her hand and then like the good bodyguard he was, he opened the door, blocking her from the cold wind with his body. He led her a few feet across the pavement and into the small building she recognized as his home.

When they got inside the foyer—it was really just a three-level town house, she realized—and up the stairs partway, she stopped him on a quiet landing.

Jacob turned to her, drawing her close. "You know what?" he asked, gazing at her.

"Wh-what?" she said breathlessly, feeling hot all over.

"Holding back my feelings—" he brushed her lips with his "—has been—" his teeth caught her bottom lip "—a mistake."

And then he kissed her. Heat coursing through her, she touched his head, running her fingers through his short, clipped hair. He devoured her with his mouth, tasting of mint.

Her heart was pounding, her breathing quickened. Her breasts felt full and heavy, and she squirmed against him.

He opened her coat, and with warm hands stroked up her leg and under her short skirt. She'd worn boots with warm knee socks, but beneath her skirt she just wore pants—*panties,* the New York lingerie store clerk called them. His palm pressed over her mound, his finger drew aside the elastic of her new cotton panties—now damp with her desire— and his thumb stroked her bare flesh.

She bucked, from the irrational shock over what he was doing—he had touched her so intimately, so publicly, where anyone could see them!—as well as from the sensation he gave her. Waves of pleasure were building slowly within her. His low voice spoke against her skin, his blue eyes, deep as the ocean, gazed into hers. "I'm not holding back what I feel for you any longer."

She shivered. "O-oh," she said.

His thumb caressed her softly, over and over, around and around that spot she could not believe he'd dared to breach. A significant barrier was coming down between them, quickly, and rather than fighting it, she welcomed it. She gasped slightly and moved against his palm. "Jacob, I…" Somewhere, her brain was trying to form words but failing.

Oh, he felt so nice. She wasn't used to this treatment. She gazed into Jacob's eyes as he lowered his mouth to hers and kissed her, his tongue caressing her tongue, his thumb creating more pleasure than she could stand.

He was destroying her composure, surely and swiftly.

He pressed his lips to her ear. "I'm not holding back anymore, Isabel."

"No. Don't. Please." That was all she could manage to gasp.

He shocked her again, where she thought she couldn't be shocked any longer. With a last gentle kiss on her lips, he withdrew his mouth and his hand. She felt naked without him.

And then he lifted her skirt and lowered his head. She gasped loudly.

After her surprise passed, she sighed and relaxed into him. He felt amazing. Amazing, amazing, amazing. Jacob was amazing. Tension was building in her—sweet, easy tension—and it was bringing her to a height she would soon fly from. She rested her fingers against his head, needing to climax with him....

Just then, a door below them opened. Jacob lifted his head and gently put her panties back in place, then smoothed her skirt down.

With serious eyes, he looked into hers. "We have to move now, Isabel."

"I...can't..."

"I'll help you." He took her hand.

Feeling more grounded in her own body than she ever had before, she reached up to him and pulled him down to her, kissing him, tasting herself in his mouth.

Wordlessly he smiled at her, slung her laptop over his shoulder and led her up the carpeted stairs.

He squeezed her hand tightly as he unlocked the door to his flat and drew her inside.

Jacob Ross did not make love to her with efficiency, with urgency, or—that first time, at least—with humor, but with all the intensity in his heart and soul. He burned for her, and he was determined to make her burn, too.

Isabel had never experienced anything like this. With his gaze locked on hers, Jacob set her laptop down and then lovingly undressed her. He kissed each part of her as though his kisses were meant to start a fire of need and want within her.

Her raincoat went first, and then her boots, her woolen socks unrolled. Then her blouse, her bra, the damp cotton panties.

He left the pleated skirt on her. The female version of the Scottish kilt she'd made him wear. And the scratchiness of the wool against her bare bum felt incredibly sexy.

But what he'd done to her on the landing had been foreplay, and she was burning hot now. She wanted him to enter her and consummate his passion. They hadn't moved five feet beyond his front door. Wearing just her short skirt, she undressed him just as carefully.

He picked her up and brought her to his bed. She felt the soft mattress beneath her, the tenderness with which he held her in his arms. He got protection from somewhere, and she drew her knees up for him; wanted him to enter and stroke her. He kissed her, gently, and when he came inside her he paused, sighing. "Heaven," he murmured.

She cupped his face. *Jacob.* Ran her hands down the length of his smooth, muscled back. Around broad shoulders that supported her.

Kissing, sighing, they made love slowly. Such a

delicious feeling flooding her entire body, from the tips of her breasts to her toes. She arched her back, crying and gasping. Isabel wasn't usually a physical person, not someone who cried out and who burned. Normally she was controlled, in possession of herself, not as in tune with her own desires.

But not with Jacob. He was entirely physical. He took her body and he brought them both to climax, a long, delicious ride that was…perfect. Sweet and fulfilling and full of tenderness and release.

There was no control left in her anymore. And it felt nice not to be in control, for once.

This was a man she could easily make love to for all her days.

Isabel woke to late afternoon sun slanting across the pillow. Jacob was sleeping on his back, a sheet covering just his waist, while she'd slept with her head pillowed on his chest.

Stretching, she glanced at the clock. They'd been sleeping soundly for four hours. She didn't need to leave yet. They still had time together.

"That's the best sleep I've had in weeks," he murmured, running his hands through her hair.

"Me, too."

"Usually, I toss and turn. Sometimes going to bed with the music on helps, but having you here is better." He turned to his side, shifting her to the mattress beside him. She leaned her head on her arm and smiled at him.

"Want to stay in bed for a while longer?" he asked. "I'm up for more hooky." He glanced at the clock and winced. "Or we could order some early dinner."

"I'm supposed to be working on the take-home final exam for my business law course," she murmured.

It didn't faze him. "Bring your books here if you want, and I'll help you."

"How?" she asked, laughing. "My exam is for business law, not criminal law."

"I know." He continued to sift her hair through his fingers. "I finished two years of law school, so let me guess—your survey course covers basic contracts, torts, property…" He paused. "What else? Corporations?"

"You mean you're a lawyer, too?"

"No. I never finished my third year or sat for the bar exam."

She sat up. "How is it that you're such a Renaissance man?"

He smiled. "I'm not." He rolled over and stretched. "I went to law school nights the first few years I worked for the NYPD, mostly to appease my mom. But I'm drawn to law enforcement. What can I say?"

She drew her knees under her arms and wiggled her toes. On Jacob's nightstand, she saw a small book beneath his iPod. She reached past the iPod and picked it up.

The back of the dust jacket had a familiar color portrait of the Scottish poet Robert Burns. She turned it over. "Burns" was all the cover said.

Inside, one page was dog-eared. Isabel flipped to it. "A Red, Red Rose" was the poem Jacob had marked.

She pressed her hand to her heart. There was so much more to Jacob than she'd realized. And here was proof that he'd been affected by her, even before they'd been physically intimate.

Overcome, she lifted the bedsheet and joined him there, stretching out on top of him. She already felt imprinted to him, to the texture and scent and taste of his naked skin. To the comforting feel of his kiss. His mouth quirked into a smile, and as she kissed him, he groaned and stroked her body.

"I can't get enough of you, you know," he murmured.

"That's what I was hoping."

They made love again. Then they ate. They talked, and the shadows lengthened so it was dark again.

A part of Isabel knew she shouldn't be doing this, that they still had issues between them. Furthermore, outside this bedroom, they each had commitments, and those commitments clashed. She knew that she was only hurting herself in the long term by bonding with him now. But she couldn't stop herself.

Partly out of guilt, while he was dressing and also on the phone with Eddie, discussing a court date they had for the next day, she dressed quickly and took heed of her uncle's advice. She walked round his flat and made note of everything she saw.

In a small, sparse kitchen area, she observed that he did not cook much. His refrigerator held mainly beverages—juice, water, milk, beer—and a stick of butter. The freezer contained only ice cubes. In the cabinets were boxes of cereal and a loaf of bread.

She moved to the living area—a couch, television and table. Serviceable and neat. He had an acoustic guitar; its case was open and some sheet music was spread across the coffee table. There were shelves stacked with books—Jacob was obviously a reader.

She felt a pang of sadness in her chest. She didn't even know what she was looking for. She just knew that she wanted to cry over having to do this.

And then, tucked between a sketchbook and a stack of spy thrillers, she found a textbook titled *Hostage Rescue*. Sinking onto the couch, she cradled the heavy volume.

"What are you doing?" he asked.

She gazed up at him. He had changed into jeans and a U.S. Secret Service T-shirt.

"Is this textbook from your work training?"

Jacob sat on the arm of the couch next to her. His voice was gentle. "Yes, it is. Are you looking for something? I've been watching you for a few minutes now."

She closed the cover of the book and tapped her finger on it. "Your father was involved in the rescuing of my two cousins. We haven't really talked about that."

Slowly he nodded. "You're right."

"Jacob, I'm sorry he was killed. That must have been horrible for you."

He smiled faintly. "Thanks. I never really knew him. My mom doesn't talk about him, either, so..."

"It must have been difficult for you growing up without him."

He shrugged slightly. "I'd always known he'd abandoned us, even before he was killed. I didn't have great feelings about him. I was angry that he'd left my mother. I wished I could talk with him and ask him why he did it."

"You never had answers?" she asked.

He shook his head. "Eventually, I just sort of put him out of my mind. When I became friends with Eddie, and we were both interested in applying to the police academy, my mom...she got really angry. That was the first time we'd ever had a rift like that. She didn't want me to join the NYPD, not after what happened to my father."

"Yes, I can see her point. But you did it anyway?"

"I...like being in law enforcement. I like being

good at it." He caressed her cheek. "I think everybody needs to be good at something."

She felt a lump in her throat.

"This," he said, "what you and I are doing now, is how honest I want to be with you. It's how I want to be." He was silent for a moment. "Do you think you can forgive me for not being more honest with you earlier? I feel bad for making you look incompetent to your uncle. And for upsetting you."

"You do?" she breathed.

"Yeah." He traced his finger along her chin. "Your feelings are important to me, Isabel."

She lowered her gaze. "Truthfully, I spent most of the weekend thinking about the wedding…especially when Rhiannon was on the monitor and I told you all those things, in confidence, about who she and Malcolm were. That would have been a good time for you to tell me everything, Jacob." Her throat tightened, and she couldn't finish. She couldn't even look at him.

He sat on the couch beside her. He was staring at his hands on his knees. It seemed he couldn't look at her, either. "Maybe…I'm learning to be more open," he said.

She thought back to their lovemaking. He'd been open there.

She put her hand on his knee. "Is this because… your family doesn't talk about things?"

"I don't think you can blame them for what I do or don't do."

"I don't *blame* anybody. I think we all protect ourselves the best way we know how, don't we?" She ran a finger over the cover of his textbook. "I mean, nobody wants to be a hostage."

Least of all her. She kept thinking about what her uncle had asked her to do—or rather, what *she* had suggested in her rush to please her uncle.

A risk assessment.

What *was* Jacob's risk to them?

She looked at him point-blank. "You said that you need to know what happened with your father because…your employer requires it."

"Yeah. That's the immediacy of it. But…" He ran a hand through his short hair. "It's become more than that to me." He tapped a finger to his chest. "*I'd* like to know. And I should know." He paused. "The point being, it's truth. And I don't want to hurt you guys. Far from it. My father—my real father, Donald Ross—hurt me and my mother more than anyone else ever could. He abandoned us, long before he died. I have no illusions about that. There's no legacy for me to rehabilitate."

He shook his head. "I just need to know. Not just for work, but for me. To give me some sense of meaning that will never be shared beyond you, me, my employer and maybe my little sister, if she asks."

Isabel curled into his lap. She wanted to give all that to him. Maybe she could help him.

"Tell me what I can do, Jacob. What specific things do you need from my uncle? Do you need a Q&A session with him? Is that what the Christmas invitation with him was all about?"

"Yes. I asked him for a talk. That's all I want. Just to find out from him what happened, because he knows."

"My cousins were abducted and held for ransom strictly for the money, because we, as Sages, owned a private company. Malcolm and Rhiannon suffered for it—they were held for eleven days. My uncle has always felt guilty, I think, over what happened to Rhiannon, especially. He has a soft spot for her and Malcolm."

"Yes, I sensed that, too, based on what I saw at the wedding and what you also told me. But, Isabel, I don't want to open any old wounds. That's the last thing I want. If I can just get an investigator's understanding, the same as any case-study class in a hostage negotiation—" He tapped the book. "Just the basics—like a diagram and layout of the facility where the incident occurred. A time line with numbers and scope of the law enforcement personnel involved. A narrative of the decisions made and operations taken. A description of the hostage-takers and their demands. The weaponry and caliber of bullets used."

"I'm not sure we can get you all that," she said, feeling overwhelmed.

"We can try, can't we?" His eyes were blazing, burning with desire and emotion.

And suddenly she knew. If she could somehow find a way to salvage this, to meet his requirements, then maybe they could salvage their relationship, too. Maybe they could find a way to make a love affair work.

It was crazy. And yet...

She turned to him. "Do you think we can make this relationship between us happen?" she asked.

He nodded, seemingly overcome with emotion.

All she could do was try.

CHAPTER THIRTEEN

"UNCLE?" ISABEL SAID into her mobile phone at four-thirty in the morning, her time. She'd come home from Jacob's flat a few hours ago, and the first thing she'd done was jot down everything they'd discussed. "I have the risk assessment you asked me to perform."

"So soon?"

"Yes. I skipped classes yesterday and spent the afternoon in a dialogue with Jacob."

Then she recited from her prepared notes, giving her uncle a sanitized version of what Jacob had requested from them.

She knew that Jacob cared for her, but that he burned even more with the quest he needed to fulfill. She understood because she also had a quest—one that she couldn't give up, either.

As they'd parted last night, snow had been falling, a light dusting under the streetlights of the city. He'd driven her home in his personal car; had parked a block away from her building and walked with her, just because she'd wanted to experience the season's first snowfall with him.

Her heart was already breaking at the thought of leaving him. They had less than three weeks together.

"Why does Jacob need this particular information with such urgency?" her uncle asked, cutting into her thoughts.

"His organization requires it of him. He can't advance without it."

"And why do you suppose that is?"

Isabel stood, leaning her forehead against the cool windowpane. Outside, the snow had stopped. The flakes that covered the ground were already blowing away in the wind. "A psychologist within his department is investigating Jacob's fitness to guard the president. Without that confirmation, he won't be approved."

"*Is* he fit? Or is he a risk?"

Jacob? She thought of her solid, protective bodyguard. "Of course he's fit," she said somewhat peevishly.

"Has he said anything else to you about us?" her uncle asked.

"No." Isabel tapped her finger against the back of the phone. "Just what I've relayed to you now."

"Given what you know of him," her uncle pressed, "how do you suppose he'll react if he is disturbed by the information he uncovers?"

What is *the information?* she wanted to ask.

But she didn't. She was so conditioned not to question him.

Isabel sat at her desk chair and looked at the sketch Jacob had drawn for her. She wasn't sure what her uncle was alluding to. The last thing she wanted was for Jacob to receive news that was any more difficult or upsetting than what he was already dealing with.

"Will he be hurt, Uncle?"

"The relevant question is whether *we* will be hurt. You and I should be concerned as to whether or not Jacob will stop when he gets his answers. Have you never found, Isabel, that answers to questions often lead to even more questions?"

She didn't have her uncle's experience in life or in business. She didn't know how to reply.

"Beware of getting too close to him," Uncle John warned gently. "You need to remain objective. It's the hallmark of a responsible CEO."

Too late. Isabel was making love with him. She was sharing confidences with him. They were helping each other in their day-to-day lives. She was as close to Jacob Ross as she'd ever been to anybody.

She was dangerously close to falling for him. Or maybe she already had. A part of her wasn't sure. She loved being with him. He was like no one she'd ever known. And yet, a part of her told her to remain cautious, as her uncle had said. But her reasoning had been different. After Alex, she needed to be sure.

"Isabel?"

"Uncle," she said, swiveling in her chair and making an impetuous decision, "could you please ask someone in our company to gather together the information Jacob requested? Send me the packet and I'll deliver it to him before I leave. I'll make sure that's the end of it, as far as Sage Family Products is concerned. Jacob will listen to me. He knows me."

There was silence on the other end of the line. "I prefer to speak with him myself."

Her uncle didn't trust her. That was what he was saying. "I've given you my risk assessment. I don't believe Jacob Ross is a threat to our company."

"My invitation for Christmas still stands, Isabel. Please pass that on to him."

The discussion was over, and she was dismissed. "Yes, Uncle," she murmured.

There was a pause. And then, "You haven't asked me about your role when you return to Edinburgh."

"I…" Hadn't she? She thought she had.

"We'll plan to talk about it at Christmas dinner as well, Isabel."

Was there to be a trade—did she need to show she could handle the "Jacob situation" in exchange for the more important role she desired at Sage Family Products? An either/or solution? "Uncle, what are your plans, honestly?"

"I'll arrange for the company jet to meet you both

at the usual place in JFK airport. Murphy will call you next week with the details." He hung up.

Isabel listened to the silence on the line for a brief moment before she reached for her laptop. If her uncle meant to deny Jacob's request, then Isabel was determined to be prepared for it. She wanted to work with Jacob, not against him. She had one more idea, one more avenue that might give Jacob what he needed even without her uncle's involvement.

She climbed into bed and fired up her internet browser. An hour later, armed with the information she'd searched for, she phoned Jacob before he left for work.

"Hey," he said in a sleepy voice. "I told you you should have stayed over last night."

"Yes, I know." She felt herself smiling. "Can we meet for dinner tonight? I need your clever help with my business law exam. I mean, I *really* need your clever help. Everything is so tightly scheduled for me before I leave New York that it's the only time I'll have left."

"Sure, I can help." He paused. "Just you and me, then?"

"Yes, just you and me," she whispered.

When she hung up, she felt like dancing. But she took a deep breath instead. It was time to get to work, but not the work that her uncle or Jacob or anybody else expected of her. This was what *she* wanted to do.

Clutching her phone with the subway instructions already downloaded, she quickly grabbed a notebook and pen, and then headed out the door.

An hour later, a television archives clerk seated her in an empty cubicle with headsets and a machine that played videocassettes from the past century.

Kidnapped from the Castle: The Rescue of the Maxwell Children flashed in a fuzzy picture across the television screen. Maudlin music played in the background, and cheesy production values showed not the MacDowall castle in the beautiful Highlands, but another, much larger castle in what she guessed to be either England or Wales.

So far, her efforts weren't getting her what she needed. She'd remembered that, growing up, her brothers had talked about the made-for-TV movie loosely based on her family's story. Her brothers had watched it at a friend's house, disobeying their parents. They'd told Isabel that the movie had changed and substituted all sorts of facts about their family, but that it hadn't mattered because everybody in Scotland already knew it was supposed to be them.

Even as a child, Isabel remembered the talk and how frightened it had made her. She remembered Malcolm, older than her, being shipped off to school in America so he wouldn't grow up in Scotland and be constantly reminded of what had happened. She remembered Rhiannon, and how doctors had recommended she be treated at hospital, given her agoraphobia, but her parents insisting she stay and be schooled in her own home—the castle.

Isabel had thought that maybe if she watched the old movie, it would provide some answers. But it hadn't. After sitting through fifty minutes of the terrible script, she shut off the program that, unfortunately, had played on both sides of the pond.

Her uncle had obviously exerted his influence over the producers. Nothing she'd just seen corresponded to the few facts of the kidnapping or rescue that Isabel knew.

The names of all involved were changed. "Matthew and Sharon" were whisked, not from an Edinburgh street by three men in a white van, but from their beds as they slept in the family's castle. The family in the movie owned a chain of traveler hotels. Uncle John wasn't there at all, and several brave Scotland Yard detectives handled the case from start to finish. One died in a burst of heroics, and she was depicted as a single-mother policewoman with two wee children of her own at home.

The movie's producers had misrepresented all these facts. But the cruelest alteration had been to Jacob, because while Malcolm and Rhiannon knew the truth of what had happened, Jacob had no idea.

He deserved to know what had happened to his father.

One thing this exercise had accomplished—it

made Isabel angry. This was Jacob's *life,* and nobody seemed to care enough to help him find answers.

She did.

JACOB HITCHED A ride from Eddie at the end of the day, hopping out of the SUV at the wrought-iron gates that led to Isabel's campus. She'd asked him to meet her at the student deli inside the business school, so he walked down a wide lane and turned into the impressive facility that was her current work turf.

He picked her out right away. She was seated at a table with one of her project groups, all four members—two men and two women—sitting with their laptops open. One of the men and both women were dressed for business; the other man was Charles— Che Guevara, himself.

Jacob tensed for a moment, remembering that Charles had invited Isabel to his home for Thanksgiving. Then again, she had chosen Jacob. Isabel was with him, not Charles.

He relaxed a bit, loosening his tie. He was glad he wore a suit because it made him fit in.

The energy of this place wasn't what Jacob remembered from his own college experience. Instead, this was a rarefied world, definitely a world-center powerhouse of future business leaders, economy drivers, bankers, venture capitalists and entrepreneurial wizards.

He looked around. All these future captains of international commerce in one room.

Out of habit, Jacob checked the layout. No windows and two exits. Securitywise, it was better designed than her residence building.

"Jacob!" Isabel got to her feet and motioned him over to her table. In a breezy style that he was starting to understand was uniquely hers, she introduced him to her colleagues. Two of them, Charles and one of the women, seemed young to Jacob, but he nodded politely without comment.

"So," Isabel asked him brightly, "would you like to walk to your flat?"

"Yeah. I have something I want to talk to you about."

"Me, too," she said.

"You go first."

It was a long walk, but a half-moon was already out and the sky was clear, not cold. After he transferred her laptop case to his shoulder, they fell into an easy rhythm.

"I called my uncle today," Isabel said, placing his hand on her arm, "and I relayed your request to him."

"You *did?*"

"Yes, I did." She grinned at him, and he couldn't help smiling back at her. He watched her long hair fan out in the breeze, loving the way the ends of it stuck to her lips.

He reached out and moved a piece, rubbing the

texture through his fingers, before reluctantly letting it go.

"Do you want to know what he said?" Isabel asked, a small smile on her lips as she watched him in the dim light of street lamps and shop windows.

"Ah…yeah." He shifted her laptop to his other shoulder. "What did he say?"

"He said that he prefers to give you the information you asked for in person." A furrow appeared on her brow, and she looked up at him hopefully, her big blue eyes just cutting him in the heart. "So…do you still want to go to Edinburgh for Christmas?"

"Will you be there?" he said in a low voice.

She nodded. "Of course." But then her smile faltered.

"Isabel, what's wrong?"

"Honestly, I'm not sure he's willing to trust you the way that you might hope."

No, Sage probably never would. That was fine with Jacob. Sage also wasn't likely to give him any information freely. Not without leverage.

He stopped suddenly and pulled Isabel close to him. His nose was in her hair, and he inhaled deeply. He hadn't expected the depth of these feelings for her. He just wanted her with him. As often as possible.

He drew back and gazed at her. "Do *you* trust me?"

"I do, but sometimes it's still hard for me." She

looked up at him. "Is there anything you're not telling me that could hurt my family or our company?"

He shook his head. He still hadn't decided what he was going to do about Sage's negotiation tactic. That was Jacob's final conundrum.

"Just so you know…" He took her hand and interlaced their fingers. "I'll never have anything to do with the media—newspapers or television—and I don't post anything on the internet. I don't do social media, and I don't want any money from anybody. I'm not going to sue people. My mother isn't going to sue people. Is that what Sage is worried about?"

She nodded. "Those are the types of risks he'd be considering."

"Nothing bad will happen," he reassured her. He kissed her earlobe, and she sighed and laid her head on his chest.

A deep contentment spread over him. "I'm proud of you, you know that?" he said, suddenly feeling effusive toward her, as if they weren't going full-blown PDA on a New York City street corner, and he didn't even care. "I love that you're strong and you're going after your dreams. Once you're where you deserve to be, you won't be subservient to anybody. I'd never want you to push aside your dreams while I live mine, do you know that?"

She'd fallen quiet, growing rigid against his chest as he'd talked.

"Did I just say something wrong?" he asked, pulling back.

"No. You respect me, and that's lovely."

"Isabel?" he growled.

She sighed. "Truthfully? I wish we had more time."

He did, too. But he wasn't naive enough to think they were going to magically find an alternate universe where he wasn't a bodyguard at heart, and she wasn't Isabel Sage of the Edinburgh Sages.

Silent again, they both began to walk.

"I, ah, got some news at work today I need to tell you about," he said. "Nobody outside my job will know this except you."

"Hmm, let me guess," she said. "You'll be guarding a very important person this week?"

"You're good. I'm impressed." And so sad that they'd made it to the point where they were starting to read each other's minds right before they'd need to say goodbye.

She smiled sadly at him, too.

"It's because of you, actually," he went on, "and because you're helping me with this thing about my father. My, ah, boss—" *actually, Diane* "—has agreed to approve me for a short-term fill-in assignment with a team that's guarding a pretty high-profile Washington protectee."

"You mean you're leaving *now?*" There was shock in her voice and in her eyes.

"Not quite. I leave town tomorrow night. I think the whole thing is a test of sorts."

"Why? What's happening?"

He shrugged. "Can't say." Because it was top secret. He leaned over and kissed her. Her cheek felt cold in the night air. "Anyway, I'll be out of town for three days total."

"And nights, too?"

"Yeah, unfortunately." He paused. He really couldn't tell her more about the mission, but there was an irony that made him wonder about Diane's motives. "When I come back, are there any special places in New York that you'd like to visit with me? I want to cram in as many experiences with you as I can, in as short a time as we have left."

"I do have something in mind," she said softly.

"Where? We have Broadway, Lincoln Center, the Statue of Liberty, Central Park. Or, knowing you business types—" he snapped his fingers "—the New York Stock Exchange."

"I prefer your flat," she said.

"My…"

"Specifically, your bedroom."

There was a twinkle in her eye that took his breath away.

"I can handle that," he said, thankful they were almost home. His leaving tomorrow night…this was going to hurt.

"Yes, and you can go on the road knowing there is

one person in this world who is thinking about you every day and every night." She stopped on the stoop of his building and gave him a heart-stopping kiss.

He was the luckiest person he knew. Later, upstairs in his apartment, they ordered a pizza, and Jacob helped her as she wrote out answers to her take-home final exam. In his opinion, she didn't need his help at all, though he didn't mind listening as a sounding board while she mused aloud. Hell, he could listen to her read anything in that musical Scottish brogue of hers, even something as mundane as the definition of a corporation versus a business partnership.

After an hour of him behaving himself so she could finish her work, Isabel put away her laptop and curled up in his arms as they sat on the couch. "Take me to bed, Mr. Ross."

He happily obliged. She didn't have to ask twice.

It was a sunny Thursday afternoon in Manhattan when the unthinkable happened.

Jacob had been assigned to guard, not quite the president of the United States, but the president's young daughter, who was leaving town after a dance performance and on her way home to her secondary school in northern Virginia.

Jacob wished he could have conveyed the pride he felt over being chosen to protect someone so vulnerable and so high-profile. This was what he'd trained for. He walked in formation with the escort team, leading the girl from a matinee at Lincoln Center, back to their motorcade.

Jacob's assignment was to ride in the vehicle beside the girl. It was a routine, everyday operation, planned, ordered and well orchestrated. Every agent was top at their game. Every risk thoroughly researched and contained.

But the shooter broke through a barricade and stepped out suddenly on Jacob's side. There was no question as to how Jacob would react. All the agents would have done the same.

Jacob did what he was trained to do. It was a split-second decision, made without thought.

He reached in front of the girl, covering her, shoving her out of the line of fire, and he took the bullet meant for her. He felt it slice into his neck, felt himself go down.

On the pavement of the New York City street, Jacob put his hand to the entry wound, and there was so much blood. He thought of his mom. He thought of his siblings and Daniel. And he thought of Isabel. He felt a great rush of love for all of these people.

But there was buzzing in his ears, and he felt weak, and the blood didn't stop coursing. The last he remembered was that all went dark.

Isabel was leaving a closed roundtable discussion in her adviser's office when she heard the news. A fellow student filing out of the office ahead of her in line turned on his smartphone and read the headlines. "Someone from the president's family was shot at," he remarked.

"That's terrible," Isabel said. "Was anyone hurt?"

"Yes. A Secret Service agent is down."

And then Isabel was shaking, fumbling with her phone, turning it on and dialing Jacob's number.

"Isabel?" A female picked up the phone, not Jacob. She was sobbing.

"Who is this? Where is Jacob?" Isabel asked.

"It's Emily. Jacob's been shot."

CHAPTER FOURTEEN

ISABEL PRESSED HER knuckles to her mouth and swallowed a scream. This couldn't be happening! She'd just seen Jacob—she'd left his home this morning, and he'd been fine. She felt a fear so terrible she'd never dared imagine it.

Her knees buckled, and she found herself kneeling in the middle of the busy corridor.

"He was guarding the p-p-..." Emily was crying so hard that she couldn't say the word.

"Where are you?" Isabel asked. "Where is Jacob?"

"The h-hospital. Saint something." A voice in the background pronounced the correct name.

"I'm coming," Isabel said.

"My mom's here, too. And my dad."

Isabel wasn't family, and she didn't have the right to go to him—but she was driven by something she couldn't explain. "Please tell them that I need to be there, too."

And then she didn't hesitate. She stood and sprinted as fast as she could to the street and craned her neck searching for an available cab.

Her phone rang, and it was Jacob's number again.

"I'm on my way," Isabel said to the person she assumed was Emily.

"This is Eddie. I'm with Emily at the hospital. Where are you?"

"I'm outside my campus trying to wave down a taxi. How is Jacob?"

"Go back to the lobby," Eddie directed. "I'll be right there to get you."

"You don't have to do that."

"Yeah, I do. Jacob would have my balls if I didn't."

She laughed nervously, desperately wanting to believe he'd be okay. "You've seen him? How is he doing?"

"Isabel, I have to go." Eddie disconnected without answering her questions.

She didn't have long to wait, though. When Eddie picked her up, he put a siren on the roof of the SUV and blasted through traffic like an emergency vehicle.

They parked in front of the hospital with the ambulances, and once on the pavement, he took her arm and hustled forward, flashing his ID as he guided her into the building.

Inside the family waiting room, Emily was crying quietly. Jacob's mom appeared shaken and pale. Daniel sat by her side, looking concerned.

"He's in surgery," Daniel said to Eddie. "We don't know any more than that. There are officials assigned to us, but…" He glanced anxiously at his wife.

"I'll bring you back an update," Eddie promised. Then he hurried away.

Isabel stayed in the background out of respect. She set about making herself useful, partly to keep her mind off Jacob and the horrible thing that had happened to him, and partly because helping was the right thing to do. Jacob would want her to be kind to his mother, especially. Isabel quietly brought drinks over and found a box of tissues.

Time passed slowly. Daniel had purposely asked for the televisions to be shut off, mainly because the news story about the shooting seemed to break into every show. Given that the reporters engaged in speculation more than fact, Isabel thought that it hurt the family more than helped. The name of the shooter hadn't been released yet, but privately, Eddie told them—in more colorful language—that he was a young man with apparent mental health issues. Politics did not appear to be a motive. Isabel felt thankful, for Jacob's mom's sake, that the only video footage they'd seen was of the empty crime scene. Blocks of Manhattan had been barricaded off, and sirens flashed everywhere. Also thankfully, Jacob wasn't identified by name.

"This is what I was afraid of," Jacob's mom murmured. She said it over and over, rocking in her seat as if comforting herself.

"Let's take a walk to the hospital chapel." Daniel put his arm through hers and led her to the door.

Isabel moved to the couch beside Emily. "Where are your two brothers?" she asked gently.

"Zach is in school and so is Danny. My mom didn't want to pull them out. But I was with my dad in study hall when the call came in, and I made him take me with him." Emily gripped Jacob's phone and scrolled through screens. Isabel realized she was looking at his photos.

"He only has three," Emily said. "He has hundreds and hundreds of songs, but just three photos. See, look."

She showed Isabel a photo of Emily in her team-uniform jumper.

"I texted him that selfie, like, on Thanksgiving night. And here he has Mom and Dad. That was from their twentieth anniversary when we all went to dinner in the city. And this…" She flicked the screen to the photo of Isabel. Taken last night, he'd shocked her. She'd posed for him in a silly head shot. They'd been laughing even though, deep inside, she knew it was bittersweet because she would be leaving for home soon.

"How did you get your brother's phone?" Isabel asked.

"Eddie brought it to me. He told me to hold on to it for Jacob."

"Eddie's a good friend."

"This is you." Emily tapped the photo on the screen.

"Yes."

"There are no pictures of Eddie."

"Well, Jacob sees Eddie every day." And he hoped to join Eddie on the job in Washington, so that would continue.

"I have about a thousand photos on my phone," Emily remarked. "Everybody does."

"You need to consider his line of work. Jacob is very aware of his privacy."

Emily crossed her arms. "This is how Jacob's father died. Doing what Jacob's doing now."

"I know," Isabel said quietly.

"It's why he does this job," Emily said. "It's so obvious."

Leave it to the sixteen-year-old to say what nobody else would. Isabel remembered being that age and having those feelings.

Isabel continued to sit with her but said nothing. Listening was what Emily needed.

"Mom wants him to use his education and do something safe and reliable. He almost has a graduate degree, did you know that? He could finish it, take the bar exam and be a lawyer. But he won't."

Isabel knew, but she remained silent.

"He knows how much Mom hates guns," Emily said. "She won't let them in the house. He locks his work gun in the car when he comes to see us. I hate that he does a dangerous job like this. It's so selfish."

"He helped that girl," Isabel murmured.

"The president's daughter, you mean?"

Isabel looked at her hands. "Yes. He probably saved her life." She waited a beat. "That's important to him."

Emily put her head on Isabel's shoulder and for once didn't speak. She seemed to be digesting what Isabel had just said. Finally she said, "Would he listen to you, Isabel?"

Isabel just kept staring at her hands. Her manicure was chipped. She'd been so busy squeezing everything into her life, including Jacob, that she wasn't perfect anymore. She didn't know who she could influence and who she couldn't anymore, either.

Her eyes watered. Jacob could influence her, that was certain. She might never go to sleep, at least for a long time into the future, without thinking of him.

Please let him make it through surgery.

"Can you make him stop this job, Isabel?" Emily pleaded.

"He loves what he does," Isabel said helplessly.

"*Does* he? Or does he feel like he *has* to do it? Does he feel like he can do it better than anyone else? Because that's what he acts like. He's so impatient and…intense with us sometimes."

Yes. That's what Jacob was…what he had been to her that first day she'd met him in her residence, before Alex had broken up with her, and Jacob, in his zealousness to get her to Vermont so he could talk with her uncle, had been forced to share the pain he'd felt when his fiancée had left him.

In doing so, and in going to the wedding with Isabel, it was as if…Jacob had calmed down. And then, these past two weeks in New York, especially since he'd confessed to her the truth about why he'd wanted to see her uncle, he'd acted…happier. More honest. More comfortable in his skin.

She could help him. He'd told her what he was looking for, and she could have done more for him. She still could do more.

Eddie roared into the waiting room dragging along a surgeon dressed in hospital scrubs. With a swift glance, Eddie took the measure of the situation. "Where are your parents?" he demanded of Emily.

"Is Jacob okay?" Emily fixated on the surgeon, with his bare arms and his serious expression.

"Yes, he is." Eddie planted his feet and addressed Emily like an adult. "Your brother is going to be fine. The bullet passed through part of his neck and damaged some blood vessels. There was a lot of blood, but the damage has been repaired. He's awake now. I'm going to bring you in to see him with your parents. Where are they?"

"They went to the chapel down the hall."

"Great," Eddie said to the teen. "Now, you lead Dr. Sharp to them. He wants to explain to them specifically what he did for Jacob. Then he'll take you all to see Jacob."

Emily stood. Eddie held out his hand, palm up. "Pass me his phone." Emily handed it back over and then left with the surgeon.

"Walk with me," Eddie muttered to Isabel. "He asked to talk to you, and I'm going to sneak you in."

"Jacob asked for me?" Isabel skipped to keep up with him. Eddie grunted at her. He strode at a brisk pace down the wide corridor.

"What happened today?" she asked Eddie when she'd caught up.

Eddie was grim-faced. "You know this is the first time we haven't been on a team together in years? Well, I was in the office doing transfer paperwork and videoconferencing with Donna, who is being led all around the mulberry bush in Maryland by a psycho real estate agent. And then the news came in." He glanced sideways at Isabel. "This—an agent down—is something we all take very, very seriously. There are dozens of us here, concerned and providing security in any way we can. There are also investigations—plural—already under way. We got Jacob's phone out for him—an EMT had it—otherwise, it would have been in an evidence locker and Jacob never would have gotten it back."

He glanced at Isabel. "I have to ask you. Did he call you from his personal phone number at all today?"

"No. He never does anything like that on work time. Other than that one occasion when we, er, went back to his flat…" She felt herself blushing. "He only phones me after hours," she finished simply.

Eddie nodded. By now they were in front of a closed hospital-room door, with a stone-faced agent guarding it.

"For the record," Eddie murmured to her, "I don't know everything that's going on between you two. He doesn't confide in me like that."

"I didn't think so. That's not important now. What I most want is just to see him so I can know he's okay."

Eddie gave a swift nod. "Great. But don't be freaked out by the bandage—it looks worse than it is, or so the doctors say."

He pushed open the door and motioned her to pass by him. "I'll wait outside. I can give you five minutes, but that's all."

JACOB STILL FELT groggy, but he was fighting for reason and awareness over the drugs they'd pumped into him. He had to tell Isabel these things he'd thought of, now, things that pressed on him, before he forgot how he wanted to say them to her.

Eddie opened the door, and Isabel came bravely inside. Other than her complexion paling, she didn't let him know how terrible he looked.

She sat on the hospital bed and took his hands in hers. She ignored the bandages and the tubes and simply smiled at him. He'd never seen anything so welcome.

"How are you feeling?" she asked.

"I'm okay."

She ran her cool fingers over his forehead. He had to concentrate to stay grounded. If he didn't, he would forget everything he needed to say to her.

"Isabel…" His voice felt so raspy.

"You don't have to talk."

"I want to." He struggled to sit up more comfortably, and she helped him by plumping up the pillows beneath him. Her gaze dropped to the bandage on his neck. It must have looked horrible, but she didn't react.

"It's valuable," Jacob muttered. "What I do is valuable. *He* would have understood."

"Your father?" Isabel asked.

Jacob nodded.

She took his hand again. "I understand."

"I know you do. You've never…criticized me for it." He lay back on the pillow because the surgery drugs were making him nauseous. "My family isn't the same way, and that's a problem for me," he labored to say.

"You don't have to solve anything right now. Your only job is to get better."

Jacob squeezed her hand. He had to get this part out, especially. "I've got to go to Scotland and get those answers. I've got to find out what happened to him. For *me*."

Isabel clasped his hand tighter, waiting.

He looked up at her, his vision somewhat swimming. "Will you help me? Take me to Scotland with you, and help with your uncle? Don't…let anything stop us."

"Yes, Jacob, I will. If you're well enough to travel, then the plans are settled. That hasn't changed."

"No…" He shook his head. "This is the part you don't know. Your uncle asked me to investigate you but I didn't do it."

She stroked her hand over his.

"Isabel, I know you idolize Sage. I never wanted to see you hurt, to hear anything bad about him."

"You shouldn't talk now," she said in a low voice.

"Yes, I should. I was quiet for too long. Your uncle wants a trade. He wants me to investigate you to see if you leaked information to the press…in exchange for…the information I need from him. I didn't do it, Isabel. Know that."

She squeezed his hand, silent for a few moments. "Thank you for telling me."

"I'm sorry I waited. Lying there in the street like that…I realized how much I love you. I love you, Isabel. I'll always love you. No matter what happens."

CHAPTER FIFTEEN

ISABEL STAYED IN New York longer than she'd originally planned, until just a few days before Christmas when Jacob was cleared to travel.

She finished her exams, her papers and her presentations, but her heart was with Jacob as he recuperated in his flat. She spent every night with him. A nurse at the hospital had shown her how to change Jacob's bandages. The nurse had also given her written instructions on caring for his wound, post surgery.

Isabel had volunteered for this duty, after conferring with Jacob and his mum. It gave her pleasure to help him bathe and put the clean dressing on each evening. He grew stronger with every passing day, and she spent every moment with him that she could.

He loved her. It was a truth that she carried around in her heart with her. Nothing dimmed the happiness and the purpose that it gave her. She didn't have to be different for him to care about her. She was herself, and she didn't have to pretend otherwise.

So much had changed with her during her time in New York. One year ago, a call from her uncle summoning her back home to the company would have been the highest item on her priority list, the one thing that would have made her happy. But instead, her growing relationship with Jacob, coupled with his revelation about her uncle, had changed everything.

Physically, her uncle's actions toward her made her feel ill. She'd never given him any reason not to trust her. Sage Family Products had started with shampoos, body creams and bath salts created by her late father. Isabel had dedicated her life to carrying the flag for his idea and growing it into an even bigger success, often at the cost of her personal happiness. These extra days with Jacob were precious—time she wasn't willing to sacrifice.

In the end, wasn't that why she'd lost Alex? Because she'd taken his presence for granted? She wasn't going to do that anymore.

As she and Jacob boarded her family's private jet and headed out of New York, Isabel knew a day of reckoning was coming. When the plane landed in Edinburgh, she would be forced into making a choice between being "Isabel as usual" or "the new Isabel." She could be safe and take her uncle's side as she always had, or she could go out on a limb and champion Jacob.

Logically, she knew that her uncle held all the cards in this situation. Jacob hadn't offered her anything permanent, and as much as that hurt, she couldn't blame him for it. If he'd asked her to give up her goals in Scotland and settle with him in America—as what? The wife of a bodyguard who might take a bullet for someone again?—no one would think that was fair, least of all him.

And so they lived in limbo. As much as she wanted to believe otherwise, wishes didn't always come true. There was no guarantee that Jacob could be part of her future. And in case she was tempted to fool herself that he'd tire of the law-enforcement life, the steady parade of colleagues stopping by to visit him only underscored that Jacob's work in the Secret Service meant everything to him.

Her uncle was wrong this time. Actually, he'd been wrong many times, in Isabel's opinion, but in the past she'd been so keen to please him, so afraid to show her true feelings in case they made her less appealing, that she'd swallowed up her own desires, to the point she wasn't even sure what those always were.

Now she knew exactly what she wanted.

A driver picked her and Jacob up at the Edinburgh airport. Being back home was emotional for Isabel. New York City had been an adventure—a wonderful adventure, once she'd met Jacob—and one that had broadened her horizons. But Scotland was where she was meant to be. She felt it more deeply as she gazed upon the Christmas decorations adorning the houses and the fairy lights shining through the windows on each street they passed, and as she listened to the warmth of their driver's familiar brogue.

Jacob took her hand, and she squeezed it, feeling herself tremble. They didn't speak; what was there to say? They were only coming closer to their final separation.

The car stopped in front of the Georgian building where Isabel's flat was located, and she carried her own luggage upstairs. From the living room, she sighed happily to see the cozy view of the chimneys of the city and the deep blue loch beyond.

Her home. Isabel spread her arms wide. Jacob came up beside her, and she couldn't help blathering, "This is it. This is where I live."

He leaned against the back of the sofa and pulled her close to him. "It's nice."

She laid her head against his chest, her cheek brushing the small bandage on his neck. With his collar raised, the bandage was hidden. But she knew it was there.

If she had her way, she'd take Jacob to the Christmas market, and maybe even a Santa's grotto, or even just put on a Christmas movie, to get in the mood for the holiday.

But all that needed to wait. "I don't want to put it off any longer," she said. "I'm going to see my uncle now."

"Do you want me to go with you?"

"Thanks, but no. This is something I want to do myself."

He kissed her, nodding gently. "Good luck."

"I shouldn't be later than dinner."

"Take your time, I'll be here."

On the kitchen table she noticed a gift hamper filled with food and a bottle of fine champagne. A note accompanying the basket was from the woman who'd leased her flat while Isabel was away in New York.

"Isn't this lovely?" Isabel said. "At least the cupboard isn't completely bare."

Jacob just smiled sadly at her. He must have known she was doing her level best to stay positive for him.

Outside, the ground was bare, but a freezing rain was spitting from gray clouds. Since they were so much farther north than New York City, the sun would set much earlier. Isabel hastened down the hill, straight to the office, which was just a few blocks from her flat, and marched into their corporate headquarters building.

After what she'd seen in New York City, the facility seemed so much smaller. There were no skyscrapers in Edinburgh. She chatted briefly with Jean, their receptionist at the main desk, and then hurried to the offices. She felt different, but the place was the same.

The "sheep's pen" of cubicles. The ringing phones. The quiet bustle of people. The conference room, where she'd held so many group meetings on the launch of their new lipstick line the summer before she'd left. The employees' kitchen, where she'd spent her earliest years, making cocoa and waiting for her father when he'd worked late.

Inside her office, she shook off her coat and dropped her handbag on her desk—cleared since she'd left—and headed back to the lift to reach her uncle's suite of private offices. She strode past his line of defense—the managers, lawyers and accountants he'd hired from outside their family.

He was on the phone. Her whole life, Isabel had been afraid of acting out or speaking her true feelings with him, and risking his disapproval. But now she felt differently. For the rest of their lives, she would have a relationship with him. Being honest with him was more important than pleasing him or projecting that perfect image. She wouldn't go back to living any other way.

Feeling calmer around him than she had in a long while, she stepped into his office and stood before him, waiting. She needed to let him know that she had limits. She was a valuable asset, but only if he treated her with trust and respect.

He hung up his phone and sighed, tapping the tips of his fingers together. "Welcome home, Isabel."

"Thank you." Without waiting to be invited, she

sat in the chair in front of his desk and leaned forward. "You need to know that I did not and will not ever speak to the media about our family or our company. Not now or ever. Is that clear?"

"The culprit has been found," her uncle said calmly. "And he is no longer with our company."

"But you investigated *me*. That's personal."

"I investigated everyone," he said gently. "It wasn't personal."

"That's unacceptable," she said, also gently. "If you have questions for me, then you have to come and ask me, and I will answer you honestly."

"Jacob told you about our agreement, I presume?"

"Yes, he did."

"Good." Her uncle nodded. "I had hoped that he would, but I couldn't be sure. You see, by asking him to do this in exchange for the information he wanted, we didn't have to give him anything without first getting a sense of his intentions and the danger he might pose."

"The danger?" she repeated. "Why do you persist in thinking that Jacob is dangerous to us?"

"Until proven otherwise, Isabel, everyone is dangerous to us. We can never let down our guard. Even one lapse can be a terrible thing." He stared at her, his voice lowering. "Remember your cousins."

"That attitude has to stop," she said quietly.

He stood. "I thought you were wiser than that. The

most important thing a leader of this family does is to provide protection to its members."

"We don't *need* to be protected, Uncle. We need to be trusted. Otherwise, we'll never be free of the past."

"Is that all?" he said brusquely, gathering together some papers on his desk.

"No. I'm here because I would like the documents, please. The plans we promised Jacob. The file on his father, to begin with."

"There is no file," her uncle said. "There never was."

She leaned back, and then recovered from her surprise. "What do we have, then? What did you promise Jacob?"

"A conversation." Uncle John tapped his head. "A recitation of what is in here."

"Did you intend to be truthful with him?"

Her uncle just looked at her.

She should have known. Jacob would never be given anything in writing. She further doubted that her uncle would reveal anything significant, no matter what Jacob did in return. Her uncle simply didn't trust, and that wasn't something she could change.

He laced his hands together. "I hope I will still see you both at Christmas dinner. I understand Jacob is here in Edinburgh with you, and my invitation is still open."

"*Why* do you want to see him?" she asked bluntly.

"I'm concerned for him—how is he recuperating from his wound? But I'm more concerned for you. Are you ready to settle back into a routine at Sage Family Products? Do you still want all that you've been working for?" He looked at her with meaning, as if waiting for her to ask him the question she'd always asked him. *Will I be the one chosen to lead the company next?*

Her father had wanted that for her. She'd gone so far as to promise to him on his deathbed that she would never stop trying.

Isabel blinked back tears. She would honor her promise, but the *way* she'd been honoring it suddenly seemed wrong.

"I will see you at Christmas," she murmured. She would; they had much to talk about. She pushed back her chair and stood. "We'll both see you at Christmas."

Uncle John looked at her. She knew she had given him reason not to trust her loyalty. "Jacob will be gone soon," he murmured. "Don't do anything rash."

But Isabel didn't answer him because she'd suddenly realized that being the top dog wasn't the most important thing to her.

It was all about love. That's all it ever had been for her. She'd wanted the job because she loved her father. Could she walk away from it because she loved Jacob, too?

"Thank you for your honesty," she told her uncle as she left.

THIRTY MINUTES LATER, Isabel walked over to the financial area and into Malcolm's office. She'd rarely ventured into his domain. Malcolm, to her, had always been the enemy—her competitor rather than her cousin.

His office was empty. A huge oil painting of a beautiful landscape greeted her from over his desk. It depicted the property in the Highlands around the family's castle, and was one of Rhiannon's masterworks. Isabel stood staring at it, so beautiful and yet so lonely and sad. The piece told much about her family, and Isabel had never realized that until now.

Malcolm stepped into the office, his dark hair slightly longer than usual and a look of surprise registering on his face. When he recovered, he smiled at her. "Welcome home."

"You, too," she remarked. "You look tanned."

"Aye. Three weeks on the beach in St. John in the Caribbean—it was heaven." He pulled out a chair for her to sit, and then he sat, too. "Thank you for coming to my wedding, by the way. How is Jacob?"

"You remember his name?"

"Of course I remember. You're my cousin."

Isabel rubbed her arms. Malcolm hadn't said so

much to her in years. Maybe he was still in a good mood after his honeymoon. Then again, she usually avoided him, which didn't give much opportunity for conversation.

He held up a mug of coffee in his hand. "Just made a pot. Would you like a cup?"

"No, but thank you for offering."

He nodded. "How did you find school in New York?"

She paused. It was strange to sit beside him and chat as if they were long-lost friends. But if she was going to change her life for the better, then she needed to start here. "Well, it gave me a bigger perspective as to our overall strategy, our place in the industry, our future direction. It helped lift my thinking beyond just our cosmetics line," she said honestly.

"That's good." Malcolm leaned back in his chair. He seemed…more of a cousin—and ally—than a competitor.

Maybe it was time she thought of him as such.

"How is Jacob?" he asked again.

She took a breath and met his gaze. "He was shot protecting the president's daughter."

Malcolm stopped, his mug of coffee inches from his lips, and choked. "That was *him?*" he sputtered, wiping his mouth.

"Yes." She waited a beat. "He's also the son of the man who was shot rescuing Rhiannon and you."

His jaw dropped. His tanned face turned pale.

"I don't want to compete with you anymore, Malcolm. We're the only two cousins interested in leading this company, and I propose that we unite in leadership and do it together—honestly and as partners."

"Yes," Malcolm said quickly.

She blinked. "I beg your pardon?"

"I said yes. That's how I want to do it, too."

"Can we shake on this, please? To a partnership between us?"

He held out his hand and took hers in his firm grip. "There, it's done. In future, we work only in harmony. Now, tell me about Jacob."

Suddenly, Isabel felt teary, which was ludicrous. She'd never shown emotion like this, especially in the business world.

She couldn't go into a long explanation of Jacob's background. She couldn't express to Malcolm how upset she felt over the way their uncle had used her. She couldn't even be sure, really, that once Malcolm heard her request, he wouldn't betray her, as well.

She had to take the chance and express herself. She couldn't live in fear or loneliness anymore.

"I need something very important from you, Malcolm," she choked out.

He nodded slowly. "I'm listening."

"I need you…to take Jacob and me to the warehouse where his father died."

Malcolm dragged his hand over his hair. He looked pained.

"Jacob…doesn't know what happened to his father, and it haunts him. He also has a dream of being part of his president's personal security detail, but his agency won't approve it yet. They want to make sure he doesn't have any unresolved feelings about his father's death. Jacob wants to know the technical details—how the rescue happened, and why it went wrong. I think it's his way of processing and understanding why his dad died."

Malcolm sat back. "They really think it's healthy to revisit all that? Because it's not a pretty story, Isabel."

"Aren't you tired of the nightmares?" she asked. "I went to Jacob's house for Thanksgiving, and I saw his family, Malcolm. This event is still rippling through two families, all these years later. I saw their sadness. I saw how it affects them, just as it affects us. Every decision we make…our family's focus on safety and security and, in Uncle's case, distrust. You know what I'm talking about."

Malcolm gazed silently at the landscape over his desk, his lips pressed together. She was sure he was thinking about his sister, self-removed from the world, painting alone in her castle.

"I want to begin to address it," Isabel said. "To stop pretending that we can't discuss it."

Malcolm forced out a breath. Then he nodded curtly. "Aye."

"I also want to do this for Jacob because he deserves to know. He's part of this, too. I know I can't have a life with him, Malcolm. I know what plans he has for his future, and I can't be part of that. I'm sure he's also reluctant to spend much time with us over here, and I don't want to leave my family, but...I can't be silent and do Uncle John's bidding anymore. I can't be an automaton. I can't toe the line and pretend that my feelings don't count. They do count. I am important, what I believe matters, and whether you like me for it or not, you know that I'm right when I say it has to stop. This...thing has reverberated through all our lives and in a sense imprisoned all of us. I want it finished. I want it addressed so it can be healed. Do you want this carried through any longer?"

"No." Malcolm stood and grabbed his coat. "Come on."

"You'll arrange a trip for the three of us?"

"Four," Malcolm said. "My wife is coming."

"Kristin?" she asked, surprised.

"She's a permanent part of my life now, and, yeah, she's affected, too. I've told her everything I remembered, and she sees how it is with Rhiannon. So yes, I want Kristin there, as well. She'll want to see it."

Had he really just agreed to do this? Isabel's hands were shaking in her lap. "Thank you," she breathed out. She stood on trembling legs, ready to go home to tell Jacob. She hoped that this would be enough to help him. There wasn't much she could offer, but this was something.

"We'll arrange the trip for tomorrow morning," Malcolm said as they strode down the hallway.

"Christmas Eve?"

"Yes. And can I tell you something I noticed about Jacob?"

"What's that?" she asked.

"After the reading you gave at our wedding, he held your hand in the pew. I saw it, and it put me on his side. I'm not worried about him betraying us, Isabel. I trust your judgment."

JACOB RODE IN the back of Malcolm's BMW with Isabel beside him. Malcolm drove and his wife, Kristin, sat in the passenger seat.

They followed a route north to a section of country that struck Jacob as lonely and forlorn. There were mountain peaks in the distance, but the terrain was relatively flat.

He was quiet, and stared out the window. In the front seat, Kristin, the lighthearted one, was talking with Isabel, asking her questions. Was she going to stay in Edinburgh? What did she think of their family's Christmas plans?

Jacob didn't know what to say. He honestly didn't how he felt. The night before, he and Isabel had made love with an intensity that had scared him. He couldn't stay here, no matter how much he wanted to be with her. They both knew that.

He needed to get the facts of his father's death, and then he needed to withdraw.

He was grateful to her for making this opportunity to visit the scene. It couldn't have been easy for her, but she'd done it—she'd made her peace with Malcolm. Now, their visit today would help him get the practical information he so desperately needed.

He could walk the perimeter. He could sift it with Malcolm's recollections, and form his own professional opinion of the operation. His way of making sense of it all.

He touched his neck. The bandage itched him again; he fought the urge to scratch it.

He caught Isabel staring at him.

"Malcolm," she suddenly asked, "how did the kidnapping start? I'm sorry to ask, but…I was so young that I was never really told the exact details." She glanced at Jacob, and he knew that she was trying to help him by getting the ball rolling. "My parents wanted to keep it from me."

Malcolm flicked the turn signal on. They were headed off an exit and into a small town; Jacob hadn't caught the name, but he would make note of it before they left.

"Rhiannon and I were walking down the street in Edinburgh, when three men in a van dashed out and threw us inside," Malcolm said. "That's how it started."

Beside him, Malcolm's wife listened. Jacob had the opinion she had heard the story of his kidnapping before. Isabel was listening as intently as Jacob was.

"I remember being furious," Malcolm continued quietly. "I fought with the attacker, but I was knocked out, and then I don't remember anything else until I woke up in the dark. I didn't know where my sister was, or even if she was still alive."

His voice cracked. "Days passed like this. When one of them came into the room, I fought him. Every time I fought, I was either knocked out again or left in the dark with nothing to eat." He made a soft snort. "All I did by fighting was make things worse."

He continued driving. Jacob noted that they were headed down a main street. They'd passed what looked like a town center; now they were headed into a small patch of woods.

Jacob felt in his pocket and withdrew the small notebook he'd started. He glanced at street names and sketched a rough map. For a while, no one spoke.

"That's strange," Malcolm murmured. He'd stopped the car, and they were parked in what looked to Jacob like an abandoned parking lot in the middle of an open field.

"What?" Isabel asked. "Are we lost?"

"No. It's true I haven't been here since…then," Malcolm said. "But I'd sworn I would never forget it. After we were rescued, I burned this place into my brain."

"There's nothing here," Jacob said.

Isabel shifted in her seat to glance behind them. "Why don't we ask someone in the pub back in the village?"

Malcolm turned the car around, doing as Isabel had suggested. They drove back to the pub and parked in a space out front. Jacob carried his notebook with him as he followed Malcolm inside the small, quaint tavern.

"That place," a woman working behind the counter told them, "was taken down years ago. Board by board, carted away."

Malcolm nodded and thanked her for her time. Jacob knew without being told that John Sage had ordered it done.

Jacob took a seat at a table beside Malcolm while the two women visited the ladies' room. "What do you make of that bit of information?" Jacob asked him.

Malcolm shook his head. "Did Isabel tell you that our uncle never paid the kidnappers their ransom demand?"

"No," he said, surprised. "I don't think she even knows."

"She probably doesn't." Malcolm sighed, and then held up his hand to the barmaid to signal four drinks be poured. Cokes, he ordered them, and she brought them right away.

"Put this down in your book," Malcolm said to Jacob. "Because I think it goes a long way toward explaining why my uncle is the way he is today. When Rhiannon and I were taken, the kidnappers phoned a ransom demand to him. But Uncle didn't have the money back then. Sage Family Products was in its infancy, and though it may have seemed profitable to outsiders because of some media interviews my uncle had given, in reality, it was a private company, and privately, it was bleeding red. So John felt he had no choice but to bring in the police, against the kidnappers' demands."

Malcolm paused to drink, while Jacob transcribed with his pen.

"All I know," Malcolm continued, "is that we were kept several days too long, longer than the kidnappers had planned, because as each day went by, they became more and more irritable. I heard them screaming at each other by the end. When the rescue did come, it was barely daybreak, and I was asleep out of pure exhaustion. I remember a torchlight shining on me and then being grabbed and hustled out of there by a policeman who deliberately kept my eyes covered."

Malcolm shook his head. "I didn't see anything. I just felt the hard pounding of him running with me, pressed against his shoulder. Bouncing and jostling, you know. Darkness everywhere, except for the beams of light from the cars. Hearing the shouts and the…"

Gunfire, Jacob silently added. But he said nothing.

Malcolm poked at the ice in his cola with a straw. "Before the whole thing had started I'd been a ten-year-old boy, too old to be picked up and carried like that, but by the time it was over, I felt diminished, stripped of all sense of safety. You know, the state of the world that most people take for granted."

Jacob nodded shortly. He understood exactly what Malcolm was saying. In the course of his training, he'd read about such things from survivors of violent acts.

In a sense, Jacob had felt the same when he'd been shot, too. Even though he'd prepared for the possibility, Jacob had been stunned by the feeling of…emotional unsettlement that came in the shooting's wake. Even now, weeks later, those feelings persisted.

"After that," Malcolm said, "I was taken in an ambulance to hospital. I asked how Rhiannon was, I called and called for her, but nobody told me anything." He stared into his drink. "I only heard later from my parents that the kidnappers all died, plus…"

"My father," Jacob finished.

"Aye." Malcolm sighed. "Though I have to tell you, even I was confused about that. There was a television movie made, you see, and in it, they changed your father into a policewoman. So, even that was a lie to me." He turned to Jacob. "What was your father's name?"

"Donald Ross," Jacob murmured.

Malcolm nodded. "Donald Ross. I won't forget that name."

The two of them sat, saying nothing. Jacob felt physically ill. Maybe the exhaustion and jet lag were catching up. He closed the book and laid down his pen, needing a rest.

The two women came back to the table and joined them. Isabel smiled tentatively at Jacob. He realized that he wished she'd been there during his and Malcolm's talk. She should have been there. Another loose end that he needed to fix before he left.

And yet, today wasn't what he'd envisioned when he'd first set out for Scotland. He wasn't feeling that composure and self-control he'd expected. The calmness required for doing his job and protecting other people wasn't there anymore.

He needed to think more like Special Agent Ross again. Open the notebook. Observe the situation. Ask questions and obtain the answers he needed, because this was the best opportunity he would ever have.

"Are we going back to that lot?" Kristin asked Malcolm.

Malcolm glanced at Jacob. "Do you want to?"

"No." Jacob shook his head. From an investigative sense, there was no point. What was there for him to draw but wide-open fields? "I'd like to talk with Rhiannon," Jacob said quietly.

"No," Malcolm said.

Everyone glanced into their drinks. Isabel was looking at Jacob nervously. Maybe she was wondering what she'd gotten herself into.

"Actually," Kristin murmured, "I think it's a good idea."

"What?" Malcolm asked her. "How can you say that? You know I'm supposed to protect her."

"I think it will be good for Rhiannon, which will protect her even more in the long run," Kristin said. "Really."

Malcolm and Kristin looked at each other for a long time. Isabel touched Jacob's arm and motioned him away from them. He got up and followed her to a window.

"You saw how Rhiannon is," Isabel murmured. "Do you really think she can help you?"

"I'll take extra care not to upset her," he said.

She still looked worried, so Jacob took her hands. "You know I have to pursue this. I don't have a choice, even though I don't like the thought of Rhiannon hurt again, either."

She blinked, gazing up at him. "I want you to be satisfied that you understand as much about what happened to your father as possible, Jacob."

"Isabel—"

But she was heading back to Malcolm and Kristin, and all he could do was follow her. Her pain was breaking him in two. He didn't see how he could stand it.

This was much too personal. He felt too much for Isabel. He wanted to see her happy, and he well understood what she wanted from him. He couldn't give that to her because something else drove him beyond the surface motions of the investigation. It was something building more and more steam the deeper he dug into the story of this… ghost that had been the father he'd never known anything about, other than he'd been a police officer and he'd abandoned them.

Jacob felt a sudden rush of compassion for the child he'd been, traumatized by the silence and sadness and pain. In a sense, he was much like Malcolm.

Jacob shook it off and went over to join the other three.

"It *will* be good for Rhiannon," Kristin was saying to Malcolm. "I really think she's ready."

"I agree," Isabel said quietly. "It will be best for all of us to finally begin to talk about this, including Rhiannon."

"Fine," Malcolm said. "We'll go."

But he turned to Jacob, and Jacob could see that he meant business. "If anything happens to her, I hold you responsible."

CHAPTER SIXTEEN

THEY DROVE FOR over an hour. Jacob kept track of their progress, staring out the window and watching the route signs change and the scenery transform into rolling hills with mountains in the distance. Technically, he supposed they were in the Highlands.

"I love it here," Isabel murmured reverently, with the accent she didn't try to hide strong in her voice.

It just made Jacob realize even more that he could never take her away from her home. But he pushed that thought aside. "Tell me exactly where we're going."

"To the castle," Kristin answered. "It's near Inverness, where Malcolm and Rhiannon grew up."

Jacob opened his notebook and jotted down his observations. They certainly seemed to be in the middle of nowhere. Since they'd left the main motorway, they'd traveled on a meandering, narrow road, wide enough for a single car. If another vehicle wanted to pass them, one or the other would have to find an open field or a farmer's driveway to pull off in.

"I spent so long in the city," Isabel remarked, "I'd forgotten how rural we are here."

From a security standpoint, a home this remote

would be more easily defended. If Jacob had a vulnerable charge that he wished to protect, he couldn't think of a more ideal location.

They came upon the castle all at once. On the outside, it was ancient-looking. A mystical fog seemed to envelop the turret. Jacob wouldn't have been surprised to see a lonely piper step out to play a haunting song. He felt himself holding his breath as the BMW slowed and made the hairpin turn.

The castle was situated in a hollow beneath the road, which seemed odd to Jacob. A wall stood guard over the grounds in a huge ring. To descend to the castle, they needed to stop at a small guardhouse.

A white-haired man poked his head outside. He saw Malcolm driving the vehicle, and a wide smile split his face. He waved them through the gate.

"Who was that?" Jacob asked.

"Jamie. He's been with us forever," Malcolm replied.

The driveway was made of gravel, and the tires crunched beneath them. Jacob studied the castle as they approached it.

Later, he intended to sketch everything he remembered; to take photos seemed disrespectful. This was not a crime scene. He felt driven to remember it, though, but for himself, not for any official investigation.

He noted that the exterior of the castle was made of gray stone and had at least two wings to the back and to one side. A small wooden drawbridge was slung over what might have once been a moat; now it appeared to be a dry ditch.

By habit—even more of a habit since the bullet he'd taken in the line of duty—Jacob scanned the windows. He saw nothing; no shadows, no people. Automatically, he felt the tension in his neck relaxing.

Malcolm parked and took out his phone. "I didn't think of it until now, but we should've called Rhiannon to warn her we were coming."

"Maybe it's better if we meet her inside," Kristin said.

"She'll be upset," Malcolm insisted. "There are too many of us."

"I'll go." Isabel reached for her door handle and climbed out. She turned to smile at Jacob before she shut the door behind her.

Gamely, he smiled back. He knew what she was doing for him, knew what this had cost her, emotionally and professionally with her uncle. But Jacob was forcing himself not to think ahead where she was concerned.

He'd compartmentalized his life again. Now was for the mission. When an agent was on the job, he kept his professionalism.

He would not falter.

Jacob got out and stretched his legs. Minutes ticked past, but he was used to waiting. This was normal for him, and he'd trained his emotions to endure it.

After a time, Isabel returned, and she looked shaken. "Rhiannon already knows we're here. The guard called her when we passed through the gate. Then she watched us through a security camera."

Malcolm made a short laugh. "Why am I not surprised?"

"There's more." Isabel looked nervously at Malcolm. "She saw us all at the wedding, as well." She turned to Jacob. "You, too. She knows who you are."

That unnerved him. He couldn't pick Rhiannon out of a lineup, and yet *he* was the professional. "She recognized me as your wedding date?"

"More than that." Isabel looked helplessly at Malcolm again. "I told her Jacob's full name and why we're here, and she said that she wants to talk to him alone."

"But that's ridiculous." Malcolm got out of the car, shutting the door. "My sister doesn't talk to strangers. She doesn't even talk to her cousins. Everyone knows this." He gestured to Isabel. "You know this!"

"Yes, but...something seems different about her this time," Isabel said. "We had a long conversation." She put her hand to her chest. "I don't remember the last time we exchanged so many words." She honestly looked astonished.

Jacob was getting a strange, itchy feeling. He grabbed his notebook. This would be the best chance he'd ever have to talk with an eyewitness; he could feel it.

John Sage would never tell Jacob anything about what had happened. Malcolm had relayed what little he could, and it hadn't been enough. But Rhiannon—she'd surely seen more.

"You don't have to worry about me," Jacob said to Malcolm. "I'm trained. I know how to talk to vics—to people who've been through traumatic situations."

Malcolm grunted; he didn't look convinced. Shaking his head, he turned to Kristin. "What do you think?" he asked quietly. "Honestly?"

"I think," Kristin said slowly, "that if Rhiannon says she wants to see someone, then she should see that person. She's a grown woman, and who are we to stop her?"

Kristin was right. It was Rhiannon's home; Jacob could just walk in. This was more than he'd hoped for—he could finally speak with an actual witness to his father's last tactical operation.

But still Malcolm paused. To Jacob, he seemed wary. He'd spent a lifetime worrying about his sister.

"Did I mention that I'm trained?" Jacob asked again. "Even more—I've just survived a trauma of my own." He pulled back his collar and showed Malcolm the bandage. "I *know* how it feels, Malcolm."

Malcolm let out a breath. Finally, he looked Jacob in the eye. "Let's go."

Jacob nodded and let Malcolm lead the way. He

stayed close to Isabel, looking all around them and taking note of their surroundings as they entered the building.

The interior of the castle was cool, though there was a blazing fire burning in a great stone fireplace in the entry hall. The ceiling was enormously high. Though the castle was decorated for Christmas, traditional hangings also adorned the stone walls: medieval swords, muskets and other such battle weapons. Colorful tartan carpeting was spread over the floors and up the stone stairway.

At the top of the stairs, a tall woman with long dark hair the color of Malcolm's stood waiting with hands clasped.

She wasn't what Jacob expected. Yes, he'd seen a glimpse of her on the monitor at the wedding, but based on what Isabel had told him about her agoraphobia, he'd expected someone frail, possibly even beautiful, like a proverbial Sleeping Beauty hidden away in her remote tower. But Rhiannon Sage looked robust, in good health, and though she might have been considered pretty by other men, she couldn't compete with the beauty he saw in Isabel.

Rhiannon was…quirky. Maybe even artistic, now that he knew she was a painter. Her fingertips were smeared with green and she was wearing a smock, as if they'd interrupted her work.

Jacob stopped two steps below her. Isabel continued to the top and smiled. "This is Jacob." Turning to him, she said, "Jacob, this is my cousin Rhiannon."

In a dignified manner, and yet with a dimple showing in her cheek, Rhiannon held out her hand. "I'm pleased to meet you, finally."

Finally? What the hell was she talking about?

His hand fell to his side. But he gathered his wits and continued up the two steps to greet her.

Her hand was warm. He glanced over to Isabel, and saw that she was smiling at him. But her lips were trembling, and he knew she was trying to make him feel at ease, though neither of them were.

Somehow, though, he was drawn forward, propelled to follow Rhiannon.

"Isabel, would you like to come with us?" Rhiannon asked.

Isabel darted a glance to him. "Yes, please," she said quickly. Her hand curled into Jacob's, and he gave it a squeeze before sliding his arm around her shoulders.

They passed through a hallway and down a set of back stairs, and then walked outside into the mist for a short bout across a courtyard. The outbuilding Rhiannon took them to wasn't easily detected from the castle entrance. It simply disappeared into the folds of the landscape, and Jacob felt as though he'd been cleverly fooled.

"Have you ever been inside here before?" he mouthed to Isabel, and she shook her head in reply.

"It's her studio," Isabel whispered into his ear as Rhiannon picked through a set of keys. "No one but her immediate family and Uncle John ever goes inside."

He felt a chill of privilege. But why him? With his left hand, he gripped the notebook more tightly. Forced himself to observe the perimeter.

Beyond the small courtyard, there seemed to be acres and acres—hundreds of acres, maybe—of raw, unspoiled Highlands. The wind blew across the trees, straight at him, and he raised his elbow to shield his and Isabel's faces.

Instinctively he knew that Rhiannon thrived here. She walked these wild lands; she drew her artistic inspiration from this environment.

Rhiannon smiled at them, opening the door and waving them inside.

They walked up another turret, shaded in darkness, with uneven stone stairs and a curving line. Jacob felt spun about. He wasn't sure what was north or south, high or low, night or day.

Rhiannon led them into her workshop—Jacob smelled the oil paints before he saw anything—and Isabel, slightly ahead of him, made a small gasp of joy.

The place was… He didn't know how to describe it. Bursts of color and light. A wide, airy window, south-facing, overlooking that Highlands wilderness.

He walked across the floor, noticing that Rhiannon had painted a woodland mural upon the boards, and dotted it with glittery designs. It looked like a fairy playground, he thought. But who was he to judge? This was Rhiannon's private space, and she'd invited them inside. Without a doubt, that was a sacred trust, and he respected that.

Jacob shoved his notebook into his pocket. Clearly, if he approached this like a technician, he would be lost here, missing what was most important. So he swallowed and kept walking, toward an easel she'd set up, facing away from the windows so the light was at her back.

"Roses," Isabel murmured beside him, a smile covering her face. "Look at that, Jacob. Red, red roses."

The entire, huge canvas was covered in an eerily lifelike, vivaciously alive panel of pure red roses. He stared, stunned. Jacob had some sketching talent; he'd taken a few art classes as a kid, but this… Rhiannon MacDowall was world-class in her talents.

Clearly, they'd interrupted her. The brush tip was still wet with green oil paint; the palette rested on a ledge of the easel.

Jacob glanced around. Where was her still-life display? He saw no photographs or pictures, either. Outside, it was winter—any rosebushes in the gardens would only contain bare, dead branches.

"Are you painting this from memory?" he asked.

"Of course," Rhiannon replied.

"You heard me sing the Burns poem," Isabel exclaimed. "At Malcolm's wedding, didn't you?"

Rhiannon smiled, clearly pleased. "Yes, and you inspired me." She put her palms together. "This painting is for you. I want you to keep it when I'm finished."

"That's…" Isabel hesitated as if tempted to refuse. But then she looked directly into Rhiannon's eyes, and Jacob saw the tears gathering in her own. "I'm honored," she said.

"No, I'm honored." Somberly, Rhiannon walked to Jacob. He let her take his hand, let her lead him to an alcove, where she sat him on a couch. "I have something for you, too," she said.

He had no idea what to expect. He glanced at Isabel, who'd also walked over to stand before him, but she simply shrugged.

Rhiannon was on her knees, digging inside a huge battered armoire. At last, she pulled out a parcel and stood, bringing it over to him.

Her expression was clear and solemn. "I drew this for you many years ago."

"For *me?*"

"Yes. I always knew you would come someday. I knew you would find me. When I saw you with Isabel at Malcolm's wedding, I knew straightaway that the time had come.…"

Jacob's hands shook. Numbly, he opened the dusty envelope that Rhiannon had brought him.

It was a pencil sketch, much like the one he'd

made of Isabel, but this was more childishly drawn, and it was of *him*.

He exhaled hard, dropping the sketch. Isabel gasped, her hand over her mouth.

"How is this even possible…?" he sputtered.

Rhiannon sat next to him. "Oh, I see. You think it's you, Jacob. But it's not. This is Donald Ross, the man who saved my life."

He whirled to face her. He picked up the sketch, studying it more closely. Emotion flooded him. He hadn't realized he looked so much like his real father. His eyes stung. It made sense, because he looked nothing like his mom.

This man—his father, Donald—wore a police officer's uniform. He had a kind face. In the sketch, he was about Jacob's age, and he was smiling.

"He told me he had a son named Jacob," Rhiannon said.

Jacob's eyes stung harder, and he blinked fiercely. "He *spoke* of me?"

"He said you were in America, with your mother, and that he thought of you every day. Someday, he hoped to go see you. He said this several times, so it was important to him."

Jacob had never expected… He'd never…

"I'm sorry, Jacob. Your father deliberately took a bullet that was meant for me, and that's all I'll ever say about that night. Can you understand?"

Wordlessly, he nodded. Jacob knew about taking bullets. He knew about that sacred trust....

"People always want to hear more, don't they?" Rhiannon said to him. "The therapists are kind, and they want to be helpful. But there are some things that are meant to be kept to ourselves, at least until the time is right. I didn't want to talk about Donald Ross with anyone else but you. Only you. Because I knew you would find me when you were ready to know."

Jacob sucked in his breath. He glanced at Isabel, and she was already crying for him. Her hands were covering her mouth and her eyes were glistening with tears. Pain welled in his chest, and he knew he was losing control. For an instant he thought of Isabel that first day when she'd vomited all over the floor in that coffee shop. He was going to lose his composure, too, and it couldn't be stopped.

"Rhiannon, I need to go...." He stood, wanting to say much more, but he couldn't form the words.

He took the sketch she'd made and rolled it as carefully as he could, then tucked it inside his jacket pocket. He wasn't letting this go, ever.

"Yes, I'll show you the way downstairs," Rhiannon said. "It's all right. Come back and see me anytime, if you'd like."

"Yes, thank you," he managed to say.

She put her hand on his. "Farewell, Jacob. As we say in Scotland, haste ye back. I do hope to see you again someday."

And then Jacob was stumbling outside, face into the mist, sinking onto the bench at the edge of the garden.

ISABEL'S HEART WAS breaking for Jacob. She went downstairs with him and watched from the doorway. He sat with his head in his hands in that dead winter courtyard. His back was to her, and his muscles moved as he took in deep breaths.

She put her hand to her chest, crushed by the sight of his pain. Waiting, she stood guard over him. Finally, she couldn't take it any longer and went to him, pressing her body over his.

She covered him as a blanket, her cheek on his back, her arms hugging him, passing him all her love. If she could take his pain into her own body, she would do so in a heartbeat.

"Jacob, I'm sorry." She kept her words close to his ear; otherwise, they would have been swept away by the wind.

"I didn't know…" His voice was faint, as though all of his intense emotion was spent. "I was wrong about him."

She hugged him tighter. "He loved you," she said softly. "He thought of you all along."

"My mom doesn't know. We thought…he'd failed us."

"Maybe he just needed more time." She paused. "He was a hero to Rhiannon."

"He was," he whispered.

"I'm glad you know now."

Jacob stood suddenly and pulled her into his arms, hugging her back, fiercely. "Thank you, Isabel. You've brought me such light."

"Rhiannon did that."

"No," he said hoarsely, "it was you. You've brought me what no one else could. I think…I always needed to hear what she said up there…." He pulled back to look at her.

"I brought you to Scotland with me because you love me," she said softly. "And I know I haven't told you yet, but I do love you back. With all my heart."

He put his forehead to hers. With a gentle hand, he smoothed her wet, tangled hair from her face. "We should get out of the rain."

"Yes, we should."

"I *do* love you, you know." He stared into her eyes. And then he led her back, into the shelter of the building that housed Rhiannon's artist studio. The heavy door shut behind them, and they were alone in the silence of the cool stairwell, smelling of damp wood beams on centuries-old stonework.

They both paused, as if not sure what came next. Isabel knew this was the moment. Soon Rhiannon would come down from her studio, or Malcolm and Kristin would wander in looking for them, and then she and Jacob would be headed back to the city again, and their time would be done.

"Jacob? I haven't said this to you because I've been afraid to think about you leaving. But I don't think that holding back is very wise for me anymore. What if I never see you again and I didn't say it to you while I still had the chance?"

Slowly Jacob exhaled, stepping back.

Her gaze dropped. He *knew* what she was going to ask. She studied a planter of leafy green holly in the corner, and nervously she reached to pluck a sprig, rubbing the sharp edges between her fingers.

When she looked at Jacob again, he was staring past her, rain and mist still on his face. He didn't want her to ask him to stay, she sensed. She was taking such a risk in doing so, and it scared her.

But not telling him the truth scared her more.

She sat on the stair beside the holly bush. "It's Christmas Eve." She gazed up at him. "May I tell you what I most want for Christmas?"

His face was a statue, the emotion unreadable on it. Jacob had fashioned himself into a bodyguard; he had been one for most of his life. But after hearing Rhiannon's story, how could any woman who loved him want him to continue that life?

"What I would most like," she said bravely, "is for you not to take bullets for other people anymore, because I selfishly want you to stay here with me."

His expression didn't change.

Her vision blurred, and she lowered her head.

After a moment, she felt his gentle touch on her

chin. "Will you wait for me?" he asked, kneeling before her.

She dared to look at him, and his eyes were compassionate. She nodded wordlessly.

"I need to go home and share what I've learned," he said quietly.

He wasn't asking her to go with him, she noticed. Neither was he promising to return. But he hadn't turned her down, either.

"Will you stay for Christmas dinner?" she whispered.

He shook his head. "It's better for you if I don't go." He cupped his hand to her cheek. "Make this about you, and what you want. You'll get more from your uncle without me there to complicate it."

She put her arms around his neck, and her forehead to his, not wanting to let him go. But he was right. She had to trust him. And trust herself.

When they returned to Edinburgh that evening, Jacob phoned the airlines and reserved himself a seat on a commercial flight to JFK the next morning. Isabel got up early with him, and she watched the taxi pull away and whisk him down the street away from her. Only then did it occur to her that it was Christmas Day, and she had forgotten to wish him a happy Christmas.

Isabel showered and dressed alone, in a red dress

with a sprig of holly in her hair. When she was ready, she drove to her uncle's home.

As she knocked on the door, and he let her inside, she felt a small triumph even through her sadness. She took comfort in knowing that she'd been true to herself. She'd done her best, her way, not only for herself, but for the people she loved, too.

Uncle John answered the door himself, and took her coat. She gave him a kiss, and he seemed surprised. "You decided to come alone," he remarked as he hung up her coat.

"I did."

He brought her into a sitting room and poured them each a small glass of sherry. "Rhiannon called me this morning," he said.

"Yes, Uncle. I know you typically spend Christmases with her and Malcolm's family."

"And I know you typically spend Christmas with your family."

"I do." She smiled at him. "But I'm glad it's just you and me for now. Perhaps you'll join me and visit my mum and brothers later, after dinner. They'll be watching Christmas movies. *It's a Wonderful Life* and *A Christmas Carol*. Maybe *Elf* for Stewart. We'd love to have you."

Her uncle smiled. He held up the glass in a toast. "Maybe I will."

"Please do."

He took a small sip of sherry. "Rhiannon told me about yesterday's visit."

"I'm glad." She took a sip of her sherry, as well. It was sweet—sweeter than she'd expected.

He nodded, lost in thought, and seemed troubled. "I'll never forgive myself for what happened to her," he said.

Isabel put down her glass and took both his hands in hers. "I wish you would, Uncle. You know she doesn't blame you. No one in the family does."

He nodded shortly. He seemed to be struggling with emotion. Finally, he met her gaze. "I'm sorry I can't name you CEO, or even president."

She had expected that. She nodded.

"Are you disappointed?"

"When I confronted you in your office yesterday, I knew I had forfeited my chances."

"But you did it anyway."

She nodded, sipping her sherry again. "I did."

"And your father," he said. "I know you made a promise to Dougal."

"In the hospital, the last day I saw him alive, yes." She lowered her gaze to the bright red sherry, their festive drink for Christmas. Her father had so loved the holiday. She found herself smiling. "But I think he's proud of me, after all."

She gazed up at her uncle. She had stood up to him, which her dad had never done. *That* would make him proud.

Last night, driving back from the castle, it had occurred to Isabel that her dad wouldn't want her to spend her life doing something that made her unhappy, just to please him. The only way she would fail him was if she denied her own heart.

"I think there's a more appropriate role for me at Sage," she said. "One that suits me. One that I think can benefit the company."

"I'm interested in hearing your thoughts," her uncle said.

"I enjoyed working in the Cosmetics Division. I'd like to head up that department. Reporting to you, if I may."

Her uncle nodded. "I'll see to it." He stood. "Well, are you hungry? I arranged for the traditional dinner. Turkey with the trimmings."

"That will be lovely," she said.

She followed him into the dining room. And at her uncle's Edinburgh mansion, all decorated for Christmas, a table set with a lovely meal for two, Isabel Sage participated in the first adult conversation she'd ever had with her uncle John that had lasted longer than ten minutes.

Away from the office, she discovered, outside of the pressure of business, he wasn't half-bad.

In any event, it was something to build upon.

CHAPTER SEVENTEEN

JACOB MADE IT to his family's house in Connecticut by midafternoon on Christmas Day. He'd slept a good part of the flight home, still shell-shocked from meeting Rhiannon, still thoughtful about all that had happened in Scotland.

He needed to tell his mom what Rhiannon had told him. That was the most important thing at the moment.

A light snow had fallen, dusting the porch, as he stamped his feet on the welcome mat. The front door was adorned with a balsam wreath like the ones his mom had made every year when he was a child, even when they'd had little to live on.

But the home was warm inside and smelled like mulled cider. Emily greeted him, skipping over and making a fuss over him. He'd forgotten he still wore a small bandage on his neck. He felt a bit stiff and he'd probably always have a scar there, but that wasn't why he'd come home.

He finished giving Emily a bear hug, and then took off his shoes in the entryway. "Where is everybody?" he asked.

"In the den. Zach is showing us his skills with his new video games." She rolled her eyes.

It was nice to know some things didn't change.

"Did you bring your gun with you?" Emily asked as she walked beside him.

Playfully, he tugged on her messy ponytail. "Absolutely not."

"Good." She led him into the alcove off the family room.

There they were, his family, snuggled on the big sectional couch and looking somewhat sleepy, except for Zach, who was jockeying with a game console.

"Hi, everyone," he said. "Merry Christmas."

"Jacob," Daniel said, rising. "We weren't expecting you."

"I know. I came back early." He glanced around. "Where's Mom?"

"She's in the kitchen, cleaning up," Emily said.

He dropped the bag of presents he'd brought onto the coffee table. "Em, you're in charge of passing these out. I'll go give Mom hers in person."

As Zach rifled through the bag, Jacob headed for the kitchen. His mom was listening to the radio. Christmas songs. The faucet in the sink was running, and she was scrubbing a pot vigorously, though it looked pretty clean to him.

He pulled up a stool and sat across from her on the kitchen island. "Hi, Mom."

"Jacob!" She blinked. "I wasn't expecting you.

Aren't you in…" She let the question drift off. Anxiously, she peered at his bandage.

"I'm okay," he said quietly. "And yes, I was in Scotland with Isabel." He paused. He'd realized on the plane that he shouldn't have ditched Isabel so abruptly, but he'd needed to do this. He needed to set this straight.

"Mom," he said. "I had to come home to see you."

She smiled slightly. "You've not done that for many years now."

"I know. I'm sorry. I've been busy working so much, away most holidays. When I was in Scotland with Isabel, I realized, well… She took me to talk with the woman who was with Donald when he died."

"You…" His mom seemed to sway on her feet. He got up and helped her into a chair.

"Mom, I just wanted you to know, he thought about us. He may have left us and made things hard, but I think he regretted how he treated us. He was sorry about it. It was the last thing he talked to her about before he died."

She shook her head at him. She seemed bewildered.

"Mom, it's okay."

"Jacob," she said, flustered. "*I* left *him*."

"You…did? Why?"

She pressed her hands to her mouth, staring at the bandage on the side of his neck. "You were only a toddler," she said, her face lined with pain. "I turned around for a moment, and when I looked back, there you were, playing with his *gun*."

Jacob stared at her. "His *gun?*"

"You were so curious, and he was so careless with it. All the time. I couldn't stay with him after that. I couldn't risk a terrible accident. I was so *angry* with him. So I took you one day, and I left."

Jacob exhaled. "Why didn't you ever tell me this?"

She shook her head. "I had hoped that he would follow us," she said helplessly. "But he didn't. He just…didn't."

She'd felt guilty for leaving Donald. Jacob saw it clearly. He drew her to him and hugged her. "You know what, Mom," he said. "I'm glad you came here. We've had a good life, haven't we?"

"You don't blame me?" she whispered.

"No, I don't blame you. I'm happy." He gave her a smile. He *was* happy.

"So…do you have any chowder left?" he asked. Daniel liked to have New England clam chowder for Christmas lunch. It had become his mom's ritual, too. "Because I'm kind of hungry."

His mom smiled at him. "I'm glad you came home."

TWO DAYS LATER, Jacob sat in a private interrogation room at the New York Field Office and steepled his hands. He gazed at Diane across the conference table.

"Thank you for meeting with me on short notice," he said.

She placed her reading glasses on the files she'd brought along with her and raised a wary eyebrow. "Jacob, I know you don't want to hear this from me, but I can't possibly expedite your case this quickly, or give you clearance to join Eddie Walsh in the Presidential Protective Division. I'm sorry, but that's my answer for now."

"Really," he said, deadpan. "That's interesting, because I asked you here in order to get your professional opinion about something else."

Diane leaned back; he'd surprised her.

"Really," she replied, echoing his tone.

"Yeah. I went to Scotland and I did the investigative work I told you I had planned. I saw the place where my father was killed. I talked with the hostage that he died protecting."

Diane was listening intently. He continued on. "I wrote the details down for you on the flight home. Everything I learned about the timeline, the hostages, my father's role."

"All right," Diane said, nodding.

"But then I threw the notebook away because I realized the details didn't matter. None of the technical aspects of the operation were even important to me. Not really."

"And why is that?"

"Because my father loved me. That's all that matters."

"He said that?"

Jacob nodded. "He said that to the vic before he died—yeah."

"Jacob, my purpose in questioning you was to assess—and more important, to get *you* to assess—your fitness, motivations and state of mind, given what happened in your family's background."

"Yeah, and I'm grateful that you pushed me. Look, I know now that the whole birth certificate quest you gave me was just to get me to talk to my mother about what happened. She'd told me he'd abandoned us, but that turned out not to be true. And the trip to Scotland—that made me confront what really happened to him and my reaction to it. I got to see it through the eyes of the people who were with him when he died.

"My dad *didn't* fail, Diane. I'd always assumed he had. The way he abandoned us and then died, well, it was pretty traumatic to me, even if I never wanted to admit it. By choosing to join law enforcement, I wanted to…I don't know…in a twisted way, maybe I wanted to prove that his life had meaning. I was going to do what he did, only better."

He shrugged, feeling embarrassed. "It didn't work

out that way," he finished. "His life did have meaning, just not in the way I'd expected."

Diane was listening, silent.

"Look, all I can do is make meaning for myself. And I have. I know I'm super lucky. I have people who love me and want me to come home to them at the end of the day, and living with that is what matters most to me at this point."

"You sound like you've made a decision?"

"I have. Remember how you gave me a choice— stay in the field office, avoiding the work you were asking of me, or explore my motivations and eventually transfer to the PPD? Well, I'm not avoiding the work you asked for, but I do prefer to stay in a field office."

"So…do you want to continue meeting with me, here in New York?"

"Actually, I notice we have a London field office," he remarked. "And since I was born in Great Britain, I figure that gives me a leg up."

She eyed him. "Did you know we have an Edinburgh field office, too?"

His heart beat faster. "No, I didn't."

"It's new. Not many protective details are involved, but we do have a burgeoning investigative office there."

"I love investigative work," he deadpanned. "Especially credit-card fraud."

She cracked a smile. "Are you asking for my blessing in preparing your transfer papers?"

"That is affirmative."

"Is moving to your father's country just another way of following in his footsteps?"

"Actually, I'm following my heart. Her name is Isabel and she lives in Edinburgh."

Diane nodded, fully smiling. "You have my blessing, Jacob Ross."

"Great. There's just one more thing."

"Oh?"

"I, ah…might want to talk with a professional now and then. Someone with a specialty in trauma therapy."

He gave Diane credit; she kept her composure. "That…is for the best, and it certainly can be arranged."

"Great." He stood and reached for his sunglasses. "I feel like we're developing something here, Diane."

She nodded, not batting an eye. He was starting to like this psychologist.

"Before I leave…" Jacob pointed to the stack of files that Diane had laid on the table before her. "May I have that original birth certificate I gave you? I never made a copy of it, and it occurs to me that I'd like to see where in Scotland my parents were born. Because who knows? Maybe I have cousins I'd like to meet while I'm over there."

Diane reached into her pile of folders. "I can certainly support that."

NEW YEAR'S EVE—Hogmanay—in Edinburgh and Isabel was solo. She had invitations to several parties, with people she liked, but in celebration of her newfound independence, she decided to spend the night taking pleasure in her own company.

Bundled up in her warmest winter coat and hat and her favorite boots, she walked through the city, alive with people. Lingering where she liked, and enjoying her own observations.

On one street a stage was set up, and she watched the comics there for a while. On another street she strolled through a festival geared toward children, with puppet shows and sing-alongs. She bought a hot cider from a vendor, and she sipped as she walked, warming her hands on the cup.

All along her meandering stroll, she made comments in her head, things she and Jacob would have noticed and discussed. A funny song. The sweet smell of cinnamon pastries. The wonder of a new year beginning.

For so long, she'd wanted to be home in Scotland, and now she finally was. She felt happy; she loved it here. And yet, with Jacob, the happiness would have doubled.

She thought about the phone in her pocket, and wondered if this was the time to call him. But he'd asked her to wait, and waiting meant being patient. And it *was* a stretch to hope he might return to Scotland, especially more permanently. Moving between countries was a major life change.

She had just made the most important life change. She had moved to the Land of Isabel. The Land of Isabel didn't need "one more year to be happy." In the Land of Isabel she could seek contentment daily. Because her decisions were hers alone.

That was why, when her phone rang, her heart leaped. She pulled off a glove with her teeth and in her haste spilled a bit of her cider in the rush to get the phone from her pocket.

"Jacob?" she said. She had to yell, because the noise on the street was so loud.

"No, it's Malcolm," her cousin yelled back.

That was good—she liked Malcolm, too. "What's going on?"

"Are you near the Royal Mile?" he shouted.

She was on it, near the bottom. "I'm working my way up the hill for the fireworks!"

"How far away are you from my party?"

The pub where Malcolm was hosting friends in a private room was only a few blocks closer to Edinburgh Castle. "Five minutes, I think," she yelled. "Maybe I'll pop in."

"Brilliant! Please join us, straightaway. Hurry!" Malcolm shouted.

"I'm coming!" She ditched the cider and pocketed her phone. Of course, there were festive crowds ahead, but she plunged her way through.

As she came closer to Malcolm's party, she heard a man singing karaoke, "A Red, Red Rose," over a microphone inside the pub.

Jacob! she thought again. She ran to the door and burst inside just in time to see the singer serenading Malcolm and Kristin. Jacob wasn't in sight.

Sighing, Isabel grabbed a glass of wine and stood along the wall to listen. How could she not think of the Vermont wedding and her first kiss with Jacob as she danced with him in his kilt?

"Isabel?" Jacob's voice was low in her ear, and she thought she must be imagining him. "Isabel, it's me."

She felt Jacob's strong arms around her and, twisting to see him, threw her arms around him, too. She hadn't forgotten how good he felt to her, how solid and strong. No person had ever looked so welcome to her. "You're *here!*"

"I'd hoped to surprise you. Are you surprised?"

She laughed. She should have known he would coordinate something wonderfully top secret. "How long are you staying?"

"Forever." He grinned at her. "I'm moving to Edinburgh, if you'll have me in the same city as you." And then he kissed her. He cupped her face and kissed her as if she were the most precious person to him.

When he finished, she was breathless.

"Yes, I'll have you!" she said.

He wiped her lip gloss that he'd smudged, smiling at her. "I'm sorry I left so abruptly, but I needed to get things straight. I transferred to the Edinburgh Field Office. I wanted to surprise you after I'd nailed everything down."

"So…" She was almost afraid to ask. "You'll still be a bodyguard, but over here instead of in Washington?"

Someone bumped into them, so he steered her by the shoulders to a quiet corner. "Nope, something entirely different. I know it's late, but here's my gift." Beaming, he pressed something solid into the palm of her hand and closed her fingers around it. Then he put his hands over hers.

"What is it?" she asked.

"Credit-card fraud."

"Excuse me?"

"Credit-card fraud. It's my gift. And if that doesn't work, there's always business law. You reminded me of my aptitude there."

She broke out laughing. "This is business law?" She shook the small box in her hand, because she'd realized that a box was what it was. Inside it, something rattled.

"No, not exactly. This is love. You love me, right? And I love you. Well, if you've decided you can carve out time for me, I've put my gun away for you. Instead, I've brought roses."

Roses? He had not. This was a ring. She shook the box again to be sure. "May I open it now?" Because it was a jeweler's box, and she was giggly with anticipation and excitement. "Please!"

"I take it you can make time for me?" He said it in a teasing voice, but she knew he was utterly serious.

"Oh, yes!"

"Even if you're CEO?"

"No, Jacob—I met with my uncle at Christmas, and we've decided I'll manage the Cosmetics Division. I'll be busy, but fulfilled-busy, happy-busy and—"

"And with a personal life?" he finished.

"Absolutely." She leaned over their hands, wrapped around the box together, and kissed him. With a slight sigh, he kissed her back.

"You're the most important thing to me," she said.

With that, he took his hands away from hers. She opened the box he'd given her. A golden ring sat on a white satin cushion, a beautiful, one-of-a-kind piece with roses sculpted around it. She grasped the significance, and held on to it tight. It occurred to her that she had everything she wanted, here at this moment.

"Which hand should I place this on?" she murmured.

"Whichever one you please."

She was the luckiest woman she knew. "The left hand, please."

He threw back his head and laughed. "I love you, Isabel Sage. How could I ever stay away?"

* * * * *

Be sure to look for the next book about the Sage family from Cathryn Parry and Harlequin Superromance in 2015!

LARGER-PRINT BOOKS!

HARLEQUIN *Presents*

PASSION GUARANTEED SEDUCTION

GET 2 FREE LARGER-PRINT NOVELS PLUS 2 FREE GIFTS!

YES! Please send me 2 FREE LARGER-PRINT Harlequin Presents® novels and my 2 FREE gifts (gifts are worth about $10). After receiving them, if I don't wish to receive any more books, I can return the shipping statement marked "cancel." If I don't cancel, I will receive 6 brand-new novels every month and be billed just $5.05 per book in the U.S. or $5.49 per book in Canada. That's a saving of at least 16% off the cover price! It's quite a bargain! Shipping and handling is just 50¢ per book in the U.S. and 75¢ per book in Canada.* I understand that accepting the 2 free books and gifts places me under no obligation to buy anything. I can always return a shipment and cancel at any time. Even if I never buy another book, the two free books and gifts are mine to keep forever.

176/376 HDN F43N

Name	(PLEASE PRINT)

Address	Apt. #

City	State/Prov.	Zip/Postal Code

Signature (if under 18, a parent or guardian must sign)

Mail to the **Harlequin® Reader Service:**
IN U.S.A.: P.O. Box 1867, Buffalo, NY 14240-1867
IN CANADA: P.O. Box 609, Fort Erie, Ontario L2A 5X3

Are you a subscriber to Harlequin Presents books and want to receive the larger-print edition?
Call 1-800-873-8635 today or visit us at www.ReaderService.com.

* Terms and prices subject to change without notice. Prices do not include applicable taxes. Sales tax applicable in N.Y. Canadian residents will be charged applicable taxes. Offer not valid in Quebec. This offer is limited to one order per household. Not valid for current subscribers to Harlequin Presents Larger-Print books. All orders subject to credit approval. Credit or debit balances in a customer's account(s) may be offset by any other outstanding balance owed by or to the customer. Please allow 4 to 6 weeks for delivery. Offer available while quantities last.

Your Privacy—The Harlequin® Reader Service is committed to protecting your privacy. Our Privacy Policy is available online at www.ReaderService.com or upon request from the Harlequin Reader Service.

We make a portion of our mailing list available to reputable third parties that offer products we believe may interest you. If you prefer that we not exchange your name with third parties, or if you wish to clarify or modify your communication preferences, please visit us at www.ReaderService.com/consumerschoice or write to us at Harlequin Reader Service Preference Service, P.O. Box 9062, Buffalo, NY 14269. Include your complete name and address.

HPLP13R

LARGER-PRINT BOOKS!
GET 2 FREE LARGER-PRINT NOVELS PLUS
2 FREE GIFTS!

HARLEQUIN®

Romance

From the Heart, For the Heart

YES! Please send me 2 FREE LARGER-PRINT Harlequin® Romance novels and my 2 FREE gifts (gifts are worth about $10). After receiving them, if I don't wish to receive any more books, I can return the shipping statement marked "cancel." If I don't cancel, I will receive 4 brand-new novels every month and be billed just $4.84 per book in the U.S. or $5.24 per book in Canada. That's a savings of at least 19% off the cover price! It's quite a bargain! Shipping and handling is just 50¢ per book in the U.S. and 75¢ per book in Canada.* I understand that accepting the 2 free books and gifts places me under no obligation to buy anything. I can always return a shipment and cancel at any time. Even if I never buy another book, the two free books and gifts are mine to keep forever.

119/319 HDN F43Y

Name	(PLEASE PRINT)

Address	Apt. #

City	State/Prov.	Zip/Postal Code

Signature (if under 18, a parent or guardian must sign)

Mail to the **Harlequin® Reader Service:**
IN U.S.A.: P.O. Box 1867, Buffalo, NY 14240-1867
IN CANADA: P.O. Box 609, Fort Erie, Ontario L2A 5X3

Want to try two free books from another line?
Call 1-800-873-8635 or visit www.ReaderService.com.

* Terms and prices subject to change without notice. Prices do not include applicable taxes. Sales tax applicable in N.Y. Canadian residents will be charged applicable taxes. Offer not valid in Quebec. This offer is limited to one order per household. Not valid for current subscribers to Harlequin Romance Larger-Print books. All orders subject to credit approval. Credit or debit balances in a customer's account(s) may be offset by any other outstanding balance owed by or to the customer. Please allow 4 to 6 weeks for delivery. Offer available while quantities last.

Your Privacy—The Harlequin® Reader Service is committed to protecting your privacy. Our Privacy Policy is available online at www.ReaderService.com or upon request from the Harlequin Reader Service.

We make a portion of our mailing list available to reputable third parties that offer products we believe may interest you. If you prefer that we not exchange your name with third parties, or if you wish to clarify or modify your communication preferences, please visit us at www.ReaderService.com/consumerschoice or write to us at Harlequin Reader Service Preference Service, P.O. Box 9062, Buffalo, NY 14269. Include your complete name and address.

HRLP13R